Peter Stephan Jungk was born in Los Angeles in December 1952, to emigré parents. He grew up in the United States and in Europe, and studied screenwriting at the American Film Institute. He began writing in the mid-seventies, and has published seven books to date. His first was *Stechpalmenwald* (1978), a collection of short stories set in Hollywood. Subsequent works include *Shabbat — A Rite of Passage in Jerusalem* (1985), based on his experiences during a year at a *yeshiva* (bible school), and the acclaimed biography *Franz Werfel: A Life Torn by History* (1990). His most recent novel, published in German, is *King of America* (2001), a fictional biography of Walt Disney's last months.

Jungk also works as a screenwriter, essayist and translator. He now lives in Paris, and is married to the photographer Lillian Birnbaum. They have a daughter, Adah.

Michael Hofmann was born in 1957 in Freiburg, Germany, and came to England in 1961. He has published four volumes of poetry and a collection of essays, *Behind the Lines* (2001). His translations of German prose, including works by Brecht, Kafka, Koeppen and Roth, have won the *Independent*'s Foreign Fiction Award, the IMPAC Dublin Literary Award and the Schlegel-Tieck Translation prize (twice).

PETER STEPHAN JUNGK

The Snowflake Constant

translated by Michael Hofmann

faber and faber

First published in Germany in 1991 by S. Fischer Verlag GmbH
This translation first published in the United Kingdom in 2002
by Faber and Faber Limited
3 Queen Square London WC1N 3AU
Published in the United States by Faber and Faber Inc.,
an affiliate of Farrar, Straus and Giroux LLC, New York

Typeset by Faber and Faber Limited
Printed in England by Clays Ltd, St Ives plc

A CIP record for this book
is available from the British Library

ISBN 0-571-20182-2

2 4 6 8 10 9 7 5 3 1

For Lillian

Even when they are asleep, people work and contribute to the totality of the cosmos.

Heraclitus

People used to think that when a thing changes, it must be in a state of change, and that when a thing moves, it is in a state of motion. This is now known to be a mistake.

Bertrand Russell

Contents

The Plant Room
page 1

Odéon
page 27

Yerevan
page 91

Ararat
page 147

The Plant Room

In the main square of the small town of Belluno, market gardeners were offering their poor produce for sale. Behind a knife grinder's stall, Tigor found a smashed wooden crate that contained two bruised, mouldering watermelons. He buried his face in the sun-warmed pulp, choked, spluttered, guzzled, crunched the seeds. The children of the stallholders gathered round him in a circle, and laughed at him. He went off on all fours, and they trailed after him. 'Lord only knows what will happen to you next, you're so irresponsible,' Viola had complained, 'even when you were a child, you used to find ways of messing things up. Here, give me those trousers, I'll sew a new seat on them.' How could I forget that, he thought, put his hand down and felt the material, felt the little ridge on the back of his right leg that he hadn't thought of since leaving Trieste. He beamed at the children, who were still dancing round him, felt money, felt the edge of the plastic gold card, don't leave home without it. Then suddenly yelped 'Home!' – it sounded like the cry of a wild animal. 'I miss my bed so much, my books, my bath, my kitchen!'

The children squealed with delight, drilled their fingers into their temples. 'Ohmm!' cried their ringleader, he had a couple of thick scars under his nose, and then the whole gang of them chorused 'Ohmm', that one sound over and over, and then abruptly stopped. Two policemen had appeared in their midst.

Making their way between rows of curious onlookers, the policemen led the man across the market square, past the Hotel Della Posta to the police station next to the church. The office had wood panelling. A coal stove added to the summer heat. A violent rainstorm had broken out, the windowpanes were lashed by torrents of water. The two *carabinieri* took their seats, one under the faded colour photograph of a pope who'd been dead for decades, the other beneath a black-and-white portrait of the president before last. They sat, shoulder to shoulder, on a wooden bench, holding their noses, as though the detainee stank to high

3

heaven. Tigor sat, fighting sleep, gripping on to an iron railing. Then his eyes fell shut, and his head rolled to the side; first left, then right. As he lost consciousness, it looked as though he were bowing in turn to the two men who had arrested him.

'Passport, papers!'

No response from Tigor.

'Passport!'

No reply.

'Surname?'

He awoke.

'First name?'

Didn't speak.

'Surname?'

Silence.

The younger of the two policemen, tired also, slightly built, went over to a desk and picked up the telephone, leaving his older, heavier colleague to carry on the questioning.

'Place of birth?'

'I was born . . . Trieste . . .'

'*Passaporto!*'

Tigor was listening to the younger policeman talking on the telephone. He was trying to get some friend or relative who was going to Vienna next week to bring him back a pound of Earl Grey tea from a shop by the name of Schönbichler, nowhere else would do, Schönbichler, on the Wollgasse, number four. The older man's insistent '*Passaporto!*' cut through the word '*quattro*.'

At that moment, it came to him that his passport was gone. He had thrown it down into the valley, along with whatever else was in his large, pale-blue rucksack. A snake, Tigor thought, I'm like a snake sloughing.

'. . . *Numero quattro! Si, quattro!*' repeated the younger policeman, and returned to the wooden bench.

'No ID on him,' barked the older one.

'Nationality?' asked the younger.

'Italian and American,' said Tigor.

The two policemen nudged each other in the ribs, twisted their lips to show they were making an effort not to laugh.

'Profession?'

'I'm a lecturer.'

4

'Lecturer in what? Vagrancy?' jeered the older.

'No. Mathematics.'

'Oh yeah?'

'Euclidean geometry.'

At that, the two of them could no longer contain themselves. They sat there, slapping their thighs, until the older one got up, brought in some colleagues from next door, to tell them about the nameless tramp who was a professor of mathematics in America. It was a case for Padua, was the general opinion, call an ambulance. Then the tired, gentle *carabiniere*, who was the senior officer present on that festive Sunday, ordered, 'No, hold on. Just a minute. We're letting him go.'

A ring of perplexed, disappointed faces. Silence, for several seconds.

'We're letting him go,' repeated Franco Sopracroda.

No sooner had Tigor walked out of the station than the man in command was assailed by complaints from his colleagues. 'Whatever did you decide that for?' they asked. 'What do you think you're doing?'

'I don't know. . .' Sopracroda replied, truthfully. 'I can't really give you a reason.'

'. . . *porca miseria!*' the policemen swore, and it took quite some time for tranquillity to be re-established in the station.

The man they had released sheltered under the overhanging roofs in an effort to keep dry. 'If you're looking for a bed for the night,' called the employee from the Manin hotel who had given him a lift into town, and who now happened to run into him again, 'then come and stay in my place, Via Venezia 22!' Tigor thanked him and waved. Under a baroque arch, he tore open the seat of his trousers, counted his money like a gambler his winnings, and stuffed it into his pockets. Near the piazza, in the narrow Dolomites Lane, there was the buzzing red-and-green neon sign of a trattoria. Dal Papagallo was its name, 'The Parrot', and Tigor went inside. His hunger by now was such that he was hardly aware of it. The tired landlord, taking him for a beggar, wanted to throw him out, but changed his tune when Tigor showed him a fistful of money. It was too late for lunch and too early for supper, the kitchen wouldn't open for another hour or so, he

5

explained to his unbidden guest. Tigor, however, would not take no for an answer, ordered a heavy meat dish and a bottle of red wine, and settled down to wait. Folded his arms on the table, and laid his aching head on them. Saw out of the corner of his eye a column of ants marching over the red-and-white check table-cloth. Leapt to his feet and paid: saw his banknote teeter off on a thousand tiny feet.

In a nearby bar, there was a wedding party in progress. Through the windows he could see the young members of a brass band, dressed in their folkloric outfits. The groom, in his fawn fireman's uniform, held his trombone at the ready. Tigor drifted on, back to the main square. Each step seemed to cost him more strength than he possessed. He was completely soaked.

Now that it was early evening and the stallholders had all gone home, there was no one in the square. Tigor knocked on the kitchen door of the town's premier restaurant, Il Veneto, and showed a twenty-thousand-lire note to the apprentice chef who opened the door. The apprentice went back to ask the head cook what to do. Tigor was ushered in. He asked if he might wash his hands, and used the opportunity to look in the mirror for several minutes. Then he tidied his hair and washed his face as thoroughly as he could in the circumstances. 'My prince!' his mother had used to say to him, 'all Petersburg lies at your feet . . .'

The cooks sat him down at one of the rough wooden work tables in the huge kitchen, and served him Dover sole, fresh vegetables and boiled rice, gave him no wine to drink, only mineral water. He had eyes only for what was on his plate, in his ears was the low hum of a ventilator and the sound of the men talking, he had no idea they were addressing him. The white-hatted ones shook their heads and withdrew. Tigor ate and drank. He tittered. A fit of laughter convulsed him. Or was it that Tigor was shivering? He began to cry. Tears poured down his cheeks. Snot dribbled out of his nostrils, mingled with his pouring sweat, and everything ended up on his plate, while the last few days passed in view before Tigor's eyes in a stream of brightly coloured cine-matic imagery.

He replayed his awakening in that Sunday's first light, bedded on whins, in between bushes and clumps of grass. It was the sev-enth day since his arrival in that crude space he dubbed the plant room. His exhaustion that morning had been so grave that Tigor's life would have drained heavily into the ground while he slept or half-slept, had he not, with the last nuclei of his remaining strength, exploded out of his cocoon. He came back to life, fitted with the sinewy wings of rebirth. He had no more fear of death. He knew that Death – soft, considerate, well mannered – would have called on him in the middle of his dream. An army of ants had filed over him, the size of lions, the strength of panthers. His craving for sleep had at first grown even stronger. Tigor felt secure with the jagged chain of mountains close at hand. The peaks emerged from the lower wooded slopes in the manner of a head and shoulders from a fur cloak. In his dream he had stood in the Marine Fauna room of the Natural History Museum in Trieste, at 4 Piazza Hortis, while twenty man-sized sharks and swordfish came jagging towards him from all sides. It was this dream that saved him: he awoke in terror. The sun climbed another ten degrees before Tigor managed to get to his feet. For a long time he held on to a tree trunk, not moving. Then he ditched almost everything, except for his logbook and his father's letter. Walked so slowly it took him two hours to reach the spring. Drank more than he had ever drunk in his life. Ripped up all the bluebells, all the clover he could find, stuffed them in his mouth, flowers, leaves and all, including the earth that clung to the delicate roots, chewed up little insects without noticing. His legs carried him, he took no part in their work, in their being. Walked with his eyes shut. Collided with trees. Bled from a gash over one eyebrow, never knew it. Reached the flaking walls of a derelict chapel. There he vomited so hard, it hurt him to the root of his penis. He pushed open an iron gate, lay down between two old wooden benches, on the cold stone floor of the chapel. Slept for no longer than a few minutes. Once more, he saw the splinters of wood and the dirty glacier ice, as far as his eyes could see.

The dream seemed unfamiliar to him, though it was one he had very often. Ever since leaving the conference centre in Trieste, he'd had a sense of being pulled on a rope in a certain direction. That Sunday morning too, he'd walked as though he had cables attached to his loins, reeling him in gently but implacably towards some unknown place. Tigor walked slowly, like someone being towed. For the first time in a week, he found himself on

7

trodden paths once more. He was afraid of seeing another human being again. Felt like someone surfacing from riverine depths: seven days in the watery kingdom of the naiads, but forty-nine years had passed in the upper world. Felt like an astronaut, steering his craft back to the earth's atmosphere: miscalculate the angle of re-entry by one or two degrees, and his little capsule would be incinerated. Having reached the banks of the river he had heard gurgling in the distance, he tried to wash off the sweat and grime of the past days. Felt the beard he had grown, the little hairs sprouting in every direction. Longed for a mirror, even a pocket mirror! He stroked his chest, felt his shoulders, rubbed his neck, fingered his full lips. A large, broad mouth, the mouth of someone who liked to talk a lot. His mother had always blamed herself, her only son had turned out too pretty. 'My Russian prince,' she'd used to say to him, 'all Petersburg lies at your feet. And don't smile the whole time, you look stupid when you smile!'

Some hours later, Tigor reached a hamlet by the name of Noach. He concealed himself behind a walnut tree, and spied on a family, four grown-ups and four children sitting round a dirty table. He saw how the youngest was picking over his sister's hair, pretending to look for lice. Then the two older boys helped their mother fish trout out of a stone basin in the courtyard with large green nets. They hit the wriggling fish on the head with croquet mallets. Before eating, they said grace, the meal was over in minutes. Hiding behind his tree, Tigor thought of his own father, how he had never taken the time, even on Sundays, to sit down and eat with his family. His mother was in the theatre every night, and his father came home late from the docks. Tigor would mostly be in bed by then, with the radio perched on his chest, sailing the seven seas on his short-wave.

On the dusty country road at the edge of Noach, a small rusty three-wheeler drew up next to him. The driver, who spoke in South Tyrolean dialect, introduced himself as a hotel porter and handyman. 'I was born in Bozen, but now I'm working for the Eyeties in Belluno. Where might you be from?' He offered Tigor a lift. His hill farmer's face was at once haggard and rosy, he would fire off four or five questions at once, not seeming to wait for a reply. He made room for Tigor in the back of the tiny vehicle, in

8

the roofed-over boot separated from the driver's cab, pitch-dark and full of noise and petrol fumes. During the drive, the handyman shouted how he knew every stone here, every fork in the road like his own overall pocket, '. . . because for the past year I've had a sweetheart up here!' He would warn everyone of the perils of the steep gorges, even Signor Bastanza, the girl's father, the local forester, would often lose his way. Up there, the other side of the peak, shouted the porter, pointing in the direction of Tigor's plant room, there weren't no house, no chapel, no hut for miles. Tigor heard the word 'gorges' and the word 'peak', but then, despite the noise of the engine, he was asleep. The three-wheeler's journey down the valley took over two hours. The passenger didn't wake up until the handyman stopped in a side street in the little town of Belluno, in front of the service entrance of the Hotel Manin. Like a dream, this re-entry into the earth's atmosphere. Hunger drove him out to the market place, where, after looking for some time, close to blacking out, he had found the broken watermelons.

'Home!' he cried out, hunched over the bones of his sole at the kitchen table of Il Veneto, 'I miss my home so much!' Only now did he take in his surroundings, see the chefs standing around him. How they smiled and looked concerned at the same time! He turned to the head cook and his assistants, thanked them for his excellent dinner. 'You must know, it's been several days since I last had anything decent to eat,' he said, in cultured Italian that sounded a little high-flown, but that was also in his character. 'You must excuse me, I had to . . . I'm afraid . . . break off my little experiment!'

'We were pleased to serve you,' replied the head cook, signalling to the young men to clear the table.

'My experiment! Like so much of what I attempt, condemned to failure from the very outset,' Tigor began, 'I'd left my pocket calculator, my watch, even my radio and all my suits behind in the flat at 25 Viale XX Settembre . . .'

'Please forgive us, but we need to get to work,' said the head cook.

'On you go, on you go, don't let me get in your way! Twenty-five is my favourite number, I call it a magical number, every number that ends in twenty-five is divisible by twenty-five! Did you know that? The only number I have similar feelings for is forty-four. Forty-four is the beauty queen among numbers. She's my guardian angel, my guide . . . have you noticed how quickly I'm speaking, it's most uncharacteristic, it just seems to be bubbling up out of me.' At first he had his arms propped on his knees, and kept his elegant hands folded. Once he began to give in to the flood of speech, they started to flutter about like butterflies.

Two waiters came in with the first orders. One lamb-chop Pompadour, one quail in Pinot Grigio sauce.

'. . . for days I've eaten almost nothing but bark, grass and nettles,' Tigor went on, 'with the exception of the flesh of that hawk, so you may imagine how I feel after the gala dinner you've served me . . . I was roughing it, living in the woods, do you understand?'

The apprentice cooks got to work, they found Tigor's spate of loquaciousness quite entertaining, and whispered to the head chef not to send the man packing whom they took to be a patient from an open institution, he wasn't really bothering them.

'. . . the inside of tree bark has a minty taste, did you know that? With a slight admixture of resin, naturally. I got to be quite fond of the taste. And clover? Are you familiar with the lemony taste of clover? It's a miracle, really! I slept in my down sleeping bag on the forest floor, in a small clearing high above the valley. My plan was to stay there for months, if I could! You may ask: why? What was he trying to achieve? Let me try to give you an answer . . . If you're interested, that is . . . If you like, I could give you an account of my days up in the forest, would you like that? Yes? My sleeping place was in a little clearing ringed by fir trees, deep in the forest, miles from any human habitation. That was confirmed to me, incidentally, by the handyman from the Manin hotel. He told me I'd been staying in an unbelievably remote area . . . but more of that later . . .

'In the middle of my plant room was a standing stone that had fallen over. Do you know what that is? A six- or seven-foot wedge of rock, against which I rested my head at night. I had intended to set it upright again, that menhir, but the necessary strength was . . . in any case, on my first morning, my first task was to establish a source of water, of course. I came across a cavern, probably the opening to some old mine workings, with narrow wooden rails on the ground. At its mouth were huge blocks of stone. I thought of building a house for myself using these stones. Crazy, isn't it, because the whole purpose of my being up there was really the exact opposite: to try to survive for as long as I could in nature – without *any* sort of roof over my head. But the impulse to erect a house, or a hut, or even a kind of lean-to, must be unfathomably deep in mankind . . . After half an hour, I had the lowest block in position, and I decided to go on building in the days to follow. (Of course, I never did any more building.) Then I climbed along a glade of thick shrubbery, with leaves the size and shape of elephants' ears. These were the leaves, incidentally, that I used to wipe myself, deliciously soft and pleasant they were, though this is hardly the place for such . . .

'At any rate, finding water turned out to be surprisingly straightforward. I stumbled upon a spring bubbling up between two flat stones. At the point where it emerged from the ground, the icy water formed a crystal bulb, and that was where I got all my water from. I knelt down on one of the stones, and replenished my battered tin flask. A weed that sprouted next to that source goes by the name of *blauwetterkühl*. Now, still on my first day, I had the following problem: each time I thought of my sky-blue nylon rucksack, which I'd left at my sleeping place, I couldn't rid myself of the feeling that it was some kind of living creature, you see, and that it was waiting for me, expecting me to give an account of myself to it – 'Where have you been? What did you find?', what the spring was like, and so on and so forth. My pack was looking to me for companionship for as long as we were up in the high forest together. No sooner was I back at my sleeping place, than I removed from the rucksack my mushroom guide, this notebook you see here, and my fountain pen, and threw everything else in a high arc over the precipice. I counted the seconds before it landed in the narrow stream bed below. I was able to calculate that the elevation of the plant room over the valley bottom was some five hundred and forty metres . . . The annoying thing was that my passport was in it, I didn't think of that until much later, and now of course I need to find a consulate, would you be able to tell me where the nearest American consulate is? I happen to have American citizenship, a compli-

11

cated business, as I'll be happy to explain, if you care to hear about it . . .'

The apprentices snickered. They were still managing to work, but hardly concentrating on the contents of pots and pans and dishes. 'Well, that was really most enlightening!' said the head chef. 'Thank you very much indeed. Perhaps you might be able to tell us a little more about your stay in the forest on some future occasion, when we don't have to work?'

'. . . but with pleasure, with pleasure,' replied Tigor, and his bushy eyebrows shot up to an unexpected height. Basically, they were in continuous motion, lending emphasis to almost every word he said. 'You see, I kept an account when I was in the forest, in that hand which I myself have some difficulty deciphering, using the fountain pen my mother gave me on the occasion of my twenty-first birthday. Here, look at it: don't you think it's beautiful? Those black and green pinstripes! Elegant, wouldn't you agree? Why don't I just translate for you from what I wrote down in my journal, which I call my logbook – that'll make it easier for both parties – except I sometimes find myself groping for words, because even though I'm a Triestine born and bred, I've lived in the United States from my twentieth year, and therefore write in English. (Though I also have fluent French and German . . .) Here we are: "First day, my terrible hunger – it was hunger that drove me all day long" – you see, right from the start, hunger was the principal theme . . . Here it is again: "hunger prevents me from understanding what has happened to me since my flight from the conference building. I climb down to a stream, in the hope of catching a trout with my bare hands. No sign of any fish. I persist in the hope for fully an hour. With icy wet hands and forearms, I pluck raspberries, pick three mushrooms of a type I've never seen before, find a gauzy silvery-grey Icelandic moss sprouting on the forest floor. Having brought matches into the forest with me, I still force myself, against the ultimate eventuality of their being used up, to strike fire from a sulphur stone instead, then I keep on striking it against the saw-blade of my penknife, two hundred and eighty-four times in all, until the first sparks fall in the tinder, and little flames light up. Boiled up the moss to a colourless, flavourless, unsustaining tea, find the mushrooms described as highly toxic in the book, the berries less than filling, so set off once more in search of something to eat . . . " You see: I keep circling round the subjects of food and drink.

'Later that evening, I noted, " . . . really should have mailed at least a couple of letters of explanation, to Reuben Davis, Patterson Van Pelt Building, 25,725 Baltimore Avenue: Dear Mr President, please forgive my sudden . . . " Am I going into too much detail for you when I read . . .? Perhaps I should confine myself to relating the highlights of my week in the forest as they suggest themselves to my memory. Perhaps all these details don't strike you as being especially noteworthy, but for someone like myself, who from childhood has hardly set foot in the wilderness, and then only, as it were, professionally, who regularly visited the same ridge in the Rocky Mountains, year in year out, for the sake of his snowflake research, the north side of Emigrant Peak, for such a person, every week like the one I've just spent . . . do you understand? At any rate, on the second day . . .'

Himself the son of quarrelsome parents, Giorgio Santini, the head cook at Il Veneto, had tried even as a child to avoid strife. Initially it had been his hope that the tyrannical guest would eventually start to flag, and go. But seeing Tigor show no inclination to leave the kitchen, Santini took off his chef's hat, mopped the sweat off his brow, and with a sigh turned to his associates: 'I've made a mistake, haven't I? But never mind, we're not all that busy tonight. Things are usually fairly quiet after market day. We'll just have to get by . . .'

'I dare say you're wondering by now (are we on "tu" or "vuoi" terms, by the way?) who this Reuben Davis is,' Tigor went on. 'Well, he's the President of the university I've turned my back on: a small but undeniably forceful character who, in spite of his physical handicap, or perhaps because of it – you see, he lost his right arm – is simply bursting with vitality. The thing about my leaving the University of Pennsylvania in Philadelphia is something I need to explain to you, otherwise you won't understand quite what it is I've done . . . The fact of the matter is this, and you should bear it in mind, people were forever telling me what to do and not to do. It wasn't just my mother either! You must understand: not one of the steps I've undertaken in my life has been entirely my own. That makes what has happened to me since the conference in Trieste all the more remarkable!

'But first let me tell you how I passed the rest of my days . . . I started to plan a series of little traps, here, see the designs? Simple constructions of wood and string, in which I intended to capture rabbits, martens, marmots. What remained to be seen, though, was: would I be able to slaughter them without being sick? I suppose you must do that as a matter of course, it's part of your job . . . but me? You need to behead the animals, and skin them and bleed them. As you probably know, all animals are edible, even caterpillars and termites, ants and stag beetles. I would have been in a position to prepare slugs, lizards, toads and snakes over my fire. Only in practice, it was too much for me. With one exception, which I must tell you about: on the fourth day of my sojourn in the plant room, there was a terrible storm. After a torrential rainstorm had left me utterly soaked, I saw a big bird sitting high up in a pine, close to my spring. Had the feeling I could see it reeling, flying up, dropping another branch or two. Reeling and coming nearer. It did that several times over, I assume it was a hawk, its feathers were spotted with brown and black. Its movements kept getting feebler and dizzier, it landed on the ground, reeling and vague. I hurled myself at the dying creature. Was terrified by the human malignity of its regard. Just like the look of an old dying woman! I hacked off its head, threw it away as far as I could, it was so disgusting to me, the memory still makes me shudder! Boiled the tough flesh for a good hour, to kill off its parasites. And then how I savoured the salty taste of it! Sucked the bones! Carried the feathers to my sleeping place, used them to pad the ground under my sleeping bag, which was still sodden after the rain . . .

'You understand: I simply wanted to prove that it was possible to survive in the wilderness, and for a long period. I wanted to do some preliminary work in the woods for a subsequent life away from human civilization. After a successful experiment, which by my definition would have been one lasting for several years, I would have gone on to write books relating my experiences as a settler in the forest. I would have become famous! A name! Do you know what that would have meant to me? And at last, something off my own bat too! Am I tiring you out with my narration? No? With every step I took in the undergrowth, I was terrified of snakes, I felt like a virgin, I kept calling to myself, "*in gamba!*" so as not to drop my guard. Picked that up from Paolo, the first husband of my aunt Viola, when walking in the Karst mountains. I'd been yearning, ever since I caught the hawk, for fish and flesh and marrow, and I had only leaves to chew on. By the by (this is quite unrelated, I just happened to think of it), I'm missing all four of my wisdom teeth, odd, isn't it? My dentist assures me this makes me highly evolved: a few hundreds or thousands of years from now, no one will have wisdom teeth any more! I was being stung to bits by mosquitoes, wasps had attacked me as well, I was feeling more and more sorry for myself. Already I felt like that criminal who was put on a prison island, a hundred and twenty-five years ago, somewhere at the end of the earth. Chewed up by flies, ambushed by vultures, he was reduced to a skeleton, and finally, in utter despair, he mixed up a brew consisting of the blood of a giant tortoise, along with some tea leaves and his own pee, and lived off that mixture in his last days . . .'

'I must ask you please', Santini interrupted, and it was clear that he was violating his own nature as he did so, 'to go now. Leave us in peace to get on with our work!'

Tigor laid twenty thousand lire on the table in front of him. Santini would not accept payment. Tigor insisted, pushed the notes towards the edge of the table. 'Absolutely no question!' said the head cook.

'Thank you very much. You've made me very welcome,' replied the guest, pocketing the money again, and not getting off his chair. 'You must know, I decided as early as the second night to curtail my daunting plant room operation . . . I don't want to detain you any further, of course, but I realized I didn't have the strength, that my hunger was getting the better of me, and that I wasn't really getting any closer to nature, however hard I tried, do you understand? When it comes down to it, I must confess I don't have any real feeling for nature. It's remained an abstraction to me . . . Day Three was probably one of the hardest days of my life to date. I felt so ashamed to be calling off my experiment prematurely! Early in the morning, I packed up my few possessions and began the descent, following the bed of a stream. A steep, savage and perilous climb. I missed my footing, tumbled over and hurt my ankle, I can show you the bruising, if you like. Found myself on an exposed rock without any way down, I could go neither on nor back. My palpitations! I felt consternation at having violated virgin terrain . . . The palpitations got worse. I was only able to turn back once I'd calmed myself slightly. Probably I was hanging between heaven and the abyss. A miracle I didn't fall. I felt too ashamed to try and call for help, ashamed in front of *myself*, if you can imagine such a thing . . . Came upon the bleached skull of a deer, it felt as soft and clean as chalk. Regretted having touched it, and tossed it away in a high arc . . . Not a sturdy heart, my heart, I should have had an operation, the specialist said it was essential when I was twelve years old, but my mother objected: we can't put the boy through something like that, she said, my only son is healthy, I'm not having him cut open and sewn up, just for you to go hacking at him . . .

'In a word, I scrambled back up the stream bed, every step was a struggle, incessantly counting my pulse, which was throbbing like machine-gun salvoes. No great distance, but it took me several hours. Returning to my plant room felt like a homecoming to me: has it ever happened to you that you were sitting in a warm bath when the doorbell rang, and you have to go and answer it? Then it turns out it wasn't for you at all, and you can get back in the bath! Such delight . . .! That's what my return to the plant room felt like. I unrolled my sleeping bag along the wedge-shaped stone. Saw myself running out of the conference centre in Trieste, halfway through the morning presentation. Running down to the port, to the covered fish market, where I took refuge to stop and think. Swimming in that sea of eyes, I resolved to look up Viola, in spite of so much family history. In the smell of fish guts and fish bones, I spotted Viola's first husband, Paolo, with his great bald dome, I hadn't seen him since my infancy, since our Sunday-morning picnics in the gardens at the edge of the Revoltella Park, but I'm straying off my subject, I'll soon be done . . . Anyway, I didn't make myself known to Paolo, I just saw he had the same creased neck he'd had decades ago, his tiny eyes were just the same, his bushy moustache . . .'

'What did you have to run away from?' asked Fulvio, the youngest of the cooks.

'Never you mind!' Santini hissed at him.

Just then, both waiters came through the swing doors at once, conveying the complaints of the clientele, who, having finished their hors d'oeuvres almost twenty minutes before, were now asking, for the second time, what was keeping their entrées.

'No wonder,' scolded Signor Pepe, the older of the two, 'you're listening to your clown in here, while we're getting it in the neck from the customers!' And they announced three further orders, one for halibut *alle genovese*, the other two for duck.

'You wanted to know what I was running away from?' Tigor resumed, turning towards Fulvio, 'I'll be only too happy to tell you. To do anything in my field, you have to be young. If you haven't notched up a mathematical discovery by the time you're twenty-five or thirty, if you haven't made your mark in "the tropical landscape of mathematics", as I like to call it, chances are you never will. It's an unwritten law that's hardly ever been broken. Whereas – what's your name? Fulvio? – I'm old enough to be your father, Fulvio. In two weeks, I'm going to be forty. I wanted to make a name for myself, nothing else mattered to me. But even eight years ago, I knew that my model of a snowflake constant, in all probability, was based on false assumptions. But the more the incorrectness of my theory was demonstrated to me, the more determinedly I clung to it, because, after fifteen years of research, I had nothing else, do you understand . . .?'

Fulvio had stopped working, his jaw dropped as he stood before the stranger. Tigor thought he saw the trainee's eyes fill with tears. It might have been from chopping onions. Sergio, too, the assistant who had first come to the door, was hardly facing the stove at all, but had turned towards the speaker.

'Fame, you understand? What I minded about was fame,' he repeated. '. . . at the end of the fourth day, I made my first nettle dinner,' Tigor continued, pleased that the young fellows were listening to him with so much attention. 'I only just blanched them over the flames in my tin pan, I was so hungry. Bit into the leaves and stalks, as though they were my favourite dish. I straight away felt fresh courage flood my veins, I'd never felt food taking effect on me in such an immediate way. Suddenly I felt I could survive in the forest for months! I drank the liquid that was left in the pan, went looking for more clumps of nettles, of course got my hands and wrists badly stung, but returned with a rich harvest. You can't imagine the agony of pissing after eating nettles, it burns to make you leap out of your skin . . . Then I lay awake for a long time afterwards in the cool breeze, each time my foot stirred in my sleeping bag, a shudder went through me. I stared up at the fir trees that ringed me, their gentle swaying, listened to the rustle of the boughs. Watched the swarms of birds that silently flew over my plant room in broad waves, flapping or darting, until darkness fell. When I awoke in the night, I was astonished by the unwonted brightness of the stars . . . I was looking at light thousands of millions of years . . .'

Once again, both waiters appeared in the kitchen at once. This time to take back the lamb and the quails they had served a few moments earlier, which were now being sent back by the diners. In one case, because the meat was oversalted, in the other because the sauce was stone cold.

'If you can't bring yourselves to turf out this tramp,' yelled Signor Pepe, while his colleague nodded vigorously, 'we're going to have to call the police!'

'. . . so I was gazing back thousands of millions of years before the beginning of calculated time,' said Tigor, 'and then to another part of the sky that had emitted its light in the months immediately preceding the Flood . . .'

Signor Pepe hurled himself at him. Santini and Fulvio had to restrain him, otherwise he would have assaulted the stranger. 'Get out!' yelled Signor Pepe. 'Get out of here!' He managed to shake off the two chefs, and stretched out his arm, jabbed his finger in the direction of the door. Tigor remained seated, perched on the rim of his chair.

'Fulvio and Sergio,' panted Santini, still trying to get his breath back, 'you've finished for today, I'll take care of everything else. Will you kindly accompany this (he struggled to find a word) . . . our friend here . . . to the station. The late train leaves for Milan at four minutes past midnight. In Milan they can furnish him with a new passport, and then . . . But I want you to see him on to his train, do I make myself clear?'

The young men grinned sheepishly. They got out of their aprons, pulled off their chefs' hats, and stood ready.

'My thanks,' said Tigor, calmly getting to his feet. He shook hands with Santini. 'You've been very good to me . . .'

*

Tigor, feeling much refreshed by the air and the walk, strode along, flanked by Fulvio and Sergio. The station was two kilometres away, and the way there led past the imposing, mostly three-storey patrician villas of the old city centre, on across the bridge over the Piave, to the memorial for the earthquake victims of 1873. Tigor, to the astonishment of his companions, did not speak, and they, for their part, knew better than to address any remarks to him.

Fully fifteen minutes later, as they reached the Church of San Stefano, with the Roman sarcophagus outside its gate in the yellow light of a street lamp, he said, 'There is a relatively new branch of mathematics, a new discipline, which I have fought tooth and nail these past years, but which is now in the process of destroying my life. It has already ruined my snowflake constant. More than that, it has made it appear ridiculous . . . I wanted to create order. I thought I could find some constant values. Over the course of fifteen winters, I have caught immaculate snowflake hexagons, and put them in a polyvinyl ethylene solution, on a black cardboard plate, at four degrees below zero centigrade, and then I took pictures of them, and compared those pictures to thousands of classic photographs, for instance to those by Wilson W. Bentley, or to those of the Japanese scientist Nakaya, you may have heard their names before? No? Never? And then I counted off the ninety-six seconds that, according to Tigor's constant, yes, gentlemen, to *my* constant, needed to elapse before an identical hexagon would appear on an area of maximally ten square centimetres . . . But what happened? I was forced to see that what will prevail is chaos. Isomorphism, yes, constants, no. Fractal geometry, yes, Euclidean geometry, no . . . Only the new geometry is capable of describing the irregular and splintered forms that surround us. And it does so by using a breed of forms to which my principal opponent, the mathematician Mandelbrot, has given the name of "fractals". Some of these "fractal quantities" that he has discovered are so bizarre that neither science nor art can come up with any other adequate descriptions of them . . .'

'We've got no idea what you're on about,' Sergio butted in with a cheeky grin.

'I would be better off myself, if I didn't know anything about fragmentation in nature, or the effective dimensions in a skein of wool, or divergence syndromes, scale invariability and isomorphism!'

'Isomorphism? What's that?' asked Fulvio, the more intelligent of the two lads, as they traipsed on towards the station.

'Isomorphic is what we call formations which are composed of structures similar to themselves, even in widely differing scales of magnitude: patterns that recur in successive enlargements, never identical but similar. An enlargement, ten-million fold, of a fish scale, say, will reveal similar shapes to those of the life-size scale . . . whatever similarities there seem to be between that theory and my own idea of the snowflake constant, it remains the explosive charge which has destroyed my life's work, three weeks ago now, during the conference in Trieste . . . I fled from the conference hall, you understand, I *fled*, I ran down to the fish market, and there, after some thought, I decided to take refuge in the top flat of number 25 Viale XX Settembre, where Viola lives. I hadn't seen her since my boyhood . . . She got quite a shock: "Your mother promised the flat to me, you live overseas anyway, Arnold has the house in Paris, and so it seemed only right that I got to keep the flat, but come in anyway, make yourself at home." (Just imagine what that feels like, going into your own flat, and being told to make yourself at home!). "You can sleep in your old room, you remember where that is, I thought I'd never hear from you again, how long have you been back in Trieste, I had no idea you were here, have you eaten today, my sugar lump, come in the kitchen, come on, how old are you now? Almost forty, that's not possible, isn't it awful how the time goes!" I explained to Viola that I didn't want to leave the site of my earliest memories for the next few days. "Are you in trouble then, my sugar lump," she laughed in her high soprano, my mother's voice. "Well, you mustn't be scared, I'll keep you safe. Or perhaps you shouldn't be here at all, this is probably the first place they'll come looking for you." I assured her no one would come looking for me, that the transgression of which I was guilty was not of a criminal nature. So I was back in my boyhood room, I didn't go back to my hotel room at the Corso until a week after the end of the conference, they were very worried about my absence. I paid for my room, took my luggage back to 25 Viale XX Settembre, and stowed my belongings in the ironing cupboard. "You need to take some deep breaths!" Viola called to me from the first day I was there. "Look in the mirror, you look like you've been chewed up and spat out, take some deep breaths, and be yourself again, here, like this, that's no way to be . . .!"'

The three of them sat in the dingy station waiting room to which the twenty-watt ceiling light lent a funereal atmosphere. It was twenty to midnight. Tigor's young companions looked shattered. When they realized they would have to keep going a while longer before they could go home, they yawned unabashedly. Sergio nodded off right away, Fulvio a few minutes later. Tigor supposed they had closed their eyes, the better to concentrate on the flow of his narrative.

'In the forest at night, I kept thinking martens, foxes or wild boar would creep up on me and take my eyes while I was asleep, or ravens would wake from their profound sleep and perch on my forehead and peck out my eyes. Sometimes I was so afraid, I would feel for branches and kindling and start a fire. The flames would calm me down, and I would go to sleep to the crackling and whistling of burning wood . . . One morning – a pity your chef isn't here, I would have liked to tell him about this – I took a longish splinter of rock and jabbed it into the ground next to my sleeping site . . . dug deeply, cut through roots, went on digging, deeper, with bare hands, with the sharp rock, ripped at the earth, searching . . . What was I searching for? – I dug with a strength I didn't know I had . . . Grubbed up earth, scratched deeper, don't ask me what was on my mind! As though I was supposed to re-arrange the entire plant room, root and branch. I crumbled every clump of soil between my fingers, tried to reach down into the heart of the earth . . . And collapsed, with my arm buried up to the shoulder in the forest floor, and slept until it was evening . . .'

The kitchen boys awoke and turned immediately to the big clock. Fulvio pretended he hadn't been asleep at all: 'Well. In the forest . . . eh? Quite something . . .'

'. . . and have you now finished with mathematics?' asked Sergio, also trying hard not to let on.

'For God's sake give it up, my father wrote to me, when I began studying, twenty-two years ago,' replied Tigor, 'he had never taken any interest in me. And then the moment I leave home, I get

21

this letter! Be as wary of your studies as you would be of a con-
niving woman, wrote my father, you cannot solve the problem
you have set yourself, it is insoluble – and this was well before I'd
begun thinking about the snowflake constant! It will only rob you
of your time and your health, and eat up your inner peace and
contentment . . . I take the letter everywhere with me, here it is!'
And he produced a crushed and stained bit of airmail paper.

'Does a man get rich in your profession?' inquired Fulvio.

'My science is founded on astoundingly flimsy assumptions, it
puts its trust in groping forward movements, and stumbles over
every line of its conclusions. Cantor's Theory of Quantity and
Peano's Spatial Curves no longer fit the foundations that were
laid by Euclid and Newton. Modern mathematics is much closer
to such things as Dadaism and Cubism, atonal music and the
writings of Franz Kafka, which, thank God, I have never read. On
our quest for absolute truth, despondency and defeat have been
our constant companions, ever since Cantor and Peano . . . Take it
from someone who ought to know: there is nothing more calami-
tous in the world than failure. Stay away from mathematics!'

'But that's not what I asked you,' Fulvio protested.

'. . . even though it all began so promisingly . . . Mama always
picked me up from school, and then we went to the theatre, had
lunch in the canteen, and after that the rehearsals began. I was
allowed to stay in the theatre all afternoon, yards up above the
stage, in the rigging loft with the stagehands. That's where I did
my homework too, on the narrow iron bridge, while Mama
rehearsed her roles. Mama as High Priestess, "*in mia man alfin tu
sei*", over and over again, and in the mean time I did my geometry homework . . . Mama as Carmen, or Tosca, or Aida, and in the
mean time I did my algebra homework. Gino, the chief rigger of
the City Theatre in Trieste, creased like an ancient trawlerman,
helped me. Since that time, music and mathematics have been
inextricably knotted together for me. Gino enthused me for mathematics, do you understand? He served for decades as second or
third steersman on various freighters and rust-buckets, before he
joined the theatre . . . He understood mathematics, he had a feeling for it, as for a living creature. I wanted to be like Gino when I
grew up! And in his afternoons off, he took me up into the Karst
with him, up the steep mountain roads on his rattling motorbike.

Gino pulled trout out of the streams with just his bare hands. Then we would light a little fire, and roast them on spits . . .

'It was he, too, who passed on to me his passion for Descartes, whom he described to me as the greatest genius who ever lived. And so Descartes became my hero too . . . I still know whole passages of his treatise, *Method for the correct use of the understanding, and the finding of truth in science*, off by heart. Against the advice of many of my colleagues, I made Descartes' geometry the basis for my own investigations . . . I wanted to help Descartes make a comeback. I had fallen for him, that was my mistake. Do you know what happened to him at the end of his life? You don't? That Queen Christina of Sweden invited him to her court in Stockholm? That she forced him, who was used to sleeping in late, to get up at five in the morning, to give her private tuition? That at the age of fifty-three, he was compelled to make the journey from his apartments in the French Embassy to the royal palace, on foot, in winter, every morning, and that he quickly came down with the pneumonia he died of nine days later, on 11 February 1650? You hadn't heard the story? . . . It borders on the miraculous that I didn't come down with pneumonia myself when I was in the forest! The number of times it rained, you have no idea. And how ice-cold it sometimes got in the early mornings . . .!'

The two apprentices sighed with relief: the Milan train pulled into the station on time. On the way from the waiting room to the platform, Tigor said, 'It's a shame I have to leave now! Ever since I can remember, I've been looking for friendship! I always suffer from these departures! And I haven't even told you how my adventure in the forest came to an end! On the seventh day, this morning in fact, or should I say yesterday, as it's now past midnight, my exhaustion was so grave that my life was on the point of draining heavily into the ground, if I hadn't decided to oppose death with the last strength in my body. I feel reborn, can you understand that? Reborn!' And he took his leave of the two apprentices as warmly as if they'd been the best friends he had in the world. As the train got under way, he hurried over to a window, opened it and waved as long as he could still see them. 'Thousand thanks for your hospitality!' he called, but they couldn't hear.

Fulvio and Sergio were left shaking their heads. It was the first time they had ever been in such close contact with anyone who was manifestly disturbed. They were too drained to laugh at him now, but several times they repeated his sentence: 'It's a shame I have to leave now!' As they parted at the bus stop, they determined to demand a hefty overtime bonus for the evening.

In slanting, heavy rain, Tigor rode through the night, thoroughly shaken about. He sat on a rock-hard wooden bench. On the threshold of the twenty-first century, there were still trains from bygone ages. A young family sat down opposite him, even though the train was largely empty. The baby was sleeping in its mother's arms. The father explained he hadn't been able to find any employment at home, and had therefore moved to Milan, where for the past year he had been working in a glass and mirror factory.

Tigor remembered Lucina's slim body, felt, as not for a long time, how passionately he had desired to possess her. Twice a week he had been allowed to call for her at the gate of her parents' house. He took her to the standing places at the Teatro Communale, didn't reveal that the celebrated Marthe Bohm was his mother; wanted, for the first time in his seventeen years, to be more than just the son of the famous singer who was the talk of the town. Was forward enough (while Mama was singing her bravura roles) to kiss Lucina. When his beloved one day learned the truth, she was so offended that Tigor was unable to placate her; she was too hurt by what she saw as his deception. Lucina finished school without seeing her admirer again. He didn't know what had become of her. He still remembered Mama's duet with the hunter in Act Three of *The Flying Dutchman*, note for note, syllable for syllable, and hummed both parts to himself. During Erik's cavatina, 'Will you not this day remember', the lofty gates at the back of the stage had opened, to reveal a view of the sea and the port of Trieste; there, in the dusk, beyond the blocked-off port road, were the wooden mock-ups of the many-masted sailing-ships of Daland and the Dutchman. And Mother cried, before throwing herself into the deep, 'Praise the commands of your angel! / Here I stand – yours to my dying breath!' He saw the Dutchman's ship subsiding in the last light of the day, saw the curtain fall, heard the applause erupt.

He missed his big warm bed. I miss my apartment so much, thought Tigor, the record player beside the lofty bed, the *Encyclopaedia Britannica* close by, the original editions of Descartes and Newton, Euler and Monge, the pale colours of their bindings, that had always greeted his eye in the instant of his awakening. The curved walls, the delicate cracks in the ceiling, 11,144 Walnut Street.

I miss my friends in the suburbs, thought Tigor, how peaceful and beautiful it is in Ashbourne and Erdenheim, the old stone houses in their gardens, the tall beech trees and tended shrubberies. I miss my students too, he admitted to himself: how will Abraham react when he hears that I've failed to return? How could I leave without letting him know? Everything is floating around in my head in such a disorderly way.

The infant had woken up in its mother's arms, now it was yelling so loud as though there was no comfort anywhere in the world. The parents, sitting facing Tigor, covered it with kisses, from its hairless skull to its plump pink knees. The father wouldn't let it go back to sleep. The mother laughed aloud. Kicked and punched the man to punish him, finally slapped him, he didn't mind, as though pleased by the blows. With his big hands, stroked and tickled the tiny soles of his newborn infant's feet, as it finally calmed itself.

Tigor knew then what his next step would have to be.

Odéon

Not only did Arnold Bohm kiss the soles of his nephew's feet and tickle them, he would spend hours massaging them, when the boy was teething or had a stomach ache, a throat infection or measles: every part of the body seemed to correspond to a certain point on the feet which only the uncle seemed to know. Arnold, who always wore polka-dot bow ties, was in the habit of travelling by train several times a year to Trieste, the city of his birth. He and his sisters Marthe and Viola were members of the German-speaking minority in the port city, the children of a wealthy coffee importer, highly regarded throughout the Dual Monarchy of Austria–Hungary, and his wife Emmy, who came from a humble background in Vienna.

Now, Arnold never came with gifts concealed in his steamer trunks, but the mere presence of the little man was a gift to the child. The uncle was as old as the century. If people asked him how old he was, he would reply, 'Look at the calendar.' He lived in Paris, where Tigor was allowed to visit him in the summer. Mama accompanied her son as far as Venice, and from there he travelled on alone, in the sleeping car, feeling very grown-up. Arnold would meet him the following morning, at the Gare de Lyon. Even so, Tigor liked it better when his uncle came to them, and slept in the nursery of the apartment at 25 Viale XX Settembre.

The feeling of having his little feet gripped in his uncle's soft, warm hands! No touch had ever seemed so loving to him in later life. And yet, when he moved to Philadelphia, he had lost touch with his uncle. He began at university. His visits to Europe became rarer. He did not write frequently. And yet, when he did, he would always get back a sheet of airmail paper, covered with single-spaced typing. The century grew older. It was ten years since Tigor had last seen Arnold.

'I'm a *toro miura*, an Andalusian fighting bull!' Arnold Bohm called from his bedroom, to himself and his nephew. 'I have occasional outbursts of rage, but I blame them on my digestion. Mind you, the odd stomach ache isn't too high a price to pay,' he said, pulling a soiled green dressing gown over his stocky, grey- and white-haired body, 'for a life like mine.'

For two weeks now, Tigor had been staying at 56 rue Monsieur le Prince, in the third storey of a dilapidated building – the staircase was in an especially parlous state – which smelled of dogshit and fresh bread, a mixture that Tigor remembered from his childhood. Arnold had moved in here before the war, when the building had been a hotel, the Medicis, and Bohm, then a young and ambitious theatre director, had rented a couple of tiny rooms under the roof. During the war, he kept his head down, joined none of the three armies that had conscripted him, and steered clear of the Resistance, whose leaders had also tried to recruit him. Then, when the Medicis was broken up into flats in the fifties and he had made a substantial fortune as a property agent, he purchased the third floor and the attic of the building. In his two original rooms he stored his life story, all the letters and papers and miscellaneous items (he referred to such things as 'impedimenta') that had accreted over the years. A third attic room was inhabited by Agueda from Caracas who, for the past forty years, had been Bohm's maid. For some time now, she had talked of returning home to her sisters and her ancient mother, but Arnold had so far always succeeded in persuading her to stay.

'Your memory can't be as good as your grandfather's, God rest him, otherwise you would remember how many times I've told you what an important day today, the fourteenth of October, is in all of our calendars,' Bohm declared, during Agueda's elaborately prepared noon breakfast. He tore the yard-long loaf of bloating white bread into pieces, and spread them with half an inch of fresh farm butter.

'That was the birthday my father shared with his older brother. They always celebrated it together at home. On the morning of 14 October 1911, your grandmother started feeling contractions, and she cried bitterly and wailed, "I'm giving birth already, I'm going to have a seven-month baby!" – whereupon my uncle just laughed. He was cross with your grandmother in any case, because she hadn't wanted to have your mother: among other

30

things she jumped off the table in order to try and lose the baby. (Just like your mother didn't want to have *you* either, not for anything, and was later overjoyed that she had!) Later, your grandmother was terribly contrite, even though she continued to say to anyone who would listen: didn't the little girl turn out to be ugly! That made us indignant, because we all thought Marthe was enchantingly pretty and lively, we introduced her to our friends when she was just three, even at that age she sang Friulian folk songs by heart, and danced to them. But what you're doing in the family is a mystery to me! None of us has ever busied himself with such improper things as you. Snowflake constant? What's that supposed to mean? Do you remember, when you were four, saying: "I'm so peculiar!" I felt sorry for you then, because you didn't have any siblings. You haven't exactly turned out cheerful, no one could accuse you of that . . . But being pretty isn't enough on its own, my dear Jakob . . .'

Agueda came in to clear the table, but disappeared when she saw the men still seated in the kitchen. She was ten years younger than Bohm, and always wore black skirts and blouses over her small, shapeless form. In the weeks since his arrival, Tigor had barely exchanged a single sentence with her, except for one evening a week ago now. That had been on his fortieth birthday: Agueda had baked a carrot cake for him, and asked him, as she was going to bed, whether he had enjoyed it. But when he ran into her afterwards, in the rooms and corridors of the apartment, she always succeeded in silently vanishing into another room. When he pursued her, or addressed her directly, Agueda would often run off upstairs, and lock herself in her room.

'. . . I've been a little concerned of late,' said Arnold, 'my Agueda's got very absent-minded. Stands there with hands spread, and can't remember what she was doing. Even forgets perfectly routine things she must have done hundreds of times. Before you got here, she would occasionally fly in like a Fury and threaten to leave for Venezuela immediately. Between you and me, I must confess I wonder whether she's still capable of travelling anywhere on her own . . . But she's looked after me for thirty-three years, and I feel a grave responsibility for her. It seems to me we complement one another: with her, it's the brain that's enfeebled, while with me it's my hearing and my eyesight that

31

are going. It's a race against time . . . By the way, yesterday, you must have popped out somewhere, I had a chat with Barbara. All you need to do now is go to her and tell her all about it, say it was your childhood dream, she won't understand right away, so just try and explain it to her, and there probably won't be any further obstacles. I must say, I find the whole business somewhat eccentric ("strangesome", as my father used to put it), but there we are, I suppose you know what you're doing . . .'

Tigor inclined over the hunched figure of his old relation, kissed him on the brow, stroked his hair, breathed in the acrid smells that emanated from the old man, especially from his dressing gown.

Not far from Arnold's house was a street corner that Tigor, from childhood, had always been particularly fond of. He felt at home there. The rue Vaugirard met the rue Medicis at the place Paul Claudel. On one side of the little square, you entered the Parc du Luxembourg, and walked past the Senate building to the shallow pond, where you could hire toy sailing boats. On the other side was the stage entrance to the majestic, sandstone-coloured, pyramid-roofed edifice of the Théâtre National de l'Odéon.

From his eighth year, Tigor had often visited this theatre with his uncle. The performances he had witnessed there were like dreams to him. When they were over, he had always gone backstage where, following the première, Arnold had paid his endless calls to the half-naked actors and actresses. The boy saw his reflection reflected in suites of mirrors, saw himself raise and lower his head ad infinitum, thrust his hand up in the air, and had it wave back at him thousandfold. Bohm's little nephew was hugged and squeezed, had his cheeks pinched, by Cleopatra and the Misanthrope, by Joan of Arc and Othello. They raved about his mother's celebrity and style. Similar things had befallen him, admittedly, backstage at the Opera in Trieste, but there was the big difference that the Odéon put on plays, and that the perfumes and eaux de toilette worn here were far more costly than their Triestine counterparts. When Tigor was asked what he wanted to be when he grew up, he would always reply, 'Rigging master at a big theatre.' 'Rigging master?' and they turned away, with furrowed brow.

'Mother's birthday, the fourteenth of October! And she's been dead for almost a whole year now,' Tigor thought, as he made his way across the place Paul Claudel, unmindful of the traffic which poured past him from all four directions. In the two weeks since he'd been in Paris, he had managed to calm down a little. He had got himself a new passport in Milan, and then crept off to a hotel to sleep. Bought shaving gear, clothes, a watch and a radio. Four days after leaving the plant room, he boarded the night train from Milan to Paris. Arnold was there to meet him at the Gare de Lyon, just as he had been twenty-five and thirty years ago.

A couple of days ago, he had sent a letter to the chef at Il Veneto, apologizing for his behaviour, which had astonished himself most of all, and thanking Giorgio Santini once again for his kindness and forbearance. In a postscript he added, 'I'm actually a very shy person . . .' Sergio and Fulvio were each sent a silk tie, from the best tie shop in the city, Charvet, off the place Vendôme.

He dived out of the glare into the cool, dark theatre. The Senegalese porter, sporting his Stetson as ever, let him pass, as though taking him for a member of the ensemble. 'When I'm gone,' Mama had predicted, 'you will want to scrape me out of the ground. You hear? Scrape me out of the ground!' Tigor felt a shudder down his spine as the word 'scrape' went through his mind. He only realized he was standing in Barbara Hathaway's little office when she greeted him in the dialect of the American South. Mrs Hathaway was the closest associate of the theatre manager, a Triestine by birth, who spent most of the year in Milan, where he had taken over the running of another theatre. Arnold knew Signor Stresa's family, his deceased father who had been the insurance consultant of a coffee import–export firm in Trieste. Stresa's mother, however, had been Arnold's first love.

'What a great man your uncle is,' said Barbara, 'we all love him dearly here. I've been your uncle's friend for years, you know. What a *child*!' she exclaimed, 'do you think he'll *ever* grow up?'

Tigor could see the cemetery with his mother's rough-hewn gravestone. On the occasion of his last visit to the Cimitero Santa Anna, it had taken him more than an hour to locate her grave.

'. . . so will he ever grow up or not, your uncle?' insisted the large-eyed assistant of the theatre manager. Tigor stammered, tried to convey that he wanted to be at the Odéon for a while, not all that long, until he had sorted out some personal issue, unpaid, if need be, the precise nature of the work didn't really matter to him.

Barbara Hathaway assumed she had misunderstood her visitor. He was asking to have a look at the stage he had known so well as a child, he wanted to be allowed to wander about backstage and in the wings, of course, why shouldn't he, and she called up Monsieur Dalland, the theatre's technical director.

'No, no . . . that's not what I meant,' whispered Tigor. He blushed like a fifteen-year-old who had just made a declaration of love to the lady in her red silk designer suit. 'I mean, I'd like to work here. Or just spend some time . . .'

'. . . but . . . you're a professor of mathematics, your uncle tells me. Well . . . aren't you?' Monsieur Dalland turned up, and she sent him away again.

Tigor started work the following week. Mrs Hathaway had had to give her word not to tell anyone too much about their new colleague. She duly promised to guard her secret like the shell its pearl. To Monsieur Dalland, she explained that Tigor was an out-of-work Italian bookkeeper, who had a great love of the theatre, and had come to her begging for a contract as a stagehand. She knew the family, and had agreed to put him on a three-month probationary period.

Dalland, a lofty man, imposing somewhat in the manner of the porter of a five-star hotel, introduced the new arrival onstage. He passed on what he had been told to a motley group of stagehands and props men. No one paid any attention. No one took a closer look at the unknown who was standing around timidly on the cracked oak planking. Tigor scrutinized the many faces for a sign. He found none.

From his gleaming new Weston shoes to his jade tweed jacket and close-shaven tanned cheeks, nothing about Tigor accorded with his new surroundings. Since his arrival in Paris, he had bought himself new clothes almost every day, acquiring forty pairs of worsted socks, which he changed several times a day. Ever since coming down from the forest, he showered and bathed incessantly, continually felt sweaty or dirty, itchy, afraid of infection.

In the next week, Treplyov's *Masha* was going into rehearsal, the revival of a production that had been extremely successful in the past season's repertoire. At the back of the bare stage, a score of men were engaged in putting together a summer forest from hundreds of metal branches and thousands of cloth leaves. Transferred from the plant room to a man-made wood, Tigor inhaled the cool, sweetish smells of timber, rope and mould. Galaxies of dust swirled through the cathedral-high space, stinging his eyes. He looked up at the rigging loft. A disorderly mass of ropes and wires hung down from the flies. Above them, swags of tulle were secured, looking like the huge sails of old clipper ships. 'Gino! Can you hear me?' Tigor thought, summoning the rigging master of the Teatro Verdi, erstwhile steersman of a long-scrapped steamer. 'Gino, please watch me!'

The workers stank of sweat, their breath of brandy and beer. They talked in scraps of language, like the gobbets a zookeeper tosses his big cats. Fragments that were incomprehensible to Tigor, even though he thought he had a mastery of French. He studied the men's clothes: the younger ones wore garish synthetics and rubber and polyester trainers, the older ones had on dark-blue cotton overalls like car mechanics. Big hammers, yellow-and-green spirit levels and collapsible foot-rules dangled from wide belts. Some had veritable tool-kits hanging off them, like bandoliers full of weapons.

Once the summer forest had been set up, the stagehands began to tie tall rushes into thick bundles. The rushes were lying in the auditorium, scattered on the sacking that had been laid over the red plush seating for the last couple of months, during which the Odéon had been dark. On his own initiative, Tigor tied up some bundles of rushes, and inserted them in little metal holders in the floor. He helped carry a leaky wooden rowing boat up onto the stage, and moor it among the rushes. He wanted to snip tinfoil into strips like the other workers, to make the reflectors that would give the illusion of lakewater between rushes and wood. No one thought to offer him a knife or pair of scissors.

'A small hotel, yeah? All night long a couple are kept awake by the noise from next door: one, two, three . . . oof!' began one of the older men, in broad Provençal dialect. He was resting both hands

on a broom handle, so as not to lose his balance. 'One, two, three
. . . oof!' he repeated. '. . . the couple are thinking: God, they've
been at it all night! The next morning, imagine their surprise
when they clap eyes on their neighbours: they're a pair of
midgets. So our couple ask the midget couple: you must have had
a good time last night? Not a bit of it, the midgets reply, we spent
the whole night trying (one, two, three) to get up onto the bed!'
He doubled up with laughter. But, apart from him, and Tigor,
who forced a chuckle, no one laughed.

The hammering and sawing all round had come to an end.
They were alone on stage, in the middle of the bundles of reeds.
Only when the overhead lights were switched off, did Tigor real-
ize that the shift was over. It was a few minutes after midnight.

Then he remained standing in Arnold's hot room, listened to
his snoring for a long time. Opened the curtains a crack to look at
the apartment on the other side of the courtyard. An old couple
lived there, they had no curtains, no blinds, so one could always
see into their domain, only a few yards away from Arnold's bedroom. They went to bed as soon as it was evening, and rose when
it got light. Their power had been disconnected years ago. They
had set some wooden crates on their shallow little balcony, where
they grew tomatoes, lettuces and basil plants, the bulk of what
they needed to live on.

What a peculiar calling, thought Tigor. To step into darkness on a
fresh, cloudless autumn morning. To spend the day like a coal
miner, in the womb of the earth, not returning to the surface till
long after dark. He descended, under the stage, into neon-lit
workshops and storage rooms. Ventilation shafts droned quietly,
as in the belly of an enormous ocean-going liner. On his quest for
friendship, he penetrated down to the fourth and lowest subterranean stratum. Reached a longish chamber with bare brick walls
like a wine cellar, full of welding gear, metal rods and rusty
hooks. No one had yet shown up for work, Tigor was early. There
was an old page of a calendar on the wall, May 1948, showing
Ava Gardner in a black lace negligee, gazing crookedly into an
oval mirror. One of the floor bricks had the figure 1783 burned
into it, the year the Théâtre de l'Odéon was built. Tigor made
himself promise not to abuse the two dates for endless, pointless

mental calculations. But went on to spend the morning accompanied by ever-changing combinations of figures.

A winter wood was being assembled up on stage, consisting of bare boughs, blackened mulched leaves and grey styrofoam snow. That would replace the summer foliage in the final act. 'They couldn't make it up onto the bed!' the man with the midget joke called out to Tigor the moment he set foot on the stage. '. . . One, two, three . . . oof!' he kept sniggering, until Monsieur Dalland appeared out of nowhere, and taking the props man, who was a good twenty years older than he was, by the hand like a child, led him out into the daylight.

Metal cables were lowered from the rigging lofts, and made fast to the four corners of the big square of summer wood. As the great weight was then slowly, centimetre by centimetre, hauled up into the air to the creaking of winches and pulleys, Tigor yearned to go up with it under the roof of the Odéon, among the thousands of hawsers and cables. But was then too timid to ask to go up, nor did he want to ask Mrs Hathaway for a further favour.

A few days passed, when a pale, blond, long-faced man addressed him. He was always sitting in the wings, tinkering with a wind machine. It was needed for the storm at the end of the second act, to produce a sudden gust that, following the amplified roll of the thunder-sheet, would set the newspaper lying by the lake shore whirling through the air. The man invited Tigor to accompany him to his regular eating-place, in the nearby rue Racine. Where in Italy did Tigor come from? He hesitated briefly, and then told him the truth. The stagehand introduced himself: Rudolf was his name, born in the port city of Rijeka, or Fiume, as was. It was just the other side of the border, in Yugoslavia, but not at all far from Trieste.

'You've made a bad miscalculation. Your clothes are completely wrong,' Rudolf explained to his compatriot, addressing him in Friulian dialect. 'How can you turn up for work in a ritzy outfit like that! My friend, the stage isn't a diplomatic reception!' He himself was wearing ancient tracksuit bottoms and a sweaty singlet. They sat under the faded colour photograph of a wedding party in a Venetian gondola. 'Where do you get hold of such stuff in the first place? Your moss-coloured tweed, today's is even fancier than yesterday's. Besides, I don't know why, but green is

37

taboo in the theatre. And people don't go around whistling either. OK, that's not so bad, but if you want to last the course with us you're going to have to dress differently. Completely differently! Also you need a first name, you can't run around under a surname, and always silent like a mummy, I have to agree with Philippe about that. Philippe's the deputy stage manager, the young bearded guy, used to be a policeman some place in the Dordogne, he has quite a tongue on him when he drinks. Which is most of the time, so watch yourself. He's really taken against you. Calls you the spy who's come back from the grave, because you're so piss-elegant and you never talk.'

Rudolf enthused about the tumbledown opera house in Fiume, where he had spent eleven years as a stagehand. He had the impression they had indeed often talked about a Triestine singer by the name of Marthe Bohm, he had never heard her sing, but she enjoyed a great reputation. As they were leaving the restaurant, Tigor had casually let slip her name, without giving away the fact of their relationship. Even with Rudolf, he kept up the act of the unfortunate bookkeeper with a small insurance company in Trieste that had lately gone bust. Only of his father's side of the family did he give a truthful account: the man who had started off as a simple dock labourer, and had gone on to be the senior union representative at the same firm, which was based in the naval dockyards of Monfalcone, outside Trieste. He had died seventeen years ago, from a congenital heart weakness. It would be good for me, thought Tigor, if I could confide in Rudolf and spill out everything that's happened to me, in the weeks since my flight from the conference . . .

'So that's what it is. Your clothes are those of a dandified bookkeeper from Trieste! And now get *rid* of them!' insisted the stagehand. As if on cue, the pale, lanky waiter was so clumsy pouring the wine that he upset the carafe, and Tigor's shirt and trousers were drenched in a theatrical bloodbath.

'One thing I beg of you: don't talk to me about the theatre!' Arnold was stretched out on the broken-down chaise longue when his nephew came home. He gazed up at the ceiling, listening to news on the BBC, which ever since the war had been his preferred station. 'I want no more to do with the theatre. It's a putrid world. I collaborated with Kokoschka on his *Orpheus* in 1922, I knew Kortner and Piscator and Felsenstein and Reinhardt and worked with them, they were my friends. They were my enemies. Take a look up in the attic, I've saved all their letters. I've no more interest in them, they're cotton-wool ghosts and cardboard!' The little short-wave receiver stayed perched on his chest, he didn't turn it off.

'I want no more to do with the theatre. It's a dumping ground for failed lives. What have I got to show for my time in it? A provincial celeb: in 1929 in Kiel I got to direct Hebbel's *Magdalena* or whatever that wretched play was called, and that was about the size of it. The following year, a production of some totally unknown piece by Pirandello, can't even remember the name of it. A total failure. Both the play and my production. And then the touring productions, in Bolzano, in Brixen, in Innsbruck! I had la Bleibtreu as my leading lady once! My parents saw Sonnenthal, though he was past his best. I've seen Moissi myself, what about that. I hated his singing Hamlet. Still, he was wonderful in *Night Asylum* and *Living Dead*. Theatre! A Babel of lies from the stalls to the gods! Half my life I've sacrificed to it, and that's enough for me. But then you come along, you move in here, twenty years I haven't seen you, only heard about you, Oh, Professor this, Professor that, and what do you go and do to me? You join the theatre! As a stagehand! I can't believe it!' Tigor began, 'I . . .' but his relative had already cut him off.

'What's that? You'd better speak up, I don't have my hearing aid in when I'm listening to the radio . . . Mind you don't say anything about the theatre!' White flecks of foam collected in the corners of the old man's mouth, and Tigor, while he felt disgusted, didn't dare tell him. 'When I was two and a half, I broke a leg playing ball. As soon as I was better, my Aunt Selly, who was an actress, insisted that we join them at Bad Freienwalde, where she was performing in the open-air theatre festival in *Sunken Bell*. I sat in the front row, and called out "Aunt Selly, Aunt Selly!" You can imagine what happened after that. On stage and in the auditorium. That was my first contact with the theatre . . . In the winter garden, I remember being very scared of wasps that were buzzing round a copper cake cloche. My aunt was sitting in a wicker chair, wearing an enormous straw hat, with a white silk veil with green polka dots tied round her chin and hat – singing nursery songs. But her voice was so tuneless and off-key, it still hurts me to think of it. She adored your mother and me. And when she hugged us, we cried, which of course made her furious with us . . . In 1914, she was already a pacifist, bold enough to protest vociferously against the glorification of war, which made things sticky for the whole family . . . Who can blame her, what with two sons at the Front! Alfons, who was especially loyal to the Emperor, would probably have been too old to be called up, so he volunteered. Fetched up in a kite-balloon detachment, only instead of anchoring his balloon with the rope, he found himself being dragged aloft by it, across woods and fields . . . I remember Aunt Selly . . . chasing me . . . round the table . . . I took an orange . . . out of the fruit bowl . . .'

Arnold had dropped off. There was a bout of klaxoning from the little street outside, people were queuing for the late screening of *Phantom of the Opera* in the local cinema. Tigor took the radio from the sleeping man's grasp, still caught the high voice of a radio actress: 'Yes, I *am* ready to do battle here.'

Tigor didn't actually go out and buy the cheapest and ugliest clothing he could find, but he did buy a shirt and trousers and socks and shoes that he would never have chosen for himself, had he not been following Rudolf's advice. He arrived late for work. No one noticed him, no one spoke to him. He looked for his new friend. From Monsieur Dalland he learned that he had called in sick that morning. There wasn't a telephone number for him, possibly he wasn't on the phone. Nor did anyone at the theatre have an address for him.

Tigor walked up and down the aisles of the auditorium, climbed through the circles, up to the topmost balconies and boxes, stood among angel statues and crossed masks. The silent expanse of velvet was as tempting as a rocky abyss. The taut groundsheets looked like the rescue blankets that firemen might hold. Tigor could feel himself leaping into the void. And slowly made his way back down to ground level.

The curving passages harboured spotlights of all types and sizes. Tigor touched their grillwork and glass and their metal hulls, stroked them as if they were alive. Pascal watched him, a young man with greying close-cropped hair. 'I've told the others as much. There's something fishy about you.' But his tone sounded not unfriendly. 'Maybe the union's put you on to us. To listen in to what we're saying. Or maybe you're from some secret service, snooping on our director. You write stuff down the whole time, and don't even bother to conceal the fact. What do you write? Show me! You don't want me to see?'

Tigor sidled past him, along the wall.

Early one evening at the end of October, the first rehearsal for the revival of Treplyov's *Masha* began. Andrei Arseniev hugged the actors and actresses, he kissed all the participants, even asked the two walk-ons how they and their families had been keeping since last season's run, when the production had been mounted for the first time. For his part, told stories about Hollywood, where he'd spent the past four months, directing a feature film. To the stagehands and the rigging men, the director had not a syllable to say.

Arseniev, whose father had written the words to the Soviet anthem in the twenties, glorifying Joseph Stalin, had made his name in the West as a film director. In his previous film, quite a remarkable piece of work, he had cast a Hollywood star as a Russian scientist, a character Tigor recognized as being based on the mathematician P. S. Morozov, whom he had revered from his student days. Though given a rigorously atheistic upbringing by his father, a loyal C.P.I. member, Tigor had always felt a spiritual exaltation at Morozov's ideas. Among his prize possessions was a copy of a lecture Morozov had given in 1964 at Moscow University, some passages of which he even knew by heart. 'At first sight, mathematics may appear to be the product of the separate endeavours of numerous individual scientists, all of them pursuing their own researches in their own continents and their own historical periods,' ran one of them. 'However, on closer examination of the history of mathematics, its innate logical development will be found to resemble the work of a single mind, developing its ideas quite systematically, while achieving its ends using a whole spectrum of different human identities. Comparing the work of the most diverse mathematicians, working completely independently of one another, but often reaching strikingly similar conclusions, it's impossible not to believe that their results are the product of a single source of inspiration. What a mysterious field of endeavour mathematics has been over the millennia! It must be more than mere coincidence, mathematics must have a meaning, a goal . . .'

For the first time since the conference in Trieste, Tigor regretted his action. He imagined the little group of his students, not knowing what had become of him. He heard Abraham addressing them, saying he should be treated as a missing person, they had to find out whether Tigor was even still alive. For the first time since the moment of his flight, he thought longingly of teaching; he felt how much he missed the science of the infinite, the world of figures and symbols, the measurement of volume, line and area. He felt the pressure of a warm hand on his shoulder. Was someone shaking him? It was Monsieur Dalland shaking him, having called him several times while he stared into space, as though sleeping with open eyes. 'Would you be kind enough to vacate the stage for us, *mon cher*,' Dalland requested mildly. 'Then the rehearsals can begin.' They laughed at Tigor in the wings.

Arseniev chortled. Called from the director's desk: 'OK, are we ready?' How Tigor longed to discuss Morozov's ideas with him! He called himself to order. But who condemned him to go on playing his part? He left the stage, not knowing where to go.

'You can do the props today,' Pascal hissed at him. 'For the first scene they need strawberries, cigars and milk. You can remember that, can't you?' He took him down to the stagehands' day-room, one storey underground. No one had even betrayed to Tigor the existence of this room where they spent the greater part of the working day. The tiled floor was encrusted with dirt and cigarette stubs. There was a smell of damp washcloths. A little blackboard had a list of what props needed to be freshly bought: cigars from Panther, asters, rye bread and honey. Daily, before start of rehearsals, a fresh carp. Next to a hotplate lay a bloodied stuffed hawk, with wings outspread. The metal lockers where the workers hung their street clothes had wrestling posters plastered over them, showing men in clinches dripping with sweat.

'What's he doing here?' came the indignant voice of Philippe, the bearded stagehand and former policeman. He was addressing Pascal, ignoring Tigor. From a wood-framed loudspeaker by the door came the first lines of Treplyov's drama, Sergei's cautious wooing of Masha. No one in the day-room paid any attention to it. An ancient black-and-white TV set was switched on, bringing news of a water polo competition, plus the efforts of a couple of hammer throwers in the final eliminator.

Tigor carried the strawberries, the cigars and the milk onto the stage. Then stopped in a side exit, watching every movement and response of the young actress playing Masha. Was shocked when she offered Sergei, the young blacksmith, the cigars Tigor had handed her only minutes before, in the half-dark, unable to see her eyes. Even as a boy, it had always given him a thrill before the curtain rose when he was allowed to touch props his mother would handle during a performance. Often Mama would not allow him to touch a particular knife or handkerchief or laurel wreath. But when she relented, Tigor felt he was touching the stuff of dreams.

Arseniev clapped his hands. He jumped up on stage, broke the concentration of Masha and Sergei, they took their chance encounter by the lakeside over again, from the top. Another handclap. From the top. Interruption, repetition, and so on. Monsieur Vial, the old actor who played Gagarin, was waiting in the wings for his cue, listening, hopping from foot to foot. Masha ran straight towards Tigor, stopped an arm's length in front of him, on the cusp between illusion and reality. She drank from a large square plastic bottle of water, oblivious of anyone. Tigor observed the moment of her recrossing the frontier: the actress tumbling back into the dream.

He handed Monsieur Vial, now about to go on, the strawberries and the container of milk, the old man muttered something indistinct back at him. He stepped out into the world of illusion, transformed into the landowner, Gagarin, driving Masha and Sergei away from his private shore.

'Aren't actors the worst?' Pascal whispered, behind Tigor. 'That's what we all think anyway. Hope you do too.'

Tigor made no reply. Looked up at the rigging loft once more. There, all was silence and darkness.

That night, Tigor rang Abraham for the first time. He stood in a glass phone box on the corner of the rue Vaugirard and the rue de

Tournon, opposite the main gate to the Senate building, and only a few steps from the back of the theatre. For some days now, he'd been carrying a shrink-wrapped pack of ten phonecards with him, but kept putting off the moment. Felt palpitations when he tapped out the Philadelphia code and then Abraham's number. Tigor could remember almost every number he had ever called, even once. The beeping of the digits echoed on their satellite journey, and constituted a nursery melody. 'Yeah?!' cried an angry old woman's voice, 'yagatthawrongnamba!' – he had misdialled, he dialled again, his heart was racing, the combination this time was less melodious. 'Yeah?!' replied Abraham, and Tigor could not speak.

'It's me . . .' he finally whispered.

'I don't believe this – I thought you was dead!' yelled Abraham, and Tigor was once again unable to speak for several seconds before, gaining in speed, volume and fluency, he described his movements, from the moment of his flight from the conference in Trieste, till he moved in with Arnold Bohm. He did not dare admit that he was presently working as a stagehand in a theatre.

'I gotta chill, Jesus, Tigerman!' groaned the most gifted basketball player at the University of Pennsylvania, specialist subject, Eulerian mechanics, who had taken up sports in order to pay his way through college. 'But why?!' he said again, 'what made you do this, motherfucker!? I think I'm goin' nuts, man!'

Tigerman had no idea how to make Abraham understand what had happened to him. He mentioned an Italian mathematician by the name of Mildor, a proponent of Mandelbrot's chaos theory. At the conference, Mildor had put forward the results of his own snowflake research, and done it so convincingly that Tigor's idea of a constant had finally become untenable. This blow was not, in and of itself, sufficient cause for the wanderings he'd since embarked on, but he did feel he'd started on a new chapter of his life, whose coordinates he hadn't yet managed to establish, let alone plumb.

'. . . plumb?! Plum crazy!' Abraham's voice cracked with disgust. 'I don't believe this!' What had possessed Tigor to run away from his responsibilities as teacher, mentor and friend? He couldn't use his personal disappointment to justify abandoning

44

people who were depending on him. 'Do you know what you've done? Paris, you idiot! Are you on vacation, or what? I don't geddit! You'd better be on the plane tomorrow, motherfucker, there are twenty-five students here with half-finished dissertations waiting for you, you must have lost it! And if you don't show, I swear I'll come and get you myself!' And Abraham hung up.

The condemned man stood in the phone box, a court of law as lofty and wide as the canopy of night. His eye lit on the Café de Tournon opposite, with the narrow two-storey hotel above it. Tigor was as rattled by his favourite student's attitude towards him as he had been by his teachers when he'd been at school. Abraham's number was engaged. Was he already ringing round his fellow students, organizing his trip to Europe? Tigor kept redialling the number, envisioning his bed at home, throned among books, his sunny apartment at 11,144 Walnut Street. After thirty minutes, still the engaged tone, after fifty.

When he finally got through, he admitted that what he had done was inexcusable. 'I beg you, please, all of you, forgive me. I love you all! You're all I have.'

'Drop the sentimental crap!'

'I can't explain it . . . it feels like there's something pulling me . . . I don't know what it is, and God knows I can't control it. But I have to find out what it is. You can understand that, can't you?'

'Crap.'

'. . . it's like a problem, a paradox I'm trying to solve. It's hard work, but I'm slowly groping towards a conclusion . . .'

'Grope away, greaseball!'

'I just sense that something . . .'

'Sure, the Great God Manitou . . .'

'Forgive me, please forgive me.'

Abraham refused to accept his apology.

'Give me time,' begged Tigor, 'to understand what's happened to me . . . Till the end of the year . . .'

'Absolutely not!'

He inserted a new phonecard, heard the familiar yowling sirens of Philadelphia's finest and throbbing rap music: Abraham lived in the ground floor of a high-rise in Darby Boro, having moved there after the sub-let he'd lived in previously was burned

45

down. A police helicopter had dropped incendiary bombs on the roof of the adjacent building, which was suspected of being the headquarters of an anarchist group. The fire, fed by the explosives that had indeed been stockpiled on the roof, spread so rapidly that, within a few minutes, the entire block of Osage Avenue, between 60th and 61st, was in flames.

The atmosphere in Darby Boro was getting more and more like a civil war, said Abraham, there were shootings every day. 'I'm less afraid of a nuclear holocaust than I am of the impending civil war. That'll eclipse everything we've seen in our lifetimes. We blacks will get the thick end of it . . . It will make Vietnam look like a tea party. And there's Tigor, safely in Europe, plucking harebells at sunrise. Wants to find himself! Well, good . . .' Tigor had forgotten to put in a further card.

He rang back, dripping sweat. Offered his friend the use of his apartment on Walnut Street. There was a spare set of keys in the bottom desk drawer. Abraham laughed: 'You talking about your office? Theodore Seville is in there now, Course 8,118, Calculations of Infinity in Leibniz and Newton. No idea what they've done with your stuff, it's probably in administration somewhere. God knows who's living in your apartment. That's what you get for always wanting to be alone . . . I'm warning you, Tigerman. All right, I'll give you a period of grace. But you watch yourself if you're not back in two weeks! I'll take your case to the President. And then I'm coming to get you, in person. Don't worry, I'll get the money together . . .'

Marie-Antoinette and her two brothers, who resembled her not at all, but each other very much, were having a game of football in a little area in front of the Odéon that was chained off from traffic. The eight-year old girl had her hair braided in narrow cornrows and stiff dreadlocks. She was bossing the two boys around, telling them how she wanted the ball passed to her. When Tigor hurried past them, the girl pursued him, kept her brow pressed against his hip, gazed up at him and grinned. He stroked the back of her neck.

Men and women of all ages would meet at all hours of the day and night in the tiny porter's lodge of her father, the Senegalese theatre porter. Napoleon, unlit cigar in the corner of his mouth,

Stetson pulled low over his forehead, fancied himself as a casting agent. He promised his visitors small parts in films by up-and-coming African directors, who hoped to realize their projects in Paris, and were just waiting for the financing to come together. As Tigor passed the tiny hut on his way in to work, a stately woman was singing a folksong from her homeland, Burkina Faso. She had on a yellow wool robe that was far too tight for her, her body swayed in all directions, and she banged her broad hips against the wooden panelling of the lodge. Napoleon clapped his hands, kept time, drove her on with eyes half-closed. A petite woman in a scarlet blouse and a rather earnest-seeming Zairean journalist, whom the porter had promised a part as a hijacker weeks ago already, were waiting their turn.

Tigor descended into the cool dark subterranean, redolent of hemp, dust and wood, on this particular Sunday bringing with him a bottle of anisette for his colleagues. 'That's not going to do you much good at this stage,' commented Pascal, 'maybe if you'd done it your first day. Not any more.' The four stagehands present were playing poker dice for astoundingly high stakes. They emptied the bottle in next to no time. On the flickering TV was a game show for hairdryers and fridges. The little loudspeaker beside the iron door was relaying the quarrel scene between Gagarin and Sergei, in which the landowner pulled a carp out of the young blacksmith's pocket to prove he was a poacher. It wasn't till the third summons that Tigor became aware of the stage manager's voice. 'Are you deaf down there? Why isn't anyone paying attention? What's keeping the fish?' By now everyone was staring at the loudspeaker.

Philippe was the first to respond: 'Well, new guy, where is it?' The men grinned.

Pascal explained: 'You see, you're the new guy, so it's your job. You should've taken care of it.'

The rehearsals were interrupted. The stage manager, an obscure but not totally unknown rock'n'roll singer from the fifties, who still wore the greasy sideburns that were characteristic of the period and a personal hallmark of his own at all times, appeared in the day-room. Jacques threatened to take the matter up with the management, it had been known for weeks that a fresh carp was required for each day of rehearsals. He demanded his fish, which none of the stagehands was able to produce.

'Why does the Russky need a fresh carp to rehearse with every day, that's just tyranny,' remarked Pascal, 'besides, it's the new guy's job to organize the props . . .'

Tigor found himself knocking on the kitchen door of the renowned fish restaurant, Méditerranée, formerly a regular haunt of Jean Cocteau and Albert Schweitzer, on the crescent-shaped place de l'Odéon, and when a cook answered the door, he begged to be let in. Tigor was asked, a little irritably, what he wanted. After delicate negotiations that lasted for some minutes (success or failure of Treplyov's *Masha* was in the balance, he begged the *chef de cuisine* to make an exception, and sell him a fish over the counter), Tigor ended up purchasing a six-and-a-half-pound carp that cost 375 francs, which he paid for out of his own pocket.

He waved to the three siblings, still playing in the middle of the square, carried the fish on to the stage and stood in the limelight. Arseniev called out effusive words of appreciation, Tigor was unable to make him out in the glare of the lights. He saw himself sitting in a maroon pedal boat on Lake Garda, trailing a length of brown string behind him, with a large hook tied to the end of it, and a chunk of bread impaled on the hook. Wanted to watch bar-bels, tench and pike suffocating, but never caught so much as a single fish. When he was a boy, there was nothing that excited him as much as the thought of watching fish die. 'I'll have to take you to the doctor if that doesn't get any better!' Mama had often threatened him, he remembered . . .

He handed the carp to the young actor who was playing Sergei. The rehearsal carried on.

A few moments later, the director called a halt. The recent interruption had broken his concentration on the scene, he claimed. Arseniev didn't want to go back to it until the middle of next week at the earliest. Pascal made a grab for the fish, carried the booty down to the basement room, and the poker-dice play-ers had themselves a feast.

A lighting rehearsal began instead. Arseniev planned to light Masha's confession and the priest's judgement in the third act in a different way to last season's production. As though steered by an invisible hand, elements of a bourgeois drawing room gently floated down from the flies. Heavy pieces of furniture, a samovar and the grandfather clock that Sergei would hide behind, were brought in from the wings. No one could quite remember where the sofa, the armchairs and the desk had been stood in the spring production. Avangard Leontiev, the assistant director, had been refused a visa this time, without any reason having been given. Tigor marked the new positions of the furniture with pieces of sticky tape which glimmered faintly in the dark. He slithered around on his knees, at the feet of the director and Mlle de Bayser, who was playing Masha. If Abraham could see me now, thought Tigor, scrabbling around in the dirt, doing someone else's bidding!

'So how are things goin', Professor?' called Mrs Hathaway in her over-exuberant screech. She was surrounded by great stacks of books and periodicals, had to stand up to look her visitor in the eye. He looked pale, decided the deputy manageress, was he quite well? She referred to the lack of oxygen in the city, which got so bad at times that one could only take shallow breaths, otherwise one would pass out.

'I should like to put in a request,' he interrupted, his heart was pounding as though he'd just completed a marathon, 'I should like to be transferred as soon as possible to the flies.' He was afraid, he continued, that the stage was not the right place for him. He begged Barbara Hathaway's forgiveness for making difficulties, but, under the present conditions, he was not able to give of his best as a stagehand.

'Are you a masochist, by any chance? I do tend to see romance in noble failure . . . but aren't you going a little too far?' She didn't understand, said Barbara, why he hadn't presented his wish to her far sooner, or even at the time of their first conversation? He was free to do as he pleased at this theatre: 'No strings attached!' He could come and go as he liked. She stepped right up to him: 'Doing what others tell you leads to death.' In fact, nothing was easier than to find room for him '*aux cintres*, as they say in French', someone there had recently gone on leave, and Monsieur Dalland would offer no objection either. She paid him for the twenty-two days he had done as a stagehand. The money was roughly what the University of Pennsylvania paid him for a single class.

'But first you should take a few days off,' Mrs Hathaway counselled. 'Pardon my saying so, but you do look awful. And then when you come back to us, honey, you can go straight to heaven.'

On the place Paul Claudel, Tigor got into the first free taxi that came his way. He asked the driver to head north-west through the city, and then take the most direct route to the Atlantic coast. It didn't really matter what place they came to. 'I need to breathe. You understand? Breathe!' The driver, who was from Asia, didn't have a clue what he was talking about. He drove off, but admitted he had no idea where he was supposed to be taking him. Tigor therefore directed him, from the back seat, via the boulevards Montparnasse and Garibaldi, and the avenue Émile Zola, through the Porte d'Auteuil. It was getting dark as they hit the motorway.

'Heaven be thanked!' exclaimed Bohm, when Tigor called from a petrol station to let him know that he would be away for the next two or three days, 'have you found a woman for yourself at last, then!? Not to have a woman of your own at the age of forty, it's high time. Also, you should not leave out of account the joys of becoming a grandfather one day. Who doesn't have a child is an incomplete person. The only woman I truly loved had an unsuitable background. When my father saw her envelopes, he simply said: she doesn't have much money. I invited her to Trieste to present her to my parents. And then I caught fright. Took her to Venice instead. When I had to do military service for a year, it was the end for us. I regret it still . . .'

Tigor attempted to bring the conversation to a close. Arnold ignored him: 'Today at the doctor's I idiotically fell in love with one of the assistants, I swear it was none of my doing! Well, it'll pass . . . You put off the visit to the doctor's from week to week, sit and wait for five hours, spend hours more on the torture rack, in all kinds of impossible positions, and the upshot is they tell you everything's normal, and they give you three new medicines to try anyway. Today the doctor examined me for two hours, blew up my stomach to the size of a football, pushed a laser round my insides while his assistant kneaded my belly. Then he wrote a page-long diagnosis, and when I finally dared to speak, all the pair of them said was: "Your health is excellent . . . " An aunt of mine, a dreadfully querulous and forever grumbling

woman, who was never short of admirers on account of her figure and her posture, used to say that going to the doctor the
whole time is a sign of untidiness! (She didn't go herself until her
eightieth year.) The only disagreeable thing is that my doctor, a
very good man, stopped taking money from me some time ago.
That's most irregular, in Paris! And then I go and fall in love with
his assistant . . . don't let me forget that being in love is never an
unmixed blessing. It's always taken up too much of my time, and
too much nervous energy . . .'

As it grew dark outside, and the light inside the taxi crumbled
away to grains of gloom, the taxi driver talked about the tyrant
who had plunged his fertile country into destruction. The dicta-
tor's stooges had taken Monsieur Khoy's father and buried him
alive, forced the son to watch. The father had remained utterly
rigid, and once he couldn't move his arms and legs any more, the
son observed tears pouring down his father's cheeks in great
streams. He himself had managed to slip away from the soldiers
during a brief moment of inattention. He had hidden in the jungle, lived alone in the forest, in constant dread of being picked up
by the despot's murder squads. At the time, he had lived entirely
on leaves, roots and small animals. Did Tigor know that every
living being was edible, even beetles, wasps, cockroaches? His
fare made no reply. To avoid becoming the prey of some wild
animal, he had built himself a type of nest in the broad trunk of a
tree. From time to time he had managed to kill a rabbit, but his
only way of making fire had been by rubbing sticks together for
hours on end. It was impossible to convey how arduous that was.
Once, he had drunk water from a nearby pond without first boiling it, and he had become so ill, he thought he was going to die.
His body was shaken by burning fevers. Monsieur Khoy told
how with the last of his strength he had forced himself to eat the
bitterest grasses and flowers he could find. Finally, through that
bitterness, he had succeeded in overcoming his near-fatal disease.
He had spent an entire year in the jungle, said the taxi driver, as
they crossed the city of Amiens, before he heard human voices for
the first time. His initial reaction was to suppose he was halluci-
nating, but the men's voices came ever nearer, until he recognized them as the voices of some men from his own village. When

he climbed down out of his tree-nest, the men had failed to recognize him, so emaciated had he become, and so heavily bearded. They had been afraid of him, and only gradually, by reciting the names of their family members to them, and his own, had he managed to win their trust. Then he learned that there was a lull in the fighting, and he had returned to civilization. He had been living in Europe now for some months, having previously spent several years in a holding camp, added Monsieur Khoy.

Tigor felt ashamed to tell the Cambodian about his time in the plant room. 'I tried to live in the woods myself once,' he told him, '. . . admittedly, it was by choice . . .' Thereupon the taxi driver had turned round and fixed him with a look of such pity, surprise and reproach, that Tigor blushed furiously, and said nothing more.

The breeze now carried the smell of the sea. Shortly before midnight, they reached the coastal town of Le Crotoy. Tigor had them stop at the very first hotel in town. It was called Aux Saumons d'Or, and in the dim neon lighting of the Atlantic promenade, it looked especially small and wind-skewed.

'You should stay here for the night,' urged Tigor, 'I'll pay for you!'

He had to return to his family, replied Monsieur Khoy, there wasn't a telephone at home, and his wife was probably worried about him by now. Before he set off, he wrote down the number of his employer on a paper napkin. 'I can always find my way to the airports,' he said, 'if you need to go to the airports, call the office.'

A black-haired woman was kneeling on the floor of the lobby, back towards Tigor. The packing paper on which she was painting with vigorous brushstrokes curled over carpets, armchairs and tables. '. . . *juste une minute, s'il vous plaît* . . . ' she said in a British accent. Her voice was low and pleasant. The dim overhead lighting reminded Tigor of the station waiting room at Belluno. He saw himself surrounded by screams of fear and fat female bodies, contorted in agony, and sexless skeleton-like torture victims whose limbs had been torn from their trunks. Smiling cherub faces reflected in pools of blood. The painter turned to look at her visitor.

'. . . Lucina?!' breathed Tigor, startled by the resemblance, after decades, to his childhood sweetheart. Her small body, high forehead, brown eyes, even the dark fluff on the top lip.

'. . . *je suis Christine. On m'appelle CriCri.*' The long, pale fingers! CriCri had inherited the Aux Saumons d'Or inn from her aunt, who had died three months before, in Cleveland, at the age of exactly a hundred. She had every intention of running it herself, she said (now speaking English with her visitor), only since she'd come to take it over, she hadn't had more than two or three visitors a week. Even though there was, to her mind, no more beautiful place to make a holiday anywhere on the Atlantic coast. She had had to let the staff go, and had performed the most essential chambermaid and cooking duties herself. Having been born in Tehran, and grown up in England, France and the United States, she had always looked on the planet as her home. She didn't, said CriCri, feel frontiers or distances to be any obstacle. The flight to Boston that she had to take several times a year, to visit her mother, actually took a lot less long, even on an ordinary scheduled airliner, than the drive from Paris or Le Crotoy to Bordeaux, where her father lived. 'My father!' she exclaimed. 'He owned the three largest cinemas in Persia. I was picked up from school every day in the heat and the incredible glare. The chauffeur took the limousine through crowds of chador-wearing market women and enormous flocks of lambs, and dropped me in front of the cinema. It was cool and shady, and the matinée would be in progress . . . That way, at the age of ten or eleven, I got to see the works of the Italian neo-realists . . .'

Tigor remarked that he was extremely tired, and would be glad to go up to his room now.

'Your room?! A kingdom for a bed!? I'm painting Prometheus tonight. You can be my model, if you like. I've been painting uninterruptedly for three weeks, it's simply pouring out of me! Promethean, son of the Titans, destiny has brought you to me, you're my portion, bring light and fire into my house!'

Tigor asked a little more forcefully to be allowed to withdraw. He said he would happily be at her disposal all the next day, but not tonight, he felt a little unwell. '. . . I'm asleep on my feet,' he added.

'Fortunate man, to have the gift of sleep! Nothing I long for

53

more than to be able to sleep! I can manage two or three hours sometimes, if I shower my legs with ice-cold water first. But when I drink alcohol, I get awful, awful fits of coughing. I'll make us some good tea, come in my kitchen, Prometheus, teacher of mankind, you whom Zeus chained to a peak in the Caucasus!'

Tigor wanted to get out, anywhere, he would walk for miles through the night and sleep rough, he thought. Just run away somewhere! And he stayed with the woman, trailed after her into her kitchen lit by candles and oil lamps. A short circuit had blacked out the rear part of the house.

'. . . what happened to her, your Lucina?' asked CriCri. 'Don't be shocked, I heard you say her name just now, under your breath, drink your nice tea, then we can go and look for a room for you, if you still want that. You know, you remind me of someone I haven't thought about in a long time too, even though you don't really look very like him. He was called Brian, and he taught me the beliefs of the Narrinyieri. The men of that tribe spend the first night after the death of a family member with their head resting on the dead body, so that their dream can reveal to them the identity of the sorcerer who brought about the death of their loved one. Brian gave me this little talisman, here, take a look at it, he brought it back for me from his visit to the Narrinyieri.'

She showed him her large collection of idols on her broad kitchen dresser. The shadows of the various stone and earthenware figures flickered up and down along the kitchen walls, finger-long women with many arms, Pan figurines with two or three towering erections, Satyrs and Molochs and a couple of garish plastic robots with protruding pincer-arms. 'These two are my house gods: during the storms four days ago, the water was almost up to the front door. I prayed to Strong and Weak to keep the floods at bay. Moments later, the wind and the hail abated, and the waves receded from my house.'

The tea tasted like a decoction of algae. They sat in the half-light of an open fire, next to the dresser with the idols. The guest felt all at once vigorous and alert. CriCri led him back to the lobby, and asked him to sit for her again. Then, to his amazement, he undressed as she requested. The painter laid each one of his garments over her arm like a silk veil, and spread them out across

54

one of the breakfast tables. With a thick rope she tied his wrists to one of the ceiling beams. Tigor resolved on no account to let himself be tied – and then let himself be tied, without resistance, without protest.

CriCri knelt down and started working on a carpet-sized piece of brown packing paper. Tigor happened to mention that he had been born in Trieste, inquired of Christine whether she had ever been there. 'Don't tell me anything about yourself,' she replied. 'I don't want to know your life story. The fact that you're here is enough for me.' Suddenly crept up to him. Kissed his feet, his knees, his thighs. He gave her a gentle nudge. She withdrew, went back to work, as though nothing had happened.

He asked if he could listen to the radio. Since childhood, the world news gave him a feeling of security, even reports of disasters filled him with a kind of momentary serenity.

'I don't have a radio' replied CriCri, without looking up. 'We can play records from my aunt's collection. I never listen to news. Recently my father was shocked because I didn't know who Benazir Bhutto was. Do you know? I know very little about the history of this century, beyond the two world wars. My cousin died in Vietnam, during the so-called Tet Offensive. I still listened to news then . . . I do know that this century is more vicious than any other in history. That's all you need to know about it.'

They listened to fado music, mild keening female voices, singing about the pain and transience of love, that had the effect of lulling Tigor to sleep. CriCri untied him, gave him more tea. He let himself be tied again, neither fighter nor victim.

At five in the morning, CriCri led her visitor, naked as he was, up to the second floor, and gave him a room with a sea view. The horsehair mattress resembled a wave-trough. Tigor slept deeply, awoke at noon, felt exhausted as after an anaesthetic. He felt hairy legs pressed against his own. He didn't move, pretended still to be asleep.

'I lay down beside you at seven o'clock,' CriCri whispered. 'You said glacier to me, or something like that, but you didn't wake up. And I slept so beautifully! Four or five hours! Sensational!' She cuddled up to him again. He leapt out of bed.

In the afternoon, they took a stroll through town. It was a cool, windy day, with scudding clouds. The locals didn't greet CriCri, a few of them crossed the road when they saw her coming. They had done the same with Christine's aunt when she was running the Aux Saumons d'Or and spent the summers here. The wind was so strong that the seagulls couldn't gain any altitude, and sat on the sandbanks looking tousled. The beach with its blue-and-white cabins had been high and dry for many years. The sea had retreated so far, that even when the tide was in, you couldn't hear the surf. The tight little streets of villas at the edge of the town reminded Tigor of a cemetery's grid-like layout. Every little house a gravestone.

CriCri told him a folk legend that went around in Le Crotoy: the towns of Lyonesse and Ys had once been swallowed up by a spring tide, and no one had survived the catastrophe. But on stormy days you could hear their cathedral bells tolling from the depths of the sea. Tigor straight away imagined he could hear the faraway ringing.

CriCri's only friend in Le Crotoy, one Madame Berck, sat perched on a headland overlooking the bay, near the statue of Joan of Arc. The old lady subsisted on crusts of bread and sugar lumps that she pulled out of a distressed plastic handbag. She had a huge telescope, made in 1881, that she rented out to passers-by and visitors at the rate of five francs for three minutes. Children paid the full price. Tigor trained it on a light aeroplane, struggling against a gust, discerned the grim expression on the pilot's face. Then he swung it over in the direction of a monument at the edge of the town. A snow-white angel was lying on its belly, with its great wings stretched out.

'. . . I would so have liked to move to Paris,' Madame Berck was saying. 'I'm very envious of you, young man. But I hear you're not going to be staying there much longer?' Tigor replied that he was perfectly happy there, and wasn't thinking of leaving it any time soon. 'Even so,' replied Madame Berck. 'Even so.'

When they returned to the small hotel in the early evening, CriCri showed her visitor the progress she had made on her Prometheus painting. A black shape squatted by the side of a tangle of strands of colours. 'The eagle', explained CriCri, 'that Zeus sent to eat your liver. Every day the liver grew back to its full extent. And every night came the eagle, every night.' She invited

Tigor to select one of the mass of paintings for himself. She asked him to stay two more days, so that she could bring the new work to completion. '. . . But of course you can stay much longer than that if you want to, it's entirely up to you . . .'

By the church on the way back, he had studied the local bus timetable, firmly resolved to leave.

'. . . you're hurting me,' said CriCri, on hearing he wanted to return to Paris. 'Don't turn away from me now. Why are you doing this to me? Say it's not true. You're not leaving me, are you? Don't do this to me.'

He kissed her on the brow. Then she went with him to the bus stop. Put her arms around him to say goodbye, pressed a small parcel wrapped in tinfoil into his hands. 'Because you didn't want to take a painting of mine, I'd like to give you this,' she said.

The bus drove off. Tigor followed the small waving form of the hotel owner as long as he could in the dusk. He unwrapped the parcel. It was the tiny Narrinyieri talisman, half fish, half woman.

Marie-Antoinette was playing with an old doll from the props department that was as big as she was. She crouched on the stone floor, in the Odéon's marble foyer, resting her temple against Tigor's leg. He stroked her braided hair. She asked him where he had been for the last two days, said she had been worried about him. 'There were so many things I wanted to ask you!' she said. 'When it rains, why doesn't everything flood? My Papa says you understand more about that than he does . . .'

When Tigor climbed up to the flies for the first time, the girl accompanied him with her platinum-blonde doll. On the fourth floor there was a half-open grey metal door, which, according to Marie-Antoinette, was the entrance to the *cintriers'* bridge, and that was as far as Napoleon allowed her to go, everything beyond that was off limits.

He cautiously shuffled forwards, twenty yards above the stage, until he felt the railing. There, dozens of numbered ropes were fastened to a broad wooden post, as though securing a mighty ocean liner to a quay. By and by, Tigor's eyes got used to the dark. There were hundreds upon hundreds of sisal and metal ropes, the sinews and arteries of the theatre's body, running along the walls from attic to basement. Here, Tigor decided, among the cogwheels and giant winches, the rope drums and pulleys, was his home, in the kingdom of swaying cast-iron counterweights, on whose draw-beams dangled forests, cathedral naves, miners' houses and dancehalls.

On the stage below, Masha went looking for the officer Andrei, persuaded him to go to Moscow with her. From up in the flies, their heads appeared tiny. Tigor listened to their love scene, which Arseniev ran through many times. The actors tried to remember their movements and steps from the previous season, the moments before their kiss, the seconds following, when they flung themselves to the ground.

A tall muscular man emerged on to the rigging-loft bridge, Tigor couldn't make him out distinctly in the darkness. 'We always get sent the idiots,' muttered the unknown man. 'The administration do it every time: anyone who doesn't make the grade downstairs, gets sent up here to us . . .'

He led Tigor into an attic room a few paces away from the bridge. It said CINTRIERS in black letters on the door. Sunlight fell through a skylight. The angled ceiling was so low that you had to duck everywhere you went in the room. Standing upright was only possible in front of the small window. If you got up on tiptoe and looked down, you could see the pond in the Jardins du Luxembourg and the children playing around it. The room contained nothing beyond a table, a few chairs, a washbasin, a broken mirror and two blue metal lockers.

Using an immersion heater, the rigging man made some fresh mint tea, which he served to Tigor in a tiny glass with a painted flower pattern on it. '. . . the thing with Italy might be true,' he said, having listened to Tigor's account of his failure as a book-keeper. 'But why don't you tell me the truth? I'm happy to tell you the truth, because I am Hakim. Some call me the waterfall, because I am a waterfall of speaking and storytelling. My name means "the wise one". I am still only a stagehand, whereas my brothers have become very wealthy. They hate their origins. They deny their origins. But even after living here for forty years, my mother hardly speaks the language. And I? Was born here, and can hardly understand my mother tongue. Mother never taught it to me, it was as though she wanted to keep it to herself. On the rare occasions when I visit her, it is all we can do to exchange a sentence or two. Sometimes we manage a brief conversation in the backslang of the Parisian suburbs, which reverses every word, so "femme" becomes "meuff", "laisse tomber" is "lesbe-ton" and so on, that suburban dialect is called "Verlen", which comes from "l'envers", do you understand? You keep staring at me like an idiot. It would be so good for you to trust me! To tell me what brought you here! Just now I'm reading Freud, the sixth volume of the collected edition, *Civilisation and its Discontents*. I tell my colleagues what I'm reading, but the name Freud doesn't mean anything to them. Except maybe Karim, who probably thinks he's the president of some country. You know Freud?'

Hakim had a great beak-like nose, light olive skin, shaggy hair and a look that was both challenging and mild. A thick book stuck out of his trouser-pocket, *Leon l'Africain* by Amin Maalouf. And he was very keen on Tahar Ben Jalloun. He read a great deal in the long hours of waiting that were part and parcel of one's life as a rigging worker, said Hakim. 'You see, we up here are the thinkers, while down there, where you used to be, there are the barbarians who hate the theatre, who don't know the first thing about the theatre, that's how unenlightened they are! Down there, with the plebs, they booze and watch TV, while up here we read and play chess.' There was no contact between rigging workers and stagehands in the Odéon, he explained, on the contrary, they deliberately kept out of each other's way, cultivating the tradition of a century-old, highly stylized enmity. 'They wouldn't dream of coming up here, nor would any of us ever go down there. Neither for personal, nor for work-related reasons. We each pass the other in the corridor, as though they didn't exist. When I first came here, ten years ago, I thought theatre was about fraternity, and we would all be like brothers. And what is the reality?'

The voice of the stage manager came through the little loud-speaker over the sink, Jacques called for a set-change. '. . . that'll be your first assignment,' determined Hakim, 'Étienne's held up as usual, Karim and Yves have got the day off . . . Now remember, hold the rope as tenderly as you would a woman. Or more. Please, never forget that!'

They tugged on hard cords whose ends were fixed to the officers' mess set. Draw-beams carried aloft the worn carpet, the wall cabinets with the files, and the back walls of the barrack room with its crossed sabres and rifles. Tigor, exerting himself to the utmost, copied Hakim's movements, and hoped the rigging man wouldn't notice just how onerous he found the work. The rough hemp tore open his palms, they burned horribly. He started to sweat, and managed the last few movements in a kind of trance.

'Stop!' cried Hakim, and again: 'Stop!' Tigor had overlooked a mark and pulled the wall-cabinet display too high, so that it was about to crash into the barrel loft. Hakim quickly turned the rope-brakes, metal wheels which looked like the kind of equipment that might be found in the engine room of a ship. 'This is all sailor's work!' he panted, 'two, three hundred years ago, almost all the Parisian stagehands were sailors who couldn't be at sea any more, either it was loved ones or the longing to feel solid ground under their feet again. And the knots we use up in the rigging loft, they're the same knots that sailors use today . . . And it's the same fiddling around with hemp and weights, block and tackle, in the theatre! And you know we don't use words like cord, rope and cable, we talk about "hemp" or "cordage". It's an old sailors' superstition!'

'. . . it's an old sailors' superstition!' cried Étienne, as though singing a sea shanty. He was a lean, fair-haired man with deep hollows in his cheeks. Now, with the help of winches and pulleys, the three of them lowered several tons of winter forest down to the depths. The stagehands secured the set to the boards.

'I've been a sailor for years, next year I'm going to dive for pearls in the China Sea,' said Étienne, once they were seated in the attic room again. 'What do you do? You a poet? A romantic? Someone like Gerard de Nerval, who calls to us: *"Maintenant je vais voyager pour voir si mes rêves existent"*?' He spoke so quickly, it was hard to follow what he was saying. '. . . I've worked at forty-five different professions, most recently I was a glove and sock seller, travelling around from market to market, before that I sold chestnuts in the Luxembourg, I've had experience of hunger in my life, I tell you there's nothing worse, nothing in the world hurts more than real hunger . . . In spite of that, there's a principle you have to follow: you have to dream a hundred dreams, so that ten of them might come true . . .'

They were called out to the rigging bridge twice more, before

60

Arseniev called a halt to the rehearsals late at night. 'Every day we have to be here at noon sharp,' said Hakim, 'and if there are no rehearsals we sit here till the evening show without anything to do. Of course the floorhands are roaring drunk by then. And we're completely exhausted . . .' Up until twenty years ago, many of the stagehands had had to stay in the theatre overnight too. They had hardly gone out into the outside world at all. At fifty-five they were let go, but they never got attuned to reality, and died within a few months, or a year or two at the most.

'Every one of us who works up here does it because he can't get by outside,' said Étienne, 'we are all living in a kind of dream world. Almost everyone lives on his own. You don't get home before midnight, you never get the weekend off, the Sunday matinée is at three o'clock, so we have to be in the theatre first thing. Show me a happily married stagehand. They don't exist.'

'Hanging around doing nothing interspersed with periods of crazy overwork. That's our life,' added Hakim. They were standing outside Napoleon's empty lodge, under the arcades where the stage workers parked their heavy motorbikes, and where, at any time of day or night, there was a reek of piss from the dossers who set up their cardboard beds here, protected from the sun and rain.

Tigor was unable to shake the hands of his colleagues, because his palms were too badly lacerated. Étienne revved up his big machine. Across the tank in red letters, it said WARBIRD.

Arnold insisted that his nephew lie down on his bed when he got home. He himself squatted on a three-legged stool by the foot of the bed, and took Tigor's clammy feet in his warm hands. Tigor was bathed in sweat. His heart was pounding. He had last experienced the anxiety that accompanied his physical condition when he was looking for a track beside the stream, up in the forest.

'Your feet are swollen! Is it your shoes? Are they too small for you?' asked the old man, pushing his thumbs deep into the tough sole. Tigor felt the pressure right up in his skull. Relief gradually flowed down through his chest, belly and thighs. 'Shoes should be bought in the afternoon, then you can be sure they won't be too small. Your feet are relaxed in the morning, and therefore smaller. Shoes you buy then are liable to pinch your feet. Tight shoes can be agony. Put them on in the morning, and pour methylated spirits over them, then they'll adapt to your foot shape. Nor should you wear the same shoes day after day, try wearing them every other day, then they'll be good as new for a long time . . . There it is, your heart-point, can you feel it? Does it hurt? They really should have operated on your heart defect, of course they should, even if your Mama didn't agree, now it's too late with this kind of congenital defect, at least that's what I assume it is . . . You're not cut out to be a worker, my gold, you have no idea about the working class . . . Your father was from the proletariat, but he left that milieu early on, and worked his way up. But what about you, mama's boy? You will certainly always remain a stranger among workers. Your relationship with the working class can only be disastrous. You're completely incapable of the most innocent dealing with a worker . . . And quite apart from all that, working is too strenuous for you. For the time being, I suppose I have to call you my favourite relative – I'm not spoilt for choice – and so I have to look after you. If you want my advice: enough is enough. You're not cut out for that sailor's life.'

It wasn't until that evening, six weeks after his arrival in Paris, that Tigor told his uncle about what had happened to him in Trieste, recounted his stay in the plant room, and only now did he talk to him about the dilemma he was in, and ask him for advice.

'You idiot!' cried Bohm, 'you could have died! You could have starved . . . What was it all in aid of? Back to nature? What were you trying to prove? That a man can survive in the wilderness? And they needed *you* for that?! I've never heard of anything so half-baked. But they tell me you often get that: a brilliant mathematician who can't tie his own shoelaces. That's my villainous sister Viola for you! Surely she must have seen what a state you were in when you fetched up! Instead of looking after you, and pampering you for a while! Sends you to your death . . . She's cheated and stolen from all of us, that crooked piece of work, together with her husband. And probably still sweet as you like, and calls you my sugar lump! . . . I thought you wanted to make a name for yourself? And you think you'll make a name for yourself in the woods and as a rigging man? It's time you woke up, my boy! You're forty years old! Tomorrow you call your students, and tell them you're on your way back. Immediately, this *week*! I thought you said you'd got a year's sabbatical? You were just lying to me?!'

He was suspended between heaven and earth, enjoyed the peaceful flight. Repaired, having crawled out of his capsule, the silvery outer skin of his spaceship. Crossed North Africa and the Near East, saw the Caucasus quite distinctly, the Black Sea and the Caspian, made out Mongolia, half covered with clouds. The horizon was a strip of pale blue, above it a darker blue and then a deep and solid blue, broad bands of colour leaking into the black dome of the universe. He adjusted his course slightly as the capsule slowly dipped into the night side of earth, the pale blue becoming orange and then red, and sank in night. Lightning, in the form of tiny diamond pinpricks of light over Japan and the island of Sakhalin. Within minutes the sun was rising again. Within minutes it sank again.

Tigor went around in his dream the whole of the next day as in a padded down coat. Took it up at noon on to the rigging bridge. The previous night, he heard, great pieces of reflecting metal foil had peeled off the broad wooden lintels at the edge of the stage. The only way of reattaching them was to have one of the cintriers lowered to the point in question. Hakim was playing chess with his friend Karim, Étienne refused to get into the flying harness, and Yves gave Tigor precedence: the first job in body harness counted as an initiation rite among the cintriers.

Barefooted Yves, a bearded wood-demon of a man, who had fought as a mercenary in Chad, draped the heavy leather waistcoat over Tigor, secured it with rusty buckles and straps, attached a metal snap hook to the back, at heart height, knotted to the end of a rope. Tigor climbed on to the balustrade, pushed off and hung suspended between heaven and earth. The rope, which Yves slowly paid out, held Tigor aloft and steered him. Reattaching the silver foil presented no difficulty. With his fingertips he touched his reflection, that in convex distortion showed him a small and round image of himself as in a funhouse mirror. Hakim and Karim quit their game for a while, Étienne too stood by the railing, the *cintriers* watched every movement of their rigging recruit. The blue-clad scene shifters and props men looked up at him, and Tigor recognized the swaying man, propped on his broom handle again. He tapped his temple with his finger when he saw Tigor.

In the kitchen that evening, Tigor told his uncle he wanted to spend a little more time at the theatre. 'Let me stay here with you a bit longer,' he pleaded. 'I really can't explain to you why it matters so much to me . . .'

'It's easy to see . . . that you're . . . in some turmoil, young man. And I'm one hundred per cent opposed to your staying here. Even though you can have no idea of how much good it does me, having you around . . . it cuts me to the quick, having to send you packing.'

Tigor inclined his head, smiled winsomely. They were eating cold cuts and scraps of cheese and vegetables. Arnold bolted his, almost without chewing, got spattered with tomato, mustard and beer, went to the fridge for more ham in its greaseproof paper. He pulled off the fatty rind with his fingers, reached for Tigor's hand, talked with his mouth full. Under one condition, he was prepared to tolerate his nephew's rigger's life until the end of the year. He plucked a hair from his nostril and went on: 'You have to inform the university where you are. And above all, you're going to have to ask your college for forgiveness, and ask them how long they're prepared to extend your leave of absence . . . Will you promise me to do that?' Tigor nodded. Even raised the index and middle fingers of his right hand to swear it. If they showed any understanding of his behaviour in Philadelphia, then he, Bohm, while not exactly approving of his young relative's emotional vagaries, would at least be prepared to put up with them a while longer.

'It's lucky for you I'm feeling rather benevolent today,' he said, picking the nails of his right hand with the ring finger of his left. 'A letter came by the afternoon mail from my friend Carlotta Meyerbeer. Next spring, with the permission of my doctors, I mean to take ship to Caracas to visit her, she will turn ninety on the first of May. And that means that Agueda will finally be able to visit her homeland again! Carlotta is still in love with me, even though I've told her she's about fifty-five years too late. But unhappily she married that shit Rolf, a nasty piece of business,

64

probably he was too small and overcompensated. He spent many years living in a remote oil-drilling camp, with a bunch of crude Americans, nothing but whiskey, poker and his pet marmoset. The only contact with the outside world was the small prop plane that brought him back to his wife for a weekend every other week. Our last time together was in 1976, when Carlotta and I travelled back from Caracas to Le Havre together, she had a young girl's figure in her bathing suit, surmounted by an ancient crone's face. She tottered along with a stick, but scooped all the prizes for her dancing on the ship . . . She writes to tell me she still dances by herself a lot, to gramophone records at home. Once she whispered sweet nothings in my ear, and when I looked at her, I swear, her expression was just like my mother's! She's a hypnotist, I tell you. She trained as a doctor, but never practised. Her father was one of the wealthiest men in all Berlin, his textile firm is mentioned in Heinrich Heine. After many years, Rolf died of a terrible illness – and Carlotta and I were in heaven . . . During the thirty-seven years of their marriage, he had forbidden her to talk to another man, or even look at one. She often said to me, "Men've found me irresistible, from when I was eight years old . . . " Do you know why I never married? I was afraid of growing old with another person. Having to watch, year after year, the wrinkles about the eyes getting ever deeper and deeper. Lustre fading, until you can't have any illusions left about the other person . . .' After a silence, he added, '. . . anyway, what I meant to say: don't forget what you promised me!'

For Tigor, the autumn was going by at an alarming rate. He was no nearer to a convincing analysis of his flight from Trieste, or a justification for his dereliction of duty towards his students. However, he did now rule out all possibility of a return to Philadelphia, nor had he kept his promise, he hadn't even contemplated keeping it, he lied to his uncle, claiming he'd been forgiven. According to him, his employers understood that he desired to leave the teaching profession until spring, and had helped himself to a six months' sabbatical.

He had, however, had several telephone conversations with Abraham, promised him to be back at the university by the beginning of next year, at the latest. His favourite student had little confidence left in Tigor, demanded the promise in writing, in the form of a sworn statement, an affidavit, mailed to himself. He in return would remain discreet with the university authorities. He even declared that, following the professor's safe return, he was prepared to play along in a little resurrection charade, according to which the runaway, following a serious climbing accident, had spent some months lying in hospital, in a coma. His papers all having been lost, the hospital administration had been unable to establish the identity of their patient. 'But watch out!' screamed Abraham, 'if you're not back by the first of January! Your apartment's all right, by the way. There aren't really any new tenants staying there . . . Don't worry about that. I've got the keys safe.'

The rigging men now trusted Tigor almost implicitly. They stayed together after work, visiting the cafés in the rue de Rennes and on the place Saint-Sulpice, one of their favourite hangouts was in the rue Bonaparte. They didn't drink alcohol, some of them for religious reasons, others because, as they particularly emphasized, their parents had been alcoholics. Hakim was especially devoted to Tigor, but Karim also was interested in the friendship of the new recruit. Born on the Algerian–Moroccan border, he was a gentle-eyed ladies' man, who each week reported on his latest, strikingly similar love affairs that were sometimes his own invention, sometimes true experiences. He was a regular reader of the best French newspaper, and relayed the news to anyone who would listen, although he tended to get continents and cities, presidents and opposition figures, parties and sects, all hopelessly mixed up. In a little kitchen under the pyramid roof, he prepared exotic vegetarian dishes for his lunch, never thinking to share them with any of the others. Only Tigor was occasionally allowed to taste one of his creations.

Étienne was an admirer of the music groups of the sixties. Their names – The Who, The Troggs, The Animals, The Small Faces, The Kinks – seemed to have magical powers when he said them. He prophesied everlasting celestial fame for the members of these bands. He sang their songs, everyone around, like it or not, was co-opted into an audience for him, he won applause in cafés and on street corners.

Supple, wiry Yves hardly slept. Beginning at six in the morning, he repaired cars in a private garage for no money. He would often talk about his time as a mercenary, cursing the brutality of the human race. The limitless moral degradation of his fellow fighters oppressed him still more than the futility of war per se. With tumid penises, the soldiers in his battalion had gone around butchering their enemies, and cutting the ears off the dead to wear around their own necks as trophies.

Tigor would sometimes spend hours in the darkness of the rigging loft, leaning against the metal railing. He picked up sentences that drifted up from the stage, got to know odd passages of the drama by heart. Waited for the moment at the end of Act Two, when Mademoiselle de Bayser dipped naked in the narrow pool that represented the lake. (From the auditorium, her stripping was barely visible, the beds of rushes were in the way.) Whispering in the dark with his colleagues gave him gooseflesh. He liked it when someone whispered near him, even more when it was himself that he heard whispering.

He clambered up a further flight of narrow metal steps, like a ship's companionway, right under the roof, where hundreds of steel ropes and wheels ran, like being inside a piano as big as a building. The *cintriers* called this rope heaven the soul of the theatre. Yves, who every day polished, greased and painted without any regard to the official working hours, showed Tigor the scribbles and etchings on the walls, left by the soldiers who, in the course of their training, had done duty here as firemen. One such inscription read 'Massacre des Boulevards 3/12/1851', referring to a popular uprising that was bloodily suppressed. Yves also took Tigor up to the roof, where they hunkered down on the lead flashing in front of the pyramid roof and gazed down at the sea of the city beneath. The barefoot man explained that the Odéon had been built in the midst of vineyards: none of the surrounding streets had existed at the time, most of what was to become the sixth arrondissement still consisted of arable land.

Tigor generally ate lunch with Yves, Étienne and Hakim in the restaurant presided over by the deathly pale, lean waiter, who contrived to be at once submissive and impertinent. One day Tigor saw Rudolf in there again. The long-faced man was the only one of the scene shifters who was on terms with the *cintriers*. 'I've looked into it,' said Rudolf, in the Friulian dialect, so that only the Triestine Tigor would understand. 'We aren't stupid in Fiume. Many years ago your father soldered rivets with a cousin of mine in the Monfalcone yard. He treated his workmate badly. And then, purely out of snobbery, he married that same Marthe Bohm you asked me about with such seeming innocence. I'm just surprised she took him . . .'

Tigor laughed: 'You're not the only one.'

Monsieur Ecoffey was often to be found sitting alone at one of the adjacent tables, but never did so much as a word pass between the actor playing the young blacksmith, Sergei, and the rigging men. He had yet to meet an actor, observed Étienne – not exactly quietly – who impressed him as being even half grateful for the work of a *plateautier* or *cintrier*. As he spoke, he picked his ear with a matchstick which he then absent-mindedly proceeded to insert between his teeth, while raking his spaghetti with his fork in his other hand. All actors and actresses behaved as though forests and meadows and entire furnished rooms came down out of the sky at the mere push of a button.

No actor, Yves chimed in, had ever grasped how much effort and sacrifice were necessary to guarantee a single performance that went off without a hitch.

'We're left standing in the dark,' added Hakim, 'while the actors are in the spotlights' beam, collecting the ovations at the end. Has anyone ever put his hands together for us? Have we, the shadow-dwellers, ever been led forth from our darkness, to bow?'

'As for Arseniev – not a clue!' said Yves. 'Knows as much about theatre technology as I do about ophthalmology! It would fit on to a postage stamp. And they're all like that, *messieurs les directeurs*. They don't want to get their distinguished paws dirty! You'd never catch them going backstage! Never mind the rigging loft . . .'

'Did you know', Rudolf addressed Tigor once more, 'that the architect of the opera in Fiume was also responsible for the theatre in Trieste and the Opernhaus in Hamburg? In Hamburg, he got the acoustics wrong, and threw himself off the theatre roof, and was dead on the spot . . .'

After lunch they regularly went on to the Café Petit Suisse, on the corner of the place Paul Claudel and the rue Vaugirard, where politicians from the Senate building opposite were to be seen drinking quantities of red wine from late morning on. Also there every day was Madame Murat, a not unattractive woman with a small mouth and thin lips, no longer in the first flush of youth, who was the senior park warden in the Luxembourg gardens. Hakim, who adored her, listened patiently to all her endless stories of *guigne* and depression, in return for spending a night or two a month with Madame in her ten-square-metre *chambre de bonne* in the rue d'Assas, where she lived with no bath, just a shower-head over the little sink. The large, prettily decorated apartment that she'd inherited in the rue de l'Université had been let out for years to well-heeled American couples, to supplement the meagre wages the municipality paid her. She chewed gum incessantly. Each time she drank a cup of coffee or had something to eat, she took a green pellet of what looked like bronchial catarrh out of her mouth, rolled it around between thumb and forefinger, and stuck it under the table or dropped it in the ashtray. Hakim referred to his friend as 'Madame Murat has her worries,' he introduced her to Tigor, and, in Hakim's absence, the senior park warden would complain instead to him, in that husky, cheerfully agitated old woman's voice of hers.

In the afternoon, Tigor holed up in pit-box number three, which was still all sheeted up, so that it felt like a tent. He crept under the legs of a pair of chairs, stretched out on the scuffed carpet, sleeping no longer than eight minutes, only a catnap like that truly refreshed him. Then sat in the auditorium till the next scene change, to watch the rehearsals. None of the riggers or *plateautiers* had ever been known to do that, didn't know the plays they worked on, at most they were familiar with little snippets of text that came to them via the softly hissing loudspeaker system.

During the protracted periods of waiting, Hakim sometimes led his friend out to the theatre's marble foyer, pulled across the heavy curtains to conceal the sacrilege from the view of the place and rue de l'Odéon, and fetched a portable table-tennis table from one of the storerooms. And there they often played for hours and hours, until Arseniev next decreed a set change.

At the beginning of the New Year, Tigor telephoned Abraham. The student seemed unsurprised that Tigerman had gone back on his word. He merely muttered: 'That's it. I've had it, motherfucker.' He had no intention of keeping their secret any longer either, anyone who cared to listen would get to hear all about Tigor's deceitfulness and lack of character.

When he inquired what Abraham was working on at present, the only answer he received was a rude belch. As though he hadn't heard, he repeated the question. Whereupon the student bellowed through the satellite link: 'I need your help, asshole!' And went on to report, very quietly, about a research project that the Navy had offered to Tigerman's doctoral students: to establish presumptive median values for the tidal variations of the Delaware Bay, close to Philadelphia, for the next twenty-five years. The problem, which at first sight had seemed perfectly capable of solution, no longer seemed so to Abraham and his colleagues.

Tigor took down some provisional data that had been collated by navy mathematicians, noted tidal density and velocity at the two points of Lewes in the state of Delaware, and Cape May in New Jersey, on the opposite side. He locked himself up in his room, having first informed Hakim and the others that he was running a high temperature. Sat hunched over stacks of paper, his hand shaking, he kept snapping off the points of his pencils. He followed a method that his friend, the mathematician and meteorologist Edward Lorenz had devised in the early sixties for global weather forecasting, but also factored in the moon's phases, sunstorms, eclipses of sun and moon, into the second decade of the coming millennium. Also incorporated into his calculations the butterfly effect, by which even the wingbeat of a mother-of-pearl moth in the south of China would affect the weather on the north-eastern seaboard of the United States.

At the end of two days, Tigor was forced to concede that he wasn't equal to the challenge without assistance from a calculating machine (in his career to date, he had used computers only very rarely and with great reluctance). After long hesitation, and in spite of serious reservations – to him, the pioneers of fractal mathematics were also the destroyers of his own line of investigation – he finally decided to apply Mandelbrot's fractal equation

$$D = \lim_{\epsilon \to 0} \left\{ \frac{\mathrm{Ln}(\mathscr{N}(A, \epsilon))}{\mathrm{Ln}(1/\epsilon)} \right\}$$

for the first time. Further, he availed himself of the so-called

Peano curves, named after the Italian mathematician Giuseppe Peano, to see the entirety of the Delaware Bay as 'plane-filling', a procedure that Benoit Mandelbrot had followed himself, particularly in his watershed and river-volume calculation $D \simeq 1.2618$. Tigor moved like a white-water kayak paddler on the flash floods of suddenly emerging data. He thought he should have entrusted himself to the fractal shapes of nature years ago, should have expunged his arrogant disdain for this new branch of mathematics. 'My whole life would have been different. The world is determined by the shapeless and the amorphous, not by regular geometrical structures and constant forces!'

Arnold was concerned for his nephew, often came to his door, from where he heard cooing and gurgling sounds. Was surprised at how rarely Tigor appeared for meals, and how exhausted he looked when he did see him. 'Don't forget', Bohm counselled him, 'to go outside for some fresh air every day. Or do some gymnastics in the morning: ten minutes of exercise at an open window will keep the body fresh and supple. Also you need at least eight hours' sleep, otherwise you'll die before your time. What are you doing in there by yourself?' When he learned that his nephew was grappling with a mathematical problem, he sounded relieved: 'At last something sensible!'

Early on the morning of the fourth day, Tigor mailed off pages of provisional results, giving his address as 176, rue d'Assas, which was where Madame Murat had her *chambre de bonne*.

Later that morning, the exhausted man was handed an express letter by Napoleon which had arrived some days previously, addressed to Monsieur Tigre. In it, CriCri said she wanted to see him again, suggested that Tigor come to Le Crotoy, otherwise (and Tigor read this as a threat) she would look for him in Paris. He had failed to leave her an address, all she knew was that he was working at the Odéon, in some capacity she didn't quite understand. 'Last night, Prometheus,' she wrote in her letter, 'exactly ten weeks after your visit, the kitchen went up in flames. The big table is charcoal. The flames went no further. The embers were crackling till morning. The talisman I gave you was my protection against fire. My life was saved by Strong and Weak.'

Tigor dreaded CriCri's visit, wondered how he might best

avoid her, nevertheless still wanted to see her, decided finally not to reply.

The première of Treplyov's *Masha* took place in mid-March. The day of the show, Étienne had installed a rudimentary sound system in the attic room that played sixties hits at top volume. Two dressers, Françoise and Nectarine, came up to visit, complaining about the moods of Mademoiselle de Bayser, and contrasting them with the warmth and modesty of Madame Praz, who was playing the general's widow. The suicide at the end of Act Four, in Françoise's opinion, was wholly unconvincing, Masha, in Arseniev's interpretation, hardly seemed capable of such an action.

'Suicide? What suicide?' asked Hakim.

And the dresser, only slightly thrown, responded: 'But Masha kills herself at the end, did you not know that, after she gets the farewell note from the officer.'

It was the first Hakim had heard of this turn in Treplyov's masterpiece, and in spite of that he professed his love for all the plays he had ever worked on. Admitted in the same breath that he had never seen any of them, accused himself of being no better than the uncultured *plateautiers*. 'It's because I work up here, and you can't see anything from up here! You hear practically nothing! When they want a set change, the stage manager flashes us a red light!'

'. . . 'cause what confused you was just the nature of my game!' boomed Étienne's sound system.

When Jacques informed them, via intercom, that there was only an hour and a half to go until the beginning of the show, the girls hurried back down to the second floor, laid out the costumes one last time, and helped the actresses dress. Only then did the five young firemen go on their control rounds, and Yves, Hakim and Karim checked that the brake-wheels were screwed tight, the lines secure, and the draw-bolts in place.

Mrs Hathaway conveyed best wishes and break-a-leg on behalf of the theatre manager who had been unable to get away from Milan to see the première, adding a '*merde*' of her own, thought to be lucky in some quarters. 'So you love it up here, in your seventh heaven, is that right?' she called to Tigor, and spat on his left shoulder, as he had always done for Mama, standing on her chair in her dressing room. The theatre, Barbara Hathaway said, was completely sold out, down to the very last tip-up seat. She left behind a dense cloud of fragrant pollen – the men held their noses, as if they were in a pigsty.

Karim had raised the curtain. The performance had begun. The riggers sat idly in their attic room, sipping mint tea. Hakim did an imitation of Madame Murat, who recently, in a voice choked with tears, read aloud the passage from the four-volume standard history of the French Revolution that dealt with the execution of Louis XVI. An event that moved the park warden as much as if she'd witnessed it herself. The way the king's blood spurted out when his head was severed from his trunk! And when it was impaled on a spike, the eyes were still rolling. For days afterwards, the people were still parading the king's head through the streets of the city. Hakim said they hadn't been able to sleep for two nights, with those pictures before their eyes.

Of course it was Louis XIV who had been taken to the guillotine, Karim insisted, and Yves banged the table, he couldn't stand accounts of bloody events, they reminded him of his time as a mercenary. Then he himself went on to give a particularly blood-curdling account of a guerrilla ambush in the plains of Chad that all those present had heard more than once already. Étienne interrupted him, said that when he was a child, he'd used to count up to a hundred as quickly as he could, twenty, thirty, forty times in succession, his record stood at thirty-nine seconds. 'When I was a child,' said Karim, 'I always thought when the train went through a tunnel, all the other people in the compartment could go on reading, but not me . . .' Then, interrupting Karim's sentence, a shrill alarm sounded, like a siren on a warship. The men ran out on to the bridge, into pitch darkness from their cramped neon-lit attic room.

The summer forest had to be hauled up, the officers' room lowered for Act Two. Tigor hauled on the ropes as though his life depended on it, pulling an adventurous proxy version of himself up out of quicksand. Heard whispering next to him, it sounded soothing, saw yellow stone configurations and the kitchen of the Il Veneto, had a sense of the butterfly effect as an endless sequence of prime numbers. I should have made Goldbach's theory that every even number is the sum of two primes my research subject, I should have spent my life investigating the phenomenon of prime numbers, that would have made me happy, 2, 3, 5, 7, 11, 13, 17, 19, 23 and so on and so forth! I would have got to the bottom of those magical numbers that are only divisible by 1 and by themselves! Between 9,999,900 and 10,000,000 there are nine primes, but only two between 10,000,000 and 10,000,100, namely 10,000,019 and 10,000,079 . . . The tangle of prime numbers is hidden in the reeds. In sheaves of reeds give me this day a seaweed taste in my mouth woody and swaying. Cardboard boxes, a pair of iron tongs and a capital-sized halibut were yesterday impounded at the frontier . . .

Two firemen carried Tigor into the *cintriers'* room, Hakim and Karim had already rigged up a provisional bed out of two chairs, on which they laid the unconscious man. Yves dashed off to bring the theatre doctor, who attended each première (along with his wife and their two ugly daughters), to pit-box number three. When Dr Chabanian entered the room, annoyed by the disruption to his evening, he was sure his assistance was too late. He called for a newspaper, which he spread out on the floor, then knelt down on it next to the emergency bed, asked for an account – which he didn't listen to – of the patient's last moments of consciousness, felt for a pulse and couldn't find one, thumbed open Tigor's eyelids and closed them again. He injected him with a powerful circulation booster, though he was quite convinced of the futility of such an exercise. He instructed the men, who had formed a semicircle behind him, to send for an ambulance. Hakim suggested the kiss of life and heart massage, but Dr Chabanian dismissed both suggestions – in his eyes was the illusionless look of experience, he knew this was a hopeless case.

Then, barely audibly, the motionless man began to murmur. Chabanian was startled, knelt down again on Karim's newspaper. 'Mountain chain. Ice caps. Embedded in the glacier wooden splinters, as far as the eye can see,' whispered Tigor. 'On the seventeenth day? In the seventh month? In the six-hundredth year of his life. And through the rocky valley begins the climb. Ahmed the bandit.' (At this point, Tigor groaned loudly and his legs convulsed.) 'And climbing, always climbing, in a south-easterly direction, Massis, mother of the world! Wooden splinters as far as

74

my eye can see.' He opened his eyelids, saw first of all the neon light on the ceiling, didn't know where he was. Recognized Marie-Antoinette who was bending down over him, in spite of Napoleon's interdiction she had run straight up to the rigging room, she had guessed which one of the *cintriers* it was who was in danger. Tigor became aware of Dr Chabanian's outline, still kneeling on the floor. He was struck by how ill and exhausted the man looked, didn't suppose for a moment he was anything other than a doctor.

'Did you enjoy your stay in the land of my forefathers, on the Holy Mountain of my people?' Chabanian asked, got to his feet, smiled wearily and tenderly at Tigor, while the riggers all welcomed their friend back to the living, all wanted to shake him by the hand, like an astronaut returned from a successful mission. 'They've taken our Paradise away from us, it grieves me that I've never even been there!' said the doctor, filling out page after page of prescriptions.

'Forgive me, I . . . don't understand,' Tigor managed to say.

'*Est-il malade?*' asked Marie-Antoinette.

'You must go to a specialist,' said Chabanian. 'You are suffering from an acute cardiac insufficiency. I fear it will be quite some time before you climb the mountain, the Massis, the one we call in our language the Mother of the World, again.'

Tigor sat up, felt his heart beating more stoutly than ever before. 'I've never been there. I don't even know', he said, drew a deep breath, 'exactly where it is.'

'You'll remember, I'm sure,' said the doctor, and handed Tigor the prescriptions. At the same moment, the alarm signal went off, calling the *cintriers* over to the rigging bridge for the second set change.

Arnold Bohm didn't get to hear what had transpired. He was struck only by how irregularly his nephew now went to his work in the theatre, hoped his passion for rigging work was now finally beginning to cool. 'Are you not feeling too well?' he asked him once. 'If you need money, borrow from me if you like, it will only reduce your eventual inheritance. You like to spend money like a millionaire, don't you? Or do you have other worries? The whole world lies before you, you're a conscientious worker, and you will always get by, so long as you don't do silly things. My generation has had a damned hard time of it, by contrast! It was 1949 before I had any experience of normal conditions . . . There's no cause for you to despair. All that counts is determination, stamina, if you want to make your way in life, the particular calling is almost immaterial. Admittedly, having a sunny disposition helps . . .'

Tigor locked himself away in his room, spent nights leafing through the writings of René Descartes, read about light and the solving of the puzzle of the rainbow, read the studies of orbiting theory and much else besides. 'When I make careful considera-tion of the subject,' he read in one place, 'then I fail to find one sin-gle proof that will dependably distinguish waking from dreaming, so much do the two conditions resemble one another, that I become doubtful, and wonder whether even this might not be a dream.' That surprised Tigor, given how much Descartes was at pains to come up with mechanistic explanations for human experience.

He spent whole days in the stagnant attic rooms of his uncle, their corners festooned with black spiders' webs and threads, sat surrounded by cardboard boxes ravened by dust and mould, torn cases and paper and plastic bags stacked up to the ceiling. He came upon old letters and periodicals and uncut newspapers from the forties and fifties. With soot-blackened hands, he pored over a frail leather folder that contained the small bundle of the typed letters he'd written to Bohm himself. 'Dear Uncle,' began one that he'd written eighteen years ago, 'forgive me for not hav-ing been in touch with you for such a long time. This morning I dreamed about you. I dreamed I was living with you, like I did when I was a child, and came and stayed with you in the sum-mers. I stayed with you for two years, I had jobs simultaneously as a park warden in the Luxembourg gardens and as a bookseller in the rue Monsieur le Prince. I have important exams here next week, I wish . . .' He put the letter in his pocket, its contents seemed entirely unfamiliar.

He wandered through the city, bought antiquarian books that he mostly gave to Arnold. He brought back little knick-knacks for Agueda, who didn't thank him. Purchased an etching of a book illustration by Grandville, showing Robinson Crusoe's first encounter with the Negro Friday. He returned often to the cash machine opposite the Opéra, in the rue Scribe. There, the gold-coloured plastic card permitted him to withdraw substantial cash sums at any time from his account in Philadelphia, the account of the prosperous man that, thanks to small and mainly unspectacular research contracts from federal sources, he had become.

He passed through the museums, the markets, the ugly suburbs, found himself in places he'd never been before, parts of the nineteenth and twentieth arrondissements that were like the casbahs of north African cities. He watched lovers and tailed them. If they went into a restaurant, he sat down at a table nearby, if they went to a cinema, he sat down in the row behind. He would sometimes follow them home by bus or Métro, and remain standing a long time in front of the doors they had disappeared into. Every day he walked in the Luxembourg. Strolled past the red grit of the tennis courts, sat amongst children during puppet shows. Watched birds far more alertly than he had ever done in the forest. The pigeons lying flat in the grass reminded Tigor of ruminating cows. He rested his back against the trunk of a huge elm, conducted conversations with a black-feathered, yellow-headed tropical bird that, in a low voice, kept calling out 'Miao! Miao!' to him. It was generally dusk before he left the park, the whistles of the park wardens came from all directions and in all ranges, announcing the impending closure of the park.

One evening, his curious eye lit on the locked display window of a small bookshop that was catty-cornered from the entrance to Bohm's house, but which he had never noticed before. That building, Arnold had told him, had once housed a brothel, and the bar in its basement had played music so loud that he had often lain awake until the not-so-small hours. In the bookshop display was a yellowed colour photograph – curling at the edges – of a geographical formation that consisted of two volcanic craters, the higher of which, a huge mountain, was snow-capped. The shop, without giving a reason, was closed for the next three weeks. Tigor also noted down the titles of two books in the display, Johann Jacob von Parrot's memoir, *Journey to Ararat, Mother of the World*, published in 1834, and *Deluge et arche de Noé*, by André Parrot, published in Paris in 1952. That night, Tigor telephoned Dr Chabanian.

*

They met the following morning in the doctor's gloomy premises on the boulevard Raspail, a suite of large brown rooms, decorated in the steel-and-mahogany style of the thirties. From the corridor, Tigor had glanced into a waiting room hung with heavy curtains – no patients were waiting there. He sniffed floor wax and freshly ground coffee. An elderly male assistant brought them brandy in small crystal glasses. After the welcoming ritual, Tigor asked Chabanian to tell him about the country he had never visited, but of which, as the doctor had informed him, he had spoken in his semi-conscious state. Dr Chabanian poured his guest more brandy, cocked his head a little in the manner of a bird of prey, and fumbled for his first few sentences.

'In your position,' he finally began, 'I would certainly want to track down a signal like that. Something as unusual and distinctive as that doesn't happen every day. Whoever finds must seek, we always said in my family. If what you say is true, and you have never been to my homeland, then I am astonished, very astonished, I must confess. In your position, I would be prepared to give a lot for the solution of this enigmatic paradox (it must be viewed as such, since it is beyond the reach of science). Would you have to make a very great sacrifice? Is your involvement with the theatre a life's work? Do you have a family?' Tigor shook his head. 'In your position, I would travel to Hajastan, which is what we call our country, the Legendary One, at whose heart is the mountain Massis, the biblical Mount Ararat, where Noah's Ark struck land. Formerly, our country stretched from the Mediterranean to the Caspian Sea, and in the north it bordered on the Black Sea. A great power, that broke up in numberless fragments, till it had no territory left to call its own. A race of people that for hundreds of years has been scattered, persecuted, deprived of its rights all over the world. A community of believers that at the beginning of this century fell victim to the first instance of state-sponsored genocide in history, a genocide that is undiminished because every one of us feels the event as though he personally had been its victim.'

Tigor tried to give the impression that the tragedy of this people he had barely heard of touched him in some way. He fixed a spot in front of him, and stared, rather moronically, he thought.

'A journey to Hajastan is a journey to hope,' said the doctor, closing his eyes, 'the hope that one day there will be peace, in this landscape that was once claimed by Noah and his family and the animals that survived: on the fertile Urartu Plains a delivered people has already once undertaken the first steps towards a new beginning.' He climbed up a ladder to reach the top shelves of his library. Handed his visitor a heavy tome, *Hajastan: Architecture and History*. He said, 'Don't be in too much of a hurry to decide. Your heart needs peace. But I think the vision you saw, during your seizure in the attic of the Théâtre de l'Odéon, must have some powerful connection with your life. If you have come to me looking for advice, then I would say to you: yes, you should undertake this journey, even though your heart has little strength. To prepare you, I suggest you visit the Basilica Saint-Denis, to the north of the City, which is the final resting place of many of the kings of France, and of Levon V, the last king of Hajastan, who died in 1375, and was a close friend of Charles VI. A visit to his sarcophagus may inspire you . . .!'

The tenth performance of the new production of *Masha* was just being given when Tigor made his return to the rigging bridge. His friends greeted him like the prodigal son. On the following days, he was even more taciturn than he had been previously. He didn't lend a hand with the summer wood. During the intervals, he often strolled about in the crowded foyer of the theatre, sweaty and unshaven, mingling with the audience. Once he heard an old woman whispering to her granddaughter: 'True experience is always so much more powerful than mere invention!' Her pupils were jittering like little glass plates on a trembling slide.

When the third act ended, Tigor as usual took hold of the rope whose draw-beam was attached to part of the silk-upholstered rear wall of Masha's drawing room. One evening, he knotted the rope to one of the wooden pegs, but only turned one of the brake-wheels all the way. Didn't know or had forgotten that there were two to each rope. Hakim and Étienne, who were busy lowering the winter forest, failed to notice that the knot, which Tigor had tied particularly poorly, was slowly coming undone. Everything after that happened very quickly: the rear wall of the drawing room, no longer held by a counterweight, dropped to the stage darkened for the scene shift, brushed the temple of Monsieur

Ecoffey who was just hurrying across the stage, and sheared off his jacket pocket, before shattering, with an unexpectedly quiet impact, on the boards. Ecoffey, who didn't appear in the final act of *Masha*, appeared unhurt. Badly shaken, he ran to his dressing room. Three stagehands cleared away scraps of wood and cloth, before making the winter forest fast to the stage. When Mademoiselle de Bayser and Madame Praz came on a moment later, no one would have guessed from their demeanour that anything untoward had happened.

Ecoffey sat in front of the mirror, surrounded by make-up girls and dressers. A hairline scratch from temple to neck was just beginning to ooze a little blood. The women cried out in consternation, and one seventeen-year-old make-up girl, from Lisbon, repeatedly crossed herself. The duty doctor (Chabanian only officiated at premières) dabbed on an antiseptic tincture. Monsieur Dalland wrung his hands in contrition, and, even before the end of the performance, made his way up to the gridiron to identify the guilty party. Every one of the five men present claimed that responsibility for the regrettable incident was fully and uniquely his own.

Marie-Antoinette kicked her father under the table when an unknown woman fetched up one day to ask where she might find one Monsieur Tigre. Ignoring his daughter's painful objections, Napoleon suggested the woman might try the Café Petit Suisse, next door. CriCri failed to recognize her Prometheus at first, he was so thin and unkempt. He was sitting over a glass of cognac, next to Madame Murat. The senior park warden was lamenting the fact that she'd ill-advisedly lent money to a young man. He had claimed to be a Boeing test-pilot, but as she knew now, he was a confidence trickster wanted by the police. She said, 'But it was always that way: my life is governed by chance – and I drift along . . .'

When Tigor spotted CriCri leaning against the bar, he ran over to her, threw his arms around her. They strolled down the rue de l'Odéon, crossed the boulevard Saint-Germain, in the teeth of noise, traffic and crowds, found themselves – without at all intending to go there – standing in front of the church of St-Germain-des-Prés. The burial place of René Descartes was in a squalid niche close to the altar. They sat down there on a wooden bench. The coffin of the mathematician had been plundered when it was transported back to France from Sweden, whispered Tigor. The thieves had helped themselves to the skull and most of the remains – the tomb now contained not much more than a few splinters of bone.

'That'll be my next painting!' said CriCri.

Tigor carried with him the big volume that Chabanian had lent him. He laid it on his knees, studied the brilliantly sharp black-and-white photographs of half-ruined chapels, grass-grown basilicas, imposing monasteries. The symmetrical foundation plans of churches were also included in the book, and Tigor worked at converting the lines and angles and coordinates of these outlandish constructions into mathematical equations. Was barely aware of what was going on around him, sank in a sea of regularity. He thought he detected a resemblance between the disposition of the churches and the crystalline forms of snowflakes. He read names like Haghpath, Aghthamar, Norawank and Sanahin, that seemed at once exotic and familiar to him, like dreams that had vanished without trace. A feeling of equilibrium filled him, he hadn't felt that way since his student days. He felt longing as he read: 'The architectural ensembles of Makarawank and Khoranashat to the north of Armenia occupy small elevated areas of the forest-grown slopes of the Bazum mountain ridge. Makarawank's structures are built of dark-pink andesite and red tufa, with occasional greenish stones; Khoranashat is built of bluish basalt . . .'

Tigor failed to hear the pale worshipper who kept whispering the same sentence to him, over and over again. He only noticed when a priest of St-German-des-Prés and two of his servers took him, a little roughly, by the arms, and dragged him out of the Descartes niche. The midday Mass could not be read while there were still visitors present in any of the side chapels.

It was only when the heavy wooden door was opened that Tigor realized CriCri was no longer by his side. She had long since left the church, and left him.

He was prepared for his uncle's pleading not to desert him now, with Agueda's thyroid operation imminent. Tigor claimed to have received, in the course of a recent phone call, the surprising news from his university that they wanted to offer him an exchange position in the Soviet Union for a year, and so, if Bohm agreed, he would be leaving very soon.

'Thank heavens!' exclaimed Arnold, 'only yesterday I was saying to Agueda that if my nephew carries on like this one more week, I'm going to call a doctor. My treasure!' Bohm scuttled round the kitchen table and, for the first time since he'd moved in, pressed a kiss on his cheek, sat down again, took vast bites, ate up a calf's liver with quantities of fried onions.

'A teaching position! Where is it to be, you say? In Yerevan? But isn't that in the Trans-Caucasus?! Excellent! Excellent! And when do you leave? As soon as possible? Splendid, my gold! Before you leave, be sure to throw off your thin skin and acquire a new thick fat one! You're too pale and thin as it is. White piccaninny is what we used to call people like you in my childhood . . . I would like you to put on a little more weight. Be healthy, then everything else will look after itself, believe me . . . It's wrong to talk about luck, luck is very unreliable. In fact, you should strike words like fortune and misfortune from your vocabulary altogether, they don't get you anywhere . . . And don't forget: people are unscrupulous the world over . . . À propos: there's a Catalan lawyer living on the first floor who's married to a poor, ugly Armenian girl; whereas he (I'm sure you've run into him on the stairs) is notably well favoured! Works at the Court of Appeal. Why not ring their doorbell tomorrow, maybe the wife will be able to tell you a thing or two about her homeland . . . Help yourself to more lemon cake . . . under Hitler, the importing of lemons was forbidden, I suppose that's news to you? He used to refer to them as "that lustful southland fruit" and that was sufficient . . . Have you really accepted an exchange professorship . . .! Bravo, my gold!'

The sensation that he was taking leave of his life accompanied Tigor everywhere during the next few days, while he was arranging his visa and plane tickets. From infancy, he'd been afraid of flying, he could enumerate every major commercial airline disaster in the past thirty years, knew the dates of the catastrophe, the numbers of dead and survivors, he kept a book on the timing of the next calamity. By his calculations, April promised to be a particularly dangerous month in which to fly. He was convinced that he would crash on one of his coming flights, not least as he was due to travel from Moscow to Yerevan on an Aeroflot Ilyushin 86, a machine that frankly terrified him.

Shapes of clouds, colours and smells in the streets, voices of people, all these he thought he was experiencing for the last time. On the place de la Concorde a great tricolour was flapping in the wind, high up on a gable-top, its sound was like the crackling of a wet log on a hearth. Tigor stopped in his tracks and listened to it for minutes. When he leaned against the trunk of the elm in the Luxembourg gardens again, he scratched open the soil, dug deeper, tore through roots, deeper, opened the earth with his bare hands, shoved his arm up to the elbow in the hole.

He hardly ever went up to the rigging loft any more. Hakim went looking for Tigor in the Petit Suisse and in their usual restaurant because he didn't know where his friend lived, many times he'd asked him for his address and telephone number, and never got a reply. Mrs Hathaway claimed she couldn't help Hakim. However, feeling just a little concerned herself, she did ring up Bohm, who told her of Tigor's plans. She was surprised at how sorry she felt that this eccentric, rather unapproachable man would be leaving the theatre. She had grown used to his pleasantly turbulent being, however little she actually saw of him.

Often, unnoticed by his friends, he would turn up in the auditorium at the end of a performance, at the moment when the applause broke out. Felt, had always felt, a particular fondness for the thoroughly archaic convention of clapping hands as a measure of approval. He bathed in the splashy sound of it, it gave him strength. When Mama had her curtain calls, again and again, he had imagined that the rapture, the wild, sometimes rhythmic applauding was, even if just in part, also for himself. 'Marthe Bohm – *un miracolo!*' was the headline in the Trieste daily, *Il Piccolo*, following the premiere of *Norma* in the autumn of 1960. And days later Tigor's classmates carried his schoolbag, and brought him cakes and flowers from their parents.

For a whole week, since his decision to leave the Odéon, he hadn't eaten a proper meal. When he got home, he would say he'd already eaten, asked his uncle for permission to retire. But one evening, Bohm called him from the kitchen: 'Come and sit down with me, I insist.' Agueda scampered off when Tigor appeared in the doorway. 'Come on, I hardly see anything of you these days, and you're about to leave me! Here, have something to eat, minute steak, excellent! Or would you rather a piece of Emmental? These peaches need to be finished . . . But remember not to drink anything after stoned fruit, or else you'll get gripe! I came across a poem of Ringelnatz's today, ha, you'll like this, where has it got to, oh the book's all spotted with grease: "On a stage there stands a tree/ Fetched from the nearest plant nursery/ Tow'ring over it on the left/ Is a papier mâché cliff/ While on the right, you may descry/ A bright expanse of tinfoil sky./ See the young Kohn in the stalls/ Heave with all this make-believe . . . " And so on and so forth . . . nice, isn't it? "*Heave* with all this make-believe"! Judging by your facial expression, you seem to have fallen out of love with the theatre? . . . Early this morning . . . what's the matter with you? Early this morning I sat in the Luxembourg gardens, and read a letter from Carlotta Meyerbeer. In the tree over my head was a sloth that might have escaped from one of the adjacent apartments, and black-and-white squirrels . . . My Carlotta! The only one of them who knows how to write me a decent letter. I suppose most of my correspondence these days is with old widows, but I never get a proper answer to anything, none of the ladies responds to what I put to them or ask them. All I get are these infantile enumerations: " . . . and an early supper and so to bed." Plus menu. I really can't get excited about what other people have eaten and already digested . . .'

He picked up the last piece of rhubarb cake, licked the cream off his fingers, ate every last crumb of it, shut his eyes, as though, still chewing, he was already asleep. 'Have you noticed', he resumed, and opened his eyelids a crack, showing only a tiny strip of white, 'that my attention span has got much smaller of late? I notice it especially when I'm reading . . . Just lately I read this quite abysmal book speculating about the future – not really a book at all, just a reflection of the author's stupidity. And now I've had it with the future. It's a long time since I was able to read Italo Svevo, never mind Thomas Mann. With Mann, there are these sentences that go on for an entire page at a time, an impertinence to the reader . . . So I'm reduced to reading four short books at a time, in four different languages . . . You should bear in mind that I'm a product of a different and intact world. In 1914, I was already a fully conscious human being, in an ambience you can't even imagine today . . . Eating on the street was completely unimaginable then . . . When I run into women sucking ice lollies on the public street, I think I must be seeing things! Eating on the street was absolutely despised in my time. A fellow student of mine was ditched by his fiancée after she caught him eating an apple on the Piazza Cavour! . . . Early 1913, we were asked in class which of us still believed in the stork. Rudi Bach was the only one to put his hand up. Mind you, none of the rest of us had any better ideas. They quickly changed the subject . . . At the age of fifteen, I was seduced by the daughter of a woman who managed a luggage shop . . . She came to me, ostensibly for the purpose of hearing me play the violin . . . She can't have been more than thirteen herself . . . Her father was away at the Front. He had a musical gift, though wholly uncultured otherwise. Played the violin by ear, stuck to the middle range. Started a mouth-organ orchestra in his famous regiment, and a Wagnerian, at that time the world was divided between supporters and opponents of Wagner, both equally fanatical . . . He called his children Ortrud, Siegfried and Senta. Names they . . . spent the rest of their lives . . .'

He had dropped off . Tigor didn't dare to budge, stayed in his uncomfortable position.

'Come along,' said Arnold, a minute had gone by, 'give me your hand. I don't suppose I'm that different to look at? People seeing me in the street still know me. Vice versa I'm not so sure. I'm forever being told I cut people dead in the street. That's supposed to be a characteristic of mine. Even as a young man, I'm supposed to have been terribly full of myself. Actually, I don't think it was quite so simple. I was shy, and that may have made me seem dismissive. I preferred to remain anonymous, attract no attention. I would say to myself: "Don't go off the deep end." And I still repeat that every day . . . When I feel unhappy, which is to say for eighteen hours out of twenty-four, then I think of the letter aria from *Figaro*, a simple triplet melody (how wonderfully your mother used to sing Susanna!) and then my mood lightens straight away . . .'

After Tigor had turned out his bedside light, Arnold came into his room once more and kissed him on the brow. He was so pleased, he declared, about Tigor's decision to accept the offer of the guest professorship. He sat down on the edge of the mattress. 'Do you remember how we used to go to the zoo together in Vienna? You were five years old . . . The tigers pissed at us from their cages, do you remember that? We used to tease them on purpose, we knew what we were letting ourselves in for. And they were very accurate too. What frightened you much more were the snakes, but most of all the baboons, who terrified you with their displays of temper, rattling the bars of their cages, and baring their teeth. We stayed at the Parkhotel Schönbrunn, not far from the zoo, and at night we used to hear the lions roaring, do you remember?' But Tigor was practically asleep, lulled by the goosedown voice of his uncle.

In the morning he awoke much earlier than usual, sneaked into Bohm's bedroom, where his uncle kept his passport in the high dresser. Needed it that day, had to go back to the Soviet Embassy, as he had asked for a visa as an independent visitor. For a while he stood by the window, watched the old couple at work on their little ledge of balcony across the courtyard, stooping down, weeding their vegetable boxes. A strip of sun fell across Arnold's bed, the old man lay completely straight under the blankets, smiling, eyes shut. His grin was so cheeky that Tigor was certain Bohm was mocking him.

'What's so funny?' he asked him.

It seemed that Arnold really was asleep.

'Are you laughing at me?' and that same instant he knew what had happened. He rested the back of his head, as the Narrinyieri did, against Arnold's chest.

Agueda woke Arnold every morning. With a start she stopped in the doorway when she saw Tigor lying across his uncle's breast.

They didn't call an ambulance and didn't telephone the doctor either. They washed the dead man and dressed him in white linen, combed his hair, and folded his hands over his belly. Arnold Bohm smiled through everything. It wasn't until the afternoon that Tigor informed the specialist.

The funeral took place at the cimetière de Neuilly, in Nanterre on the southern perimeter of Paris. Tigor and Agueda were the only mourners, Barbara Hathaway had ordered a thick wreath of cut flowers to be delivered by motorbike. The local priest spoke a blessing over the coffin, but there was no eulogy. At the time that Bohm had bought his grave, forty-five years ago, the cemetery had been surrounded by fields and meadows. Now, in the grip of trunk roads and motorway segments, surrounded by the numbing din of automobiles and construction sites, the graveyard seemed like an accidentally spared bit of an allotment garden. Right beside the cimetière de Neuilly was one of the biggest building sites in the country, a megalopolis of banking, petroleum and government skyscrapers, whose trademark had just been finished in skeleton form: an enormous triumphal arch, as tall as the Eiffel Tower, as massive as the Opera, conceived of as a window on the world, looking out into the coming millennium. Arnold Bohm had found a final resting place at the foot of the Grande Arche.

The following day, Tigor, in the company of Agueda, called on the Catalan lawyer on the first floor whom Bohm had mentioned to him. Maître Josep-Maria de Sagarra declared himself willing to serve as notary. As Arnold had died intestate, Tigor appointed Agueda as sole beneficiary. Sagarra attempted to dissuade him from this spontaneously taken decision, but the nephew remained adamant: what Bohm had owned, Agueda was to inherit. She appeared neither happy nor unhappy about such a turn of events, locked herself away in her attic room, without having set her signature to any of the documents.

Tigor found himself once more in Napoleon's porter's lodge. Took receipt of a letter from CriCri, full of bitter reproaches and a demand for the return of the Narrinyieri talisman. He had brought along a large kite for Marie-Antoinette, she was confused when he gave her the present. 'Can you tell me', she wanted to know, 'why can I remember the things that have already happened, and not things that haven't happened yet?'

He climbed down to the levels under the stage, hid among the old sets that were stored there, half rusted and mouldering away in the damp. A pair of wings of real swans' feathers had collapsed into several grey-brown fan shapes. Cowering under the stage, he listened one last time to the four acts of *Masha*, waited after the performance till all the stagehands and riggers had left the theatre (he had not said goodbye to a single one of his former colleagues) and was duly locked into the theatre by the unaware porter. When everything had gone dark, he crept up onto the stage, had brought a little torch with him, looked for a place in the winter forest where he could lie down. Stretched out in the middle of the reed-beds next to the rowing boat, and shivered with cold. Draw-beams and ropes, perspectives and bits of scenery hung down without rhyme or reason. A diluvial rain was pelting down on the pyramid roof, it sounded like a Caribbean percussion ensemble playing to vast applause. In the small hours, Tigor dreamed that the aeroplane he was on was failing to gain altitude, minutes after taking off, it was back at treetop level. The machine broke apart. Tigor heard the screams of the one hundred and ninety-four passengers and crew, all, like himself, being thrown through the air. He succeeded in grabbing hold of the crest of a pine tree. It swayed in the wind. He saw pieces of wreckage burst into flame very close to him. The local peasants were swarming towards the site, looting the ruins, robbing the dead. Burning fuselage and dancing peasants still before his eyes, Tigor woke. Decided straight away to postpone his departure by a day.

It was still raining. Tigor looked for the switch for the work-lights, found it in the wings, where the thick red fire hoses were all coiled up. He returned to his sleeping place, and sent a powerful stream of piss down next to the boat, at the very spot where, at the end of the play, Gagarin found Masha's dead body. Stayed to watch the slow dissipation of the liquid into the floorboards. The safety curtain hadn't been lowered at night, so from the back of the stage, Tigor was able to look into the feebly illuminated auditorium. The rows of red velvet seats, boxes and balconies had something extraordinarily decent, comforting and regular about them, as opposed to the rough, grey-brown expanse of stage. To think that at the end of the second millennium of the Common Era, scenery was still dragged up into the air by hand! And he bowed to the emptiness, and left the stage.

After rebooking his flight, he sat down, in the early afternoon, under the mighty elm. The storm had passed, but the ground was still drenched. Great pools of water lay around. Tigor had Arnold's short-wave radio with him, listened to the news headlines every hour, expecting to hear of the crash of the flight that would have taken him to Moscow. He dug deeper into the hole in the ground, bloodied his fingers on splinters of wood. Children took him for a tramp, circled round him on bicycles and skateboards. In the depths of the hole, Tigor struck a toy wooden steamship, the size of a matchbox, edged in washed-out yellow-and-blue stripes. The name on the bow was no longer decipherable. The boys made a beeline for the stranger, demanded to see what he had found. They even helped him to fill up the little mineshaft.

He had the little boat in his pocket, his bleeding fingers clenched up in a fist, the horde of children following him like a sort of Pied Piper. It was just then, as he was leaving the park by the rue Bonaparte gate, that he encountered the tall and gaunt form of Samuel Beckett, staring, as ever, at the ground.

At the same moment, a few hundred yards away, Marie-Antoinette was crossing the busy place Paul Claudel. She had her new kite tucked under her arm, hadn't unpacked it yet, was just going to fly it for the first time with her brothers, who were waiting for her in the park. A motorcyclist on a large and powerful machine roared down the rue Medicis, leaned across to take the corner in front of the Petit Suisse. Didn't see the little girl crossing the street, struck Marie-Antoinette's shoulder with his rear-view mirror. She was spun right round, and slammed on to the asphalt, face first. The motorcycle skidded a little, but its rider quickly had it under control again, and he went on his way, without even a look over his shoulder. Not one of the following cars stopped for the girl lying on the road. The ripped kite fluttered across the square. A park warden who had observed the whole incident, a young man from Dahomey, lifted the girl onto the pavement. He knew Napoleon, who had once got him a walk-on part in a film, and had him sent for right away. Radioed for an ambulance.

Tigor reached the spot just as the ambulance men were putting the little girl on to a stretcher. Marie-Antoinette tried to smile at him. He felt in some way responsible, that he had started the chain of events that had culminated in the accident. If he had been on the Moscow plane that morning, as had been his original intention, then Tigor believed everything subsequent would have transpired differently. Every individual was like a thread in the complicated weave of reality. By remaining in Paris, taking his breakfast in the Petit Suisse, and spending the day in and around the Luxembourg gardens, he had upset the delicate equilibrium of the machinery of destiny in the city. As he saw it, the consequences of the mild displacement he had caused had gone out, like echo waves, to the periphery, and then bounced back to their starting point. The motorcyclist, if Tigor had indeed left as planned, would have reached the place Paul Claudel a split second sooner or later.

Moments before the ambulance left, Tigor dropped the little wooden boat on the stretcher, next to Marie-Antoinette.

Very early the following morning, he had himself driven to the airport by Monsieur Khoy, whose radio-telephone number he had kept. At the subterranean post office in the Charles de Gaulle airport, he mailed the Narrinyieri talisman back to CriCri without an accompanying message of any kind.

On his way to the departure gate, on the opposite side of the passage, separated from him by a thick sheet of plate glass, in the midst of a whole herd of passengers who had landed in Paris moments earlier, he was passed by the athletic figure of his favourite student, Abraham Porter. So shocked was Tigor by this that he briefly had to sit down to clear his head. Abraham, making rapidly for the luggage carousel, had failed to spot him.

On the flight to Moscow, Tigor felt distinctly euphoric. The middle pages of the in-flight magazine showed the network of the airline's routes, dozens of blue threads spanning the globe in orderly chaos. Tigor sat and studied the picture for a long time. He could feel it making him happy. Forced himself to feel grief for Arnold, but was unable to. Forced himself to feel alarm over whatever Abraham might be purposing. Felt no alarm.

Yerevan

In the reception of the Hotel National in Moscow, near Red Square, the staff were unable to find any record of Tigor's reservation. They didn't have a bed free anywhere in the whole mammoth building. In a small bare neon-lit office on the first floor, a tour guide was endeavouring to find alternative accommodation for the guest. But in the whole city there was no other room to be found, not even in the Ostankino skyscraper with its six thousand billets.

He was looking in his torn address book for the name Morozov, had trouble making out his own writing. Then dictated the number to the uniformed girl, who dialled it for him. Her large fingernails looked like the back armour of stag beetles. At the maths seminar in the Sorbonne, he had telephoned a sullen Russian exile more than a dozen times before the man had been prepared to let him have his former professor's home telephone number. A young woman answered. She was his housekeeper, she explained, cried out: '. . . professor stay year away, away.' While Morozov was spending a year as guest lecturer at the University of Southern California in Los Angeles, she was looking after his apartment for him. Tigor was disappointed. Since his student days, he, who looked up to hardly anyone, had been hoping to make the personal acquaintance of P. S. Morozov. 'I know parts of your 1964 Moscow lecture off by heart!' was how he had been going to greet the revered mathematician.

The tour-guide suggested he go on an evening tour of the city. 'You luggage stay here, return later, try, is possible: found room!' She took him down to the front of the hotel, where an orange minibus was parked. 'Wait a little hour with driver Igor, probably more peoples come. Wait!' said the uniformed woman, and she vanished back into the hotel's labyrinthine corridors.

Tigor and Igor sat in silence in the valerian-scented, clearly leftward-listing vehicle. The burly driver stared expressionlessly into space. After a few minutes, two men and a woman got on.

'Let's go, c'mon, let's go, move it. What are we waiting for? I wanna see somethin'!' cried the elder of the two men, a character wearing a brown suit, with a round red tomato face. The younger, contrastingly ashen-faced, was sweating profusely. He looked like an ex-footballer, an impression his lilac-and-yellow striped tracksuit top did nothing to diminish.

'Judy and me, we're just damn hungry, Mike, that's all *I* care 'bout!' replied the younger, and grasped the shoulder of a bull-necked woman with short hair and a greasy complexion sitting next to him.

'C'mon stupid, let's go see some sights!' retorted the elder man. 'Half-baked ignorants, the pair of you. Why don't you get out, if you don't like it. Go *eat*!'

It was dark as they set off, and raining heavily. They drove along six-lane highways, past fog-grey high-rises. They came to Gorky Park, which they couldn't see and on which Igor wasted no words. He drove past the Donskoi monastery without a commentary. No one noticed the magnificent five-domed cathedral, lit up by powerful spotlights, not even Tigor, who had slipped into a velvety half-sleep. After crossing in complete darkness a park that was as big as a middle-sized town, they found themselves on the banks of the Moskva river, close to the Kammenyi Bridge. They could barely make out the red brick walls of the Kremlin, on the other side of the river.

'Reminds me of the Ohio River, down in Paducah, round by the glassworks,' observed the elder of the two men, also seeming to emerge from slumber. 'Driver's not tellin' us where the damn we are, is he?! Hey, Russky, where the damn are we?' And after a two-second pause: 'The guy's deaf-mute!'

The younger man concurred: 'Could've stayed at the hotel just as well. They had some food there. Gruesome stuff, sure, okay, but who cares? God*damn* I'm hungry!'

'Oh, Danny, c'mon, shut up!' his bull-necked girlfriend growled, 'quit makin' such a fool of yourself . . .'

'He gets very angry when he gets very hungry, do you understand?' The older man attempted to explain the impetuosity of his friend, in easy English, lowering his head as if in apology. And asked his fellow passenger whether he too were attending the international trade union conference.

94

He was working as a rigger in a big theatre presently on tour in the Soviet Union, came Tigor's reply.

'What's he say?' asked the man in the tracksuit.

'Guess he's an actor or somethin' like that,' replied the trade union delegate. And, turning to Tigor, he continued: 'You're an actor, right? And we, we're from Illinois, Il-li-nois. It's a first, you know, us visiting the Soviets. Unheard of. Amazing. Do you understand what I'm saying?'

Tigor nodded politely.

High above the city, they passed the Lomonossov University, this construction too swathed in fog and darkness. They saw crumbling concrete walls. A few pillars, staircases and battlements emerged from the gloom. Not far from the mighty, thirty-storey building was an esplanade where Igor let the little group stretch their legs. He himself remained at the wheel, flapping his arm vehemently towards the terrace rail, as though shooing away some annoying insects. That Napoleon Bonaparte had once viewed Moscow in flames from this very spot was well known to the driver, but he chose not to share his knowledge.

The four passengers went over to the wooden rails, were unable, apart from a little stand of trees that was lit up by the headlights of their minibus, to see anything at all. Shivering and soaked, they hurried back to their crooked conveyance.

'This guy's completely wacko if you ask me!' said the young woman.

Igor drove on, none of them had any idea where. Tigor only awoke on the brightly lit Nachimovsky Prospect. 'This is the factory where, in the summer of 1918, Vladimir Ilyich Lenin was shot by the Jewish counter-revolutionary Fanny Kaplan as he was leaving,' the driver suddenly announced as they passed a long, low building. 'She was practically blind, that demigoddess, and so she only succeeded in wounding Comrade Lenin, instead of killing him. Because if she had succeeded, that saint, the history of the world would have been different. By way of reprisals, eight hundred so-called counter-revolutionaries were shot out of hand. Lenin's death, six years later, was a delayed consequence of that tragically failed attempted assassination . . .'

'. . . so he knows English! . . . What a jerk! . . . I can't believe this! . . . Why didn't ya tell us some more?! . . .' the members of the

Illinois trade union exclaimed. 'Probably a Jew 'n' all!' the woman whispered.

'I suspect', Tigor put in, 'that that may have been the only sentence the gentleman knows in English . . .'

Igor suppressed a quiet laugh. And then was once more mute. He stopped in front of several restaurants. None of them had room for them. The seventh attempt was crowned with success: the two liveried doormen of a co-operative establishment in the Planernaia district allowed themselves to be dazzled by the banknotes that were flashed at them by the trade unionists from the United States of America. To the blaring brass of an eight-piece combo, the sightseers guzzled smoked sturgeon and lamb kebabs with tomatoes from a private source. The music grew louder, the sports hall of a room ever rowdier. Pilots from the state airline were dancing with policewomen, black marketeers with casual prostitutes, male bus drivers with lady taxi drivers. A small, perfectly spherical woman grabbed Tigor by the arm, dragged him (still clutching knife and fork) out on to the dance floor. She pressed herself tightly against him, knife and fork clattered to the floor. She wore a stained white blouse and black skirt. Her ears were protruding, her grey hair thin and lank. She smelled of the glycerine balls in public conveniences. Tigor resisted, and she tightened her grip. Rubbed her belly against his pelvis. Let go of him for an instant to stamp to the music, shook herself like a wet dog, bent way down and shot up again, reached for Tigor's hips. 'I love you!' she moaned to him. He broke free of her. The little old woman went on dancing alone, even more wildly than before. Her pinky-brown slip showed with every move, it looked like a wide expanse of tongue.

At one o'clock in the morning, Tigor and the other travellers on the bus found themselves all alone on the brilliantly lit, airfield-sized expanse of Red Square. Even though there was no wind, the flag on the onion dome of the Supreme Soviet building was flapping, kept taut at every hour of day and night, all the year round, by wind machines at the foot of its flagpole. The travellers shielded themselves from the rain under pages taken from large newspapers. Suddenly three lorries turned up, loud, droning, tank-like street-cleaning carts, built more than forty years ago, and in continuous service ever since. In spite of the heavy rain, their water jets rinsed the whole of Red Square from St Basil's Cathedral to the Historical Museum, and from the Kremlin walls to the GUM department store, cleansed the Krasnaya Ploscad' so swiftly and so thoroughly that the little group had some trouble staying out of their way. Tigor was slow to realize that they were already rattling back towards him, aiming streams from their gigantic tin tanks. In front of the Lenin Mausoleum, he took evasive action so clumsily that he knocked over one of the two élite soldiers who were standing guard.

They returned to the hotel. 'Bye now, so long, sir, whatever it is at the theatre, we wish you good luck. See ya around!' called the elder of the two men while he stepped out of the bus.

And the younger muttered: 'Nice trip, hey? Couldn't see the darnedest thing, could we?'

'Oh, Danny, c'mon, shut up! Course you did!' chided his companion.

The tour guide with the stag-beetle fingernails was still working. She was sorry and announced: 'Nyet room. Nix bed. Sir like sleep with me?!' And when she laughed, Tigor noticed she had gold teeth where vampires have their sucking fangs. He saw himself reflected in them, the size of a pinhead, bobbing along in a stream of prime numbers, upright and lost as a buoy at sea.

For a quite fantastic price, Igor drove Tigor to the domestic airport at Domodedovo. He was a Balt from Riga, spoke in a beautiful Nordic singsong. It was his feeling for numbers, he volunteered not apropos of anything, that had determined his life from childhood on. 'In my schooldays,' he said, 'my teachers were always careful of me, for some reason they had a high opinion of my gifts. I was permitted to arrive late for school, I slept in late in the morning, in bed I lay and thought about life, tossing from side to side. I hurried from lamp post to lamp post, stopping at each one, felt for its serial number, wrote it down in a loose-leaf notebook. Kept adding up the serial numbers, I was certain that I would find the secret of the universe by means of these constellations of figures.'

'. . . and were you proved right?'

'I think I know the riddle of the world. Nothing and no one rules alongside the tyrannical King Chance. You won't have come across the saying, "That isn't mathematics, that's theology," but . . .'

'That's what Paul Gordon wrote on Hilbert's proof that every system of algebraical forms has a finite base.'

'You're one of us!' exclaimed Igor, his astonishment rendered him speechless for seconds. 'But the moment you climbed on the minibus, that was what I hoped! You got on the bus, and straight away, I don't know why, I began thinking about Hilbert's Paris lecture of 1900, with its twenty-three unsolved problems, above all I had in mind the one about the irrationality and transcendence of certain numbers. And I wanted to ask you a first, somewhat more cautious question, when these other . . . people came along. And then everything was kaput. And then you told those people some story about being in the theatre. You see, I listen carefully. And I was so disappointed! Because I believed that theatre stuff! So where do you teach? Where are you travelling to now?'

In the airport building, which resembled an outsize nineteenth-century railway station rather more than a state-of-the-art airport, Igor never left Tigor's side. Even though it was three in the morning, Domodedovo was thronged: people from all the different language groups and ethnic allegiances of the Soviet Empire swarmed round the numerous ticket counters. There was no place to sit down anywhere. It smelled of ammonia and formaldehyde.

'. . . airports are our equivalents of Babel!' shouted the Balt. 'The masses that inhabit them, at every hour of the day and night, none of them speaks the other's language. They are the ones who were scattered over the globe. They wanted to reach up and touch the sky. They are bewildered and bedevilled by language, till the end of time . . .!'

They stood in a group of Kirghiz, Mongols, Belorussians and Armenians, all waiting at ticket counter 132, for their turn to come.

'Now, sir,' said Igor, tapping Tigor on the shoulder, 'can you explain the following to me: in his work *On the Infinite*, Hilbert writes, "Let no one drive us out of the paradise that Cantor has created for us." Do you understand that? What did he mean by it?'

Then something quite extraordinary happened. When such things occur in films, one quite inevitably thinks: this can't be. That's not how things happen, not like that. A well turned-out elderly gentleman who was standing immediately in front of them in the queue turned round, looked them both up and down the way an army doctor might give new recruits the once-over, and said, 'My grandfather, Georg Cantor, was, as no doubt you know, the founder of set theory. At your service, Ernst Cantor is my name.'

'Your grandfather?!' Tigor was incredulous.

'And so you're Georg Cantor's . . . *grandson*!?' Igor blurted out, he too quite flabbergasted.

'. . . but the huge significance of his ideas never made my cele-brated forefather vain or conceited in any way,' the old man con-tinued, 'and if you ask me what Hilbert meant by that "paradise" reference, I think we may safely assume that it was Cantor's dis-covery of set theory, by which the infinite was fully enfranchised in mathematics, and that Hilbert justifiably considered this one of the most marvellous intellectual feats of the human race.'

'. . . if you will allow, I am speechless,' whispered Igor.

'Consider, gentlemen: my grandfather made the discovery, to content myself with a single example, that every point on a line cannot be described as a whole number, but that the number of such points is actually infinity times infinity more infinite than the number of whole numbers. You will bear me out: set theory is among the most comprehensive revolutions in the entire history of mathematics.'

Cantor's grandson, himself a professor of mathematics at the Humboldt University in East Berlin, who had spent the emigra-tion years in Princeton, New Jersey, was presently, as he informed them, on his way to Leningrad, his grandfather's birth-place. 'I have never been there, constrained by my sense of awe. "*Le cœur a ses raisons que la raison ne connaît pas*," as Pascal quite rightly observed. In 1856, my grandfather, then a boy of eleven, moved with his parents to Frankfurt. I have not been there either, this time for political reasons. Are you familiar with the sentence Cantor spoke during his doctoral defence in Berlin? "In mathe-matics, the art of putting questions is more important than the art of finding answers to them." Those words to me are an expression of the purity and nobility of our science! "In mathematics, the art of putting questions is more important than the art of finding answers to them."'

Igor and Tigor were still numbed with the shock of the chance meeting. They were like a couple of apprentices who, encountering the immense personality and the revolutionary theories of a major scientist, are made aware of their own inadequacy and insignificance.

When Professor Cantor reached the front of the queue, after half an hour's waiting, he took his leave of them with a deep bow. 'Gentlemen, at the conclusion of our unexpected and enjoyable meeting, I should like to leave you with an insight of my grandfather's that would appear not to have anything to do with mathematics, except that it matches it for global significance, with the request to you both to give it as much currency as you can: that the true author of the so-called plays of Shakespeare was not Shakespeare at all, rather (and let us not forget it!) it was the statesman Francis Bacon, born in 1561, died in 1626, who made mankind the divine present of these thirty-seven works.' He bowed once more, deaf to the noisy grumbling of the queue, oblivious to the furious tapping of the airline employee on the grease-spotted glass in front of the ticket counter.

At four in the morning, Tigor was able to secure one of the last remaining seats on the morning flight to Yerevan. There were five hours before it was scheduled to leave. Igor reckoned they should both stretch out in the departure lounge, and try to get some sleep.

'Why both of us?' asked Tigor.

'I'm certainly not letting you out of my sight before your plane leaves.' They lay down in the Intourist lounge of the airport. Igor kept watch over his friend, kept an eye on the milling hordes of people as they drifted back and forth, or spent the night huddled up in a foetal position. An icy draught sliced through the huge windows, Tigor tried, half asleep, to cover himself with the tatty plastic cushions of the sofa, didn't notice that Igor had draped his own yellow-brown imitation leather car-coat over him.

When Tigor woke at first light, the Balt was sitting cross-legged to his left. To his right, however, was the seemingly endless expanse of airport. Dozens upon dozens of aeroplanes were parked here in orderly chaos and random arrangement, machines of all types and sizes from propeller planes to wide-bodied jets, roomy as arks. It was raining in thin, regular threads. Tigor did not often use his little pocket camera, but to mark their parting, he shot off a whole colour film, showing the driver, who had been a professor of mathematics at Lomonossov University before losing his job over some political kerfuffle, waving and sadly smiling in ever new poses, waving and smiling and smiling.

'. . . don't forget now: Francis Bacon!' Igor called out to the departing voyager.

During the descent, Tigor could see the twin volcanic peaks of Ararat out of the windows of the gigantic Ilyushin 86. The crowded aeroplane spent more than a minute flying parallel to the snow-capped higher of the two peaks, before suddenly plummeting down, sending a gasp of horror through fifty rows of seats.

Rubble and ash covered the airfield. The noise of construction mingled with the whining of jet engines was almost unbearable in the tiny airport of Zvartnotz. The hot spring air was difficult to breathe. It was orange-yellow in colour and smelled of sodium chloride. The pall of smog that hung over the landscape obliterated the antediluvian mountain, even though it was only a few miles away. However near it might be, it remained unattainable. A death-strip, sprinkled with fine sand, intervened between the double peak and Yerevan, separated the Soviet Union from Turkey.

A group of Scandinavian archaeologists had deplaned from the same machine, nine bearded men, all roughly the same age, who assembled in the dingy building site of an arrival lounge. Tigor, not especially knowing why, joined them. A large, heavily perspiring man hurried up to the delegation from the high north, introducing himself as Johann Wolfgang Oganessian, director of the Archaeological Institute of the University of Yerevan.

'Permit me to improvise a welcome speech for you,' he said, 'forgive me for availing myself of the German language, I know no other strange language. This may appear to you astounding, but my father was an amateur of German arts and musics, a scintillating Wagnerian, and worshipper also of the literary classics, hence my perhaps for these regions rather unwonted name. Final consequence of such an education: I have mastery of German vocabulary far exceeding her grammar! Put in a nutshell: we welcome you with whole hearts to Yerevan, the capital of the Soviet Republic of Armenia, and wish you extremely fruitful days one and all, in the exploration of our common past. The exchange plan, my visit to you projected for year after next is integral component of our friendship between peoples. I hope with whole heart that you may have good memories of Armenia, lasting longer than present year!'

The nine nodded back as one. Their own spokesman, one August, responded (also in German) that he and his team of colleagues felt extremely privileged to be visiting a country that had already been settled way back in the palaeolithic era, and whose role as one of the cradles of civilization still received insufficient attention. 'What were we at the end of the Iron Age?' asked the Scandinavian. 'Savage huntsmen, with a few weapons. The reindeer was everything to us. Meanwhile, on your territory, esteemed Director Oganessian, there were already rock-drawings! Depictions of snakes, signifying fertility! Depictions of cranes, signifying liberation! Let us then do good work together!'

Tigor climbed on to the bus along with the members of the delegation, and drove into the city with them. The men supposed him to be part of the welcoming committee; Oganessian took him for one of the Scandinavian visitors, and smiled warmly in his direction. Large herds of sheep were encamped along the highway. Goats grazed among rusted hulks of lorries. The city was characterized by crumbling high-rises in pink tufa, and by wide avenues lined with purple-brown coarse-leaved trees. Johann Wolfgang, who had taken off his crumpled jacket and loosened his black tie, stood swaying in the aisle. '. . . in 1920, we had twenty thousand inhabitants and two factories. And how many, would you guess, today? Today we are one million three hundred thousand inhabitants, and two hundred and eighty factories.' He covered thousands of years of history in a sentence or two, brushed the sweat off his brow with the ball of his thumb.

As the bus curved into the huge oval expanse of Lenin Square, Oganessian nominated the study group's first objective: 'Today we visit the fortress of Yerebuni on the edge of the city, is built by

King Argishti I, in the year 782 before Common Era, thither we will go in three hours after you have deeply deserved rest.'

The colossal Armenia Hotel lay at the edge of the stadium-shaped square, across which sped streams of ancient cars and motorcycles, hooting loudly. Brilliantly polished limousines made their way through the traffic. Great blocks of pedestrians scurried this way and that. In the cool hotel lobby, however, a majestic silence prevailed. Dark marble created an official minis-terial atmosphere. Tigor waited for the delegation to move off to their rooms, waited for Johann Wolfgang to go, before he pur-sued the matter of accommodation for himself. In the outsize guest book he entered his name as a single traveller.

'Alone', observed the young porter, drilled a finger into his nostril, gulped down whatever he found there, 'is not possible!'

'I am alone, though,' countered Tigor.

'Not Swedish also?'

'. . . just happened to be on the same bus . . .'

'Not possible.'

'Couldn't you make an exception?'

'No single tourist.'

'I'm here for research purposes.'

'Not allowed.'

'An exception!'

'Only delegations!'

'In four days' time,' Tigor then said, 'my group will be arriving. Would you kindly reserve seven quiet single rooms for us.'

'No problem. Welcome to Yerevan! Your papers please.'

And Tigor entered seven names (CriCri, Bohm, Porter, Hathaway, Davis, Santini, Hakim) in the large, leather-bound book.

Room 6,625 was on the sixth storey of an annexe building. It could only be reached after walking down five long corridors and taking two glacially slow-moving lifts. An old floor-lady was sit-ting in front of a radio that was playing martial tunes. Tigor looked out of the window of his little cubbyhole. In the middle of the courtyard there was a fountain bubbling away. He found a tourist leaflet on the bedside table. 'Among the most striking symbols of the Armenian capital', he read there, 'are its fountains.

One of them is made up of 2,768 individual jets of water, symbolizing the age in years of the city of Yerevan.' He unpacked his few belongings and sat very upright on the narrow bed. Stared into space for an hour or more, lost in thought. Had the big jet fly back to Moscow, tail fin first, Arnold's coffin was lifted out of the grave, then the hearse backed into the rue Monsieur le Prince. Tigor watched as the set wall that had hurt Ecoffey floated up into the rigging heaven, and how the dying falcon, gaining strength, fluttered back up to the treetop, saw himself standing in the fish market in Trieste, and then running back, neck and heels first, to the conference building. Even the crucial sentence in the paper of his colleague Mildor lost its destructive implications when played backwards.

The bathroom was finger-deep in dirty water. Tigor tried to summon the chambermaid.

'. . . afternoon, never!' the porter cried indignantly. Thereupon, the guest unblocked the floor drain himself, lifted out bunches of hair, swabbed the tiled floor with the thin, worn scrap of towel. When he began running the hip bath, the tap spat out boiling-hot brown water. Tigor contemplated his nudity in the shot mirror over the sink. Clambered up onto the rim of the toilet bowl for a better vantage point.

He decided to go home the next day: 'Mister President, I beg your forgiveness. I guess I just really *needed* a sabbatical . . .' 'Go see a doctor,' the College President would reply, without even deigning to look at him, 'you're unfit to teach.' 'Sir! I beg you, give me another chance,' he heard himself cry out. His voice bounced back off the tiles.

Suddenly, the floor-lady was standing in front of him. She had come in without knocking. Even though the bath water was perfectly opaque, he was still shocked to see her so close to him. 'No! No!' he scolded, flapped the backs of his hands at her in an unmistakable gesture. The floor-lady beamed back at him, said politely 'Nerezek chentrem!', laid a piece of paper on the side of the bath, and tiptoed out again.

'Highly esteemed man of the theatre! I await you in the square outside. Your Johann Wolfgang Oganessian,' he read. How did Oganessian know about him? Tigor's heart beat erratically. Meanwhile, the director of the archaeological institute paced impatiently back and forth in the shadow of a bust of Lenin as big as a house.

As Tigor approached him, Johann Wolfgang spread out his arms. But when the stranger stood in front of him, he dropped them again. 'It's *you*! Aha! Surprise!' said Oganessian. 'Was it your intention to inveigle yourself, like smuggled goods, into the Scandinavian delegation?'

'How do you know who I am?' asked Tigor, with pounding heart.

'I know nothing. You will tell me.'

'How did you know when I . . . How did you know my name?!'

'So my tormenting of you is to end already?'

'What's that?'

'These torments to which I am subjecting you are hereby to end?'

'. . . absolutely!'

'Guess!'

'I can't.'

'Is easy.'

'I give up.'

'I fear you have lazy brain.'

Tigor was forced to laugh. It was what his father had always told him.

'Go, make effort,' insisted Johann Wolfgang.

'I don't know . . .'

'Task is elementary!'

'. . . I really don't.'

'Chabanian! Logic, you hero! Can you not put one and one together? Doctor Chabanian and I, we were friends at school. We went to school in Aleppo, Syria. Chabanian wrote to me about you. About your collapse and all. And that you would be travelling in April to Yerevan. I must take you under my wings, he wrote. For past week, I go day by day to main hotels, looking for you. Is logical, no? Well!' He opened his arms again, pressed Tigor firmly against the coarse nylon weave of his suit. The embraced Tigor felt Oganessian's sweat drip onto his neck. 'Doctor Kevork Chabanian instructed me to look after you as strongly as possible and as long as your stay continues.'

They sat down on a narrow bench in the little Shahumian Park, behind the Lenin Monument. Groups of schoolchildren passed them, staring at the stranger as if he were a visitor from another planet. His formal clothes struck them as other-worldly. Some of the children remained rooted to the spot, to follow the two men's conversation as closely as they could.

'. . . you will naturally want to go on a pilgrimage forthwith to our playhouse-cum-opera,' said Johann Wolfgang, 'for eighty-five weeks, they have played *Othello*, I go there with you, possibly tomorrow, acquaint you with the technical personnel.'

Tigor shook his head. He would be leaving the following morning, there was hardly enough time to get in a theatre visit. And by the way, he was not, as Doctor Chabanian had not unnaturally assumed, a rigging worker at all, but a professor of mathematics at Philadelphia.

'Ha! Now kindly draw a line!' Oganessian seemed irate. He feigned a dry laugh: 'Ha! Haha! I don't fall for so many fairy tales. Kevork told me when, where and how he met you. And that's that. No discussion of leaving. You have here a great task. I don't know precisely what, Chabanian remained silent shtum about it. As long as this task is not accomplished, he writes, there can be no question of your leaving.'

The heat of the spring afternoon oppressed Tigor. He found it impossible to breathe properly. No leaf, no fragrance of blossom in the city.

'Drop your disguise,' said Johann Wolfgang.

'You are mistaken about me . . . thank you so much for your trouble.' He stood up.

'Tonight you shall be my guest. My wife has been cooking for you for past several days. 19A, Acharian Street. We expect you. Third floor, left-hand side.'

'I won't be able to come . . .'

'. . . half past seven.'

'. . . I'm afraid I can't . . .'

'You will most certainly be there.'

Situated on the roof of the Armenia Hotel was a terrace with a bar. Access to it was blocked off by pieces of timber. It wasn't difficult to overcome the obstacle. For years the viewing point had had no visitors. The stone underfoot was crumbling. Only the bare bones of the espresso machine were left. On the rust-blackened bar there was a telephone that consisted of the dial and three wires. The page of a notepad trembled in the breeze. On it was a half-faded reckoning, in pencil: two cakes, two teas, one rouble eighty-five kopeks.

He went up to the edge of the roof, secured by no wall or fencing. All around him were clusters of high-rises and strings of outsize pylons that wandered right through the city centre; he made out equestrian statues, radio transmitters, fountains, railway stations, factory chimneys, a football stadium to the north of the city. Bare ochre hills ringed the metropolis. Olive orchards and greybrown fields lay to the south. In the west of Yerevan, though, in the late afternoon light, the silhouette of the double-peaked mountain loomed through the grime: the taller of the two peaks conical, wrapped in ice, and the other shorter and sharper. Tigor felt a pain in his right wrist that he hadn't felt since childhood. A dull glow, like a deep electrical throbbing. I first felt this pain, Tigor thought, when I was holding the bars of my cot, as a three- or four-year-old, in the dark apartment at number 25, Viale XX Settembre. I was holding on to the struts, and pushed my head through the bars like a little zoo animal, trapped and closely guarded at the same time.

He walked out into the dusk, down a narrow, dirty street that led directly off Lenin Square, between rows of houses that were two or three storeys high, skewed by the wind, crumbling their colourless plaster. Children were playing in the muddy puddles in front of the entrances, between piles of wood and pieces of broken furniture. Rats scurried hither and thither. Through a small, grimy window, he watched an old man walking round and round a room in rapid circles, spitting at each of his four walls in turn.

At a crossroads, three men came up to Tigor, asked him to sell them anything he had, or alternatively to exchange it, his shirt, his shoes, his watch or his cigarette case. '. . . here no shops . . .,' said one of them. '. . . here no buy . . .,' said the second. '. . . here no good . . .,' the third. 'You good man. America?' asked the first. 'Chicago, Spiderman, Phantom-Jet?' He looked strong and bold, his eyes were very large and pale blue. He wanted to know the stranger's name, but didn't volunteer his own. 'I most important man of Wild East,' he claimed. Asked how it was that he knew English, the fellow replied: '. . . oh! I collection comic books . . .'

There was nothing to which Tigor was more attached than his gold-nibbed, black-and-green-striped fountain pen, from which he had been inseparable these past twenty years. It surprised him that it was this he was now parting from. That it felt easy to abandon his pen. The street pirates had never had such a magnificent item in their hands.

'See you later, alligator!' called their leader. Then (not out of ignorance, but for the sake of justice) they carefully divided the fountain pen into its six component parts, and shared them out fraternally among themselves.

Not owning a street map or having a plan for the evening, Tigor somehow wound up in front of Oganessian's apartment block in Acharian Street anyway, fully two miles away from Lenin Square. The staircase, its windowpanes without a single exception smashed, stank of festering rubbish. On the third floor, laughter issued from one of the apartments, and low voices were audible. Tigor stood motionless in front of the door for several minutes, before ringing the bell.

He was led straight away into the dining room of the comfortable, generously proportioned apartment, where the nine bearded Scandinavians were pressed together at a long table together with Oganessian's three daughters. Silva, the lady of the house, served the food, kept going back to the kitchen for more dishes, plates and pots. Johann Wolfgang was enthroned at the head of the table, flung his arms in the air when he saw Tigor come in. He introduced him as an Italian theatre man who had been sent to him by a doctor in Paris, his school-friend Kevork Chabanian.

At the other end of the table sat a grinning man who looked like the spit and image of Oganessian. '. . . not blench – it is but Friedrich, my twin soul!' cried Johann Wolfgang, and the Scandinavians laughed like a tuba nonet.

'My friends and I, we could hardly credit it!' explained August, the spokesman for the archaeologists.

'. . . my twin brother Friedrich, he is fifteen-fold national champion in weightlifting! All the youth of Hajastan swear by him, under his Armenian name of Aristakes!' He ushered the newcomer to the place next to Aristakes. 'Our youth', he added, 'doesn't swear by the beard of the prophet, that is the preserve of those criminal peoples, with whom we have the misfortune to be neighbours. Our young people, and may I be split by lightning if what I say is false, they like to swear by the name of my twin here!'

Aristakes shook Tigor by the hand. His grip was unexpectedly gentle. Where Johann Wolfgang had pudgy fingers with dirty, chewed fingernails, the hands of his twin brother were carefully groomed, and seemed altogether finer. Where the one was forever dripping with sweat, at any hour of day or night, the other was always cool, and he smelled of imported eau de cologne. The weightlifter was, like his brother, going bald, but he tried to cover his bare scalp with his few remaining strands of hair, dunked in hair oil, and of a similar thickness to packing twine.

Silva kept bringing new outlandish appetizers to the table. Johann Wolfgang took a couple of mouthfuls of the stuffed vine leaves and a couple of mouthfuls of aubergine paste, then filled his glass with vodka, and rose to make his first speech. In it, he gave expression to the hope that his guests might enjoy a long and healthy life. He stressed the immeasurable joy to his family and himself of being accorded the privilege of welcoming to his home both the delegation of his colleagues and the visitor from Paris. 'Until very, very recently,' he cried joyfully, 'it was not thinkable to be able to offer welcome to foreign visitors from abroad within four walls here. Not a little has history changed our country! Not a little! Previously, for every good-honest word, I must have had to go to Siberia. Previously, I had to lie all-the-time. Today I need no longer to lie.' He emptied his glass. 'To the friendship between the peoples of the Caucasus and the people of Europe!' He proceeded, without any transition, to enthuse about a new drill recently developed in Sweden, with the help of which his own research would be greatly simplified, if only he were able to afford said piece of equipment, 'let alone in its sweet entirety'.

Aristakes muttered incomprehensibly. Tigor slid his chair nearer. '. . . a coarse violation of manners,' whispered the weightlifter, 'talking to you while our *Tamada*, our host, is still speaking. But I must tell you one thing: there is good connection, having you in our midst, here in Yerevan. In the apartment of my brother, on this third floor! Let it be as it is. No coincidence without desire. Everything that befalls is equally meaningless and miraculous. I welcome you!'

'Brother heart!' Johann Wolfgang's voice boomed down from the other end of the table, 'I am almost finished with my speech. Your whisperings reveal to me that you, too, desire to speak. As our *Tamada* here, I hereby cede the floor to you.'

Thereupon the fifteen-times weightlifting champion got to his feet, similarly held his glass in his extended hand, called out: '... *kenatzed!*' And then, when the other fifteen persons present had responded: '... *kenatzed!*', he drew a huge breath, as though about to jerk a two-hundred-and-fifty-kilogram weight. 'Let us drink to this ceremonial occasion! Health, happiness and fertility to you assembled here! It is destiny with her fine ropes that brings us together now, we who have never known each other before. Far distant things are carefully and fatefully brought together to this city and this table. But we are no puppets! Currents flow about us and invisible reins direct our footfall. Our father often said to his children: "The more irregular the net thrown by the bold fisherman, the more blest the catch!" On how many occasions we do things, not knowing why we do them. But then when we one day look back on these actions, we may discern something like an internal landscape, a pattern, a coded message, that tells us why we have taken this step or that one, why we have permitted this decision to prevail over that one, when we found ourselves standing at a crossroads. Everything is changing, everything is in movement. Sometimes the movement is so slow that it doesn't appear. But there is always change, and always movement ... At every point of the earth, there is a point of possible connection to every human being. But a man needs time to find these points of connection, for them to disclose themselves to him . . . This evening here and now will remain in my memory, I will often see it before me. Like the repeating of some sporting event on the television, I will see this evening again and again: in slow motion! I drink to the kindly circumstances that have brought us all together! *Kenatzed!*'

Milk soups and meat dumplings were served, and fresh trout from Lake Sevan and mutton on skewers. After every course, one of the members of the delegation was obliged to make the ritual speech and toast. Generally, they were more stammering than suave about it, some of them were pitiful and barely audible, one or two rose to the occasion rather gracefully. Knut, a paleontologist from Malmo, with a large pointed head, astonished his hosts by requesting permission to ask for the hand of the oldest Oganessian daughter, who had just turned twenty-one. Takuhy, who was sitting next to him, and didn't grasp what was happening to her, blushed beetroot. She then turned pale, as her father failed to reject the request out of hand.

In his own speech, August stressed that he would personally do all in his power to see that the Swedish state would make Johann Wolfgang a present of the drilling equipment he so unambiguously craved. '. . . a more explicit instance of nudging and winking, my dear friend Oganessian,' he added, to general merriment, 'than you gave in your welcoming speech is hard to imagine!'

By the time the great array of desserts had been eaten, the guests, with a single exception, had all had their say. All eyes were on Tigor. He remained seated. Instead of holding his brimming glass out to the assembled company, he drained it. 'Forgive me!' It sounded as though he were speaking to himself. 'Forgive me: I'm a man of few words,' he began by claiming. 'The circumstances that have brought me to Yerevan, and hence to this gathering tonight, and this table, were thrown up from a plane of existence that I have done everything to deny. These circumstances are emissaries from a grey area that I was always afraid of coming into contact with, fearing, as I did, that if I gave in to their blandishments, then they would lead me down to unplumbed depths, and rupture all my ties with so-called reality. I lived, to put it briefly, by Newton and Descartes: in the conceit that our life, our world, followed a strictly determinist path, one that observed natural laws as immutable as the trajectories of the planets, and as predictable as the eclipses and tides. I clung to these venerable traditions, even though the way new ground is broken in mathematics is when established laws are *violated*. Only rarely did I ponder whether it wasn't high time for this axiom or that theorem to be reconsidered . . .'

Johann Wolfgang, who continued to see in Tigor the rigging worker he had first been presented as, gesticulated to his brother: a jiggling movement of thumb and forefinger in front of his temples as though shaking an invisible test tube. Aristakes, however, indicated that he wanted to follow their guest's discourse undisturbed, and certainly didn't desire it to be curtailed.

The speaker rose, steadied himself on the armrest of his chair. His eyes went round the room. Little pictures decorated the pale green walls. Storm at sea with sailing boat. Lagoon in fog. Fishing port in pink evening light. Behind Johann Wolfgang's back, a tall display cabinet in which various finds from the crust of the Caucasus were displayed on seven glass shelves, among them pieces of rock crystal and fossilized snail shells. A bunch of red-and-white carnations in a tall vase. 'I am anxious not to burden you needlessly by these personal revelations,' he carried on, 'though of course the glasses we have drunk together . . . one more thing I want to say: I have given – I occupied a Chair in Mathematics at the University of Pennsylvania in Philadelphia – I have given years of my life to the elaboration of one particular mathematical theory . . . I had entered, perhaps this is familiar to you too from your own discipline, a quasi-matrimonial relationship with the topic of my research. I was obsessed by a single idea. I gave everything to it that I had. Every minute not spent in the pursuit of my objective seemed an unbearable sacrifice to me.

'However, several months ago, I was forced to witness the final demolition of my quest for knowledge, it was in the course of a mathematical conference, held in, of all places, my birthplace of Trieste – that too certainly not by chance, or, if you prefer, purely by chance, seeing as what is decreed to befall us in life, is our lot, as my neighbour so eloquently suggested just now . . . I was compelled therefore to confront the irreversible destruction of my life's work, for which I had worked myself into the ground, and which, on top of everything else, has also kept me from the society of my fellow-beings for the past fifteen years and more. One rainy Tuesday changed my life and showed me the spectacle of a self in ruins. I have always belonged to that school of mathematicians to whom the utility of their investigations was an essential element, I was never one of those to whom mathematics was an art form, whose usefulness outside the convent walls of mathematics was not considered. My students not infrequently reproached me for the humdrum objectivity of my approach. One of them said to me once, Professor, he said, the First World War was made possible by chemists, the Second World War by physicists. The Third World War will be the one that will be fought out by the knowledge and the gifts of us mathematicians. I don't want to live under that sort of responsibility any more. And he abjured mathematics . . .

'Following my personal experiences of the last few months, please forgive me for talking about myself like this . . . following a certain chain of events, I am now in the process . . . to transform my entire relationship with mathematics . . . That plane of hypothesis, intuition, guesswork . . . I no longer exclude the possibility, as I used to, that the gates of the unconscious may afford us better access to reality than the gates of pragmatism. *Perhaps the unconscious has a secret method of calculating which is better than any known method* . . . Do you understand me? The way I see it today, mathematics is a *terrain vague*, neither more true nor more unreal than our dreams. The ideal mathematician grubs for his finds, the way archaeologists dig for traces of the past, we need to make our way through layer after layer, to feel our way towards the secrets, we need to entrust ourselves to feelings and intuitions and leave set formulas alone, because they will only diminish and hinder us, in all the sciences they are brake blocks . . . And so I raise my glass to our host and his family, rarely in my life have I eaten and drunk as well as here with you, I drink to your health and the health of your children and your children's children!'

Those around the table held out their glasses towards him. They made a kind of dove-like murmur that might indicate agreement, or then again demurral. Johann Wolfgang thanked his guest, welcoming his words as a sign of deep confidence, as they had given the company an insight into profoundly personal conflicts. Yerevan, he assured him, was the ideal place to bring the inner struggle he was evidently engaged in to a victorious conclusion. 'Yerevan has healing powers, believe me. Our city is related to the ancient cities of Jerusalem and Jericho,' he said. He admitted that his friend Chabanian couldn't have told him all there was to know about Tigor's identity, because he now saw that the ostensible stagehand was in reality an internationally renowned mathematician, and he therefore now felt doubly proud to have had a man, as he put it, 'of such calibre' as his guest.

'*Such* a Philistine, my dear brother!' cried Aristakes, from the other end of the table. 'What if your visitor had turned out to be the finance minister of the republic of X, would you have crawled under the table, and nuzzled his feet? Our guest is a man of great heart. To anyone with eyes, it takes just a glance to see that. And *basta*! Who cares what the profession might be! "Calibre"! It makes my blood cook!' Tigor laid a hand on his neighbour's arm to calm him, to thank him.

The company around the table began to loosen. People yawned, stretched. Knut asked Tigor whether he happened to know his friend, Professor Joshua Dellman, the Rector of the Archaeological Institute of the University of Pennsylvania?

'I know him well. He's not a particular friend of mine, in fact I find him quite repellent,' replied Tigor. Heavy with cognac, he stumbled through the rooms, wound up in front of the tall bookcase, reached for the cloth-bound first edition of Novalis's *Fragments*. Looked up the page headed 'Magical Mathematics'. 'Miracles, being facts against nature, are amathematical,' he read, 'but there are no miracles of that type, and what are called such are made graspable by mathematics, because to mathematics nothing is miraculous.' And a few lines later: '. . . in the time when numbers were new, certain commonly occurring numbers that corresponded to real things, characteristic, lasting numbers, as for example, ten fingers, and other striking numerical phenomena, must have engaged the imagination of people with especial vividness, and caused them to sense in the science of numbers a buried trove of wisdom, a key to all the locked doors of nature.'

He returned to the gathering. '. . . I'm so sorry: I mean . . . when you asked me just now . . .' he stammered as he faced Knut Mertens. 'I don't know Professor Dellman at all well. That's the truth. He is very well regarded. I just want to say, if you could please . . . I'd rather people didn't know . . . that you've seen . . . that we met here. It might create difficulties for me.'

'Let me set your mind at rest on that,' replied the man from Malmo, sounding very jovial. 'I give you my word – as a gentleman!'

The twin brothers escorted their guests back to the city centre. The gaggle of men strode through pitch darkness: the city centre had street lighting, but not the suburbs. Aristakes slowly removed himself from the group, a step at a time, taking Tigor with him. After a quarter of an hour or so, they were on their own, following narrow alleyways and gloomy covered passages that only a native would know.

'. . . my brother can sometimes get on my nerves a little,' he explained, 'and I rejoice that I can speak to you as man to man. In my eighteenth year, I became a father, I have two sons and two daughters. Unfortunately my children, of whom I am fiercely proud, could not be with us tonight. You shall be my guest in my house, in my big garden, and there you will be able to meet them. You shall drive with me and my family to Lake Sevan, and spend the night in my dacha. And early in the morning we will take rowing boat to go fishing! . . . Are you father yourself?'

In his exhaustion, it seemed to Tigor, if only for a moment, as though the weightlifter's words had been bundled up into lasers, which an imaginary projectionist was flashing onto an endless screen. He imagined he could see the colour of the sons' eyes, the cleavages of the daughters, the wife's carmine lipstick, and he could make out the pollen on the apple blossoms in Aristakes' garden.

'. . . are they apple trees in your garden?' he asked.

'Apple trees I don't have, I regret. They are nut trees, my whole pride.'

'Nut trees . . .?'

'And you? A father to children?' Aristakes would not be deflected.

'Is your apartment on the ground floor?'

'That is so. Has Johann Wolfgang told you? . . . With us men, is never too late, right to our dying day! Take my uncle Astig: seventy-nine, he has become a father, week before last.'

'. . . who doesn't have a child isn't a whole man, my uncle always used to say to me.'

'He spoke truly, your uncle . . . Tell me more about the woman who did not want children!'

'What about your wife – does she have black hair?'

'Dyed red. Why do you ask that sort of question?'

'Forgive me . . .'

'She is my entire pride, my little angel!' cried Aristakes. 'Only a couple few years ago, I was in a knife-fight over my adored one, because a stranger spoke to her insultingly, she was still so attractive though she was already fifty-five years . . . My opponent stabbed me in the middle of the heart, here! They performed operation, and I was saved. But ever since, my pulse has beat irregular, it goes tatac-ta-tactacatac, and so forth, at first it was a grave difficulty for me, I become very feeble and faint, till step by step my body accustoms itself. Now I live with it fairly passably. Only I need to take rest a little from time to time. And that incident, how could it be otherwise, meant the end of my career in active sport . . .'

Tigor divulged to Friedrich that, a matter of weeks previously, he had blacked out as a result of heart insufficiency. At that, the one-time national champion weightlifter put his arm through Tigor's and pressed the stranger to himself. 'You don't have many friends, my friend. Am I correct?' he asked.

'You are correct.'

'You may assuredly address me as "Du". To find a friend, you had to jump through many hoops, am I correct?' The light of a half-moon lit their way through ramshackle alleys and paths paved with duckboards. '. . . in me, though, you have a friend for life. And a friend, furthermore, not without influence in this magnificent country. If you like it here, I can organize it that you stay as long as your panic-struck heart desires. You see, I lay my cards out on the table. I am the director of the only state-owned mirror factory. I took over this proud post from my father-in-law, the veteran Communist Aram Ohandjanian. You will visit me there, in my factory, you will learn from me many things, if I am not mistaken . . .!'

Outside the hotel he gave Tigor a crumpled city map that he carried with him. Pink high-rise apartment buildings protruded from toxic green parks, and on the edge of the colourful map there was the snow-capped peak of the double mountain. 'I expect you without fail, tomorrow afternoon at four o'clock. In my factory at 25th Street, Nor Aresh district!'

There was no wind, and with the window open Tigor could hear the water splashing in the fountain. The past day hung over the exhausted man. The sheets smelled of moth powder. No sooner

116

had he reached the first, shallowest level of sleep than there was a loud knocking on his door. The floor-lady (she hadn't been relieved for the night shift) handed the visitor an envelope. 'I fear I can't wait till tomorrow with what I have to tell you. Come downstairs please. I must talk to you. Your friend, Friedrich/Aristakes.'

They sank into a couple of worn armchairs in the deserted hotel bar. 'I have something to tell you,' the champion began, 'but you must promise me in advance that you will believe me. Can you do that?' Tigor said nothing. 'It began when I was five years old . . . I beg you not to laugh . . .' He told him how from early childhood on he had only had one aim in mind: to search for remnants of Noah's Ark on Mount Ararat. He had never questioned the literal truth of the story of the Flood. Ever since he'd been capable of thought, he'd suffered from the fact that men were dragging 'the words of Heaven' down in the dirt. As a stripling, he had formulated a plan for his life: '. . . to proceed with the search at any cost, regardless of losses. Then however I become a family man early, and that marks a decisive change in the feelings of a man. But still I cling to my conviction: that if traces of the Ark be found, that is proof of the historical truth of the Flood. And from there it is only a short step to the constatation that the Tower of Babel actually stood, that Jacob's Ladder is the truth, that Abraham was indeed instructed to sacrifice Isaac, his firstborn, that Pharaoh's armies were overwhelmed in the waters of the Red Sea, that the Ten Commandments were engraved in stone, and that the Saviour has risen. I supply, and this is from childhood my unappeasable desire, the incontrovertible proof for the veracity of the Divine Books. I bring to the world the proof positive, as you mathematicians like to say when you prove your hypothesis . . .'

'But the idea of a proof is so mendacious!' Tigor shot back. 'There's no such thing as a complete proof. All we can ever do is *demonstrate* something, never conclusively prove it. Strictly speaking, there is no such thing as a proof in mathematics,' he said, hunching his back as he always did when teaching. 'Proofs are illusions, rhetorical devices, tricks of the light, the kind of thing we use to excite the imagination of students at our lectures, so they don't run off right away, and study some other subject . . .'

'. . . but a weightier factor is this: under my nationality, it is forbidden to me to visit the land west of the border, the land that belongs to our people,' Aristakes carried on, indomitably, he probably hadn't even been listening. 'No Hajastani is permitted to travel there! And I, as a father many times over, could not have risked it either, my body riddled by machine guns or thrown behind bars. The dream had to be set aside, put in the icebox. But I knew the day would come, the weather would turn, a new day would dawn. And then my dream would finally be realized . . .'

Memories rose in Tigor, obscured by thick banks of clouds, of the dangerous ascent he had undertaken in the *cintriers'* room in the Odéon. 'With my heart, I'm not capable of climbing a mountain like that . . . should you happen to have been thinking of me.'

'You have been brought here', responded Aristakes, 'by some mysterious and providential force, surely you sense that . . . We both talked about it before, at dinner!'

'I've been brought here by my damnable rudderlessness. Nothing else. Nor do I believe in those . . . books of yours. Religion is tying down and fixity. There's none of that in my life . . .'

'That's a somewhat scanty basis, I'd say, no?'

Filthy half-collapsed workbenches and ancient grindstones, rusted taps fully a yard long, thousands upon thousands of shards of glass in all colours and shapes on the bare brick floor – Armenia's premier state-owned mirror factory looked as though it had been neglected for decades and then left in a kind of Sleeping Beauty trance. Stannic chloride, silver nitrate and caustic soda fumes rose from unstoppered jars, mingled and fogged Tigor's head, he felt instant dizziness. He had only come in order to take his leave of Aristakes. Had lain awake all night till his mind was made up, not to permit himself to be catapulted from place to place any longer. He would go back to his life in Philadelphia.

'You look as if you've just had a heart attack!' the mirror manufacturer greeted him. 'So: an inspection of the enterprise which is my entire pride and joy is now planned for tomorrow, this afternoon is devoted to fresh air, we are going on a motorbike excursion!'

Tigor shuddered. 'I want to say goodbye to you, Aristakes.

What you were looking to me for . . . has nothing to do with . . . my life. Please don't bear me any ill will.'

Oganessian hesitated briefly. 'I bear you no ill will,' he said. 'One shouldn't use compulsion. Perhaps I have been a little heated at times.'

'Where was the excursion to?' Tigor heard himself ask, unwillingly.

'To the monastery of Khorvirap. There is no place in our country that is nearer to the frontier. The three old people are waiting for us, the last representatives of the Ten Tribes. I have asked them to be there . . . No matter . . .' The big man, several hundred pounds of him, stood lost on his factory floor, a frail monster, a brute angel, and his voice sounded very sorrowful.

'I should like to . . . see this monastery,' said Tigor.

The mirror manufacturer flung his arms around him.

Aristakes steered the primordial, infernally noisy motorbike over potholed roads, through tan-coloured plains. Tigor perched in a yellow canoe-shaped sidecar, his elbows propped on the pale-blue mudguards either side.

Khorvirap was situated on a hill that afforded a wide view of the flat borderlands below. They could see the river meadows of the Araxes, where the early-warning equipment was concealed. The watchtowers of both states could be seen. The light was murky, even at this proximity Ararat was obscured from sight. In the cloisters, a group of people stood together as though posed for a formal photograph. In front of them, on unsteady legs, they had a thick, dirty sheep with a red cloth tied round its neck. A girl with a long blonde pigtail had it on a rope. The end of the rope was made fast to one of the animal's hind legs. The little girl was in festive dress, white blouse, black skirt and black waistcoat. She had white plastic sandals on her bare feet. When she saw the stranger coming, she called out: 'Hey, hello, mister!' And again: 'Hello, hey, you, mister!'

Aristakes began by introducing Tigor to the priest, Sagatel, and then to the little girl and her parents. Her father, a turner in a heavy machinery plant in Yerevan, no longer young, was unable to suppress a continual grin. His wife was bigger, fatter and altogether more sure of herself than her husband. She had once been a train driver, and had given up her job when Seda was born. She tugged at her father's robe, to get him to shake hands with the visitor. The old man was blind, but gave the impression of being otherwise hale and cheerful. Round his waist he wore an ammunition belt with bronze bullets in it as big as fingers. Tigor was also presented to Artem, the older brother of Samvel, the blind man, who had been, before his retirement, a well-known geologist and geochemist. A little to the side stood an old, brightly made-up woman who was evidently waiting to be approached. 'Don't come too near me!' called the turner's mother, when Tigor was just a step away. 'I am very tired and I have the flu!'

Aristakes said, '. . . Madame here has been travelling ever since World War One. She has lived in New York and in Hollywood. She feels equally much at home in Prague and Budapest as in Tashkent or Tiflis!'

The priest cut into the sheep's left ear with a rusty knife. Seda allowed the warm blood to dribble across her finger, then painted a cross on her forehead in blood. Sagatel crammed a fistful of salt into the mouth of the tired animal, and chanted a benediction.

'. . . so that the sheep is blessed . . .!' explained the mirror manufacturer.

Tigor assumed the ceremony, whose purpose he did not understand, was thereby concluded. He wanted to inspect the dome structure of the little seventh century church, which he remembered from depictions of it contained in the volume that Chabanian had lent him in Paris. Aristakes seized him by the wrist: 'There's no way in the world you can leave now!'

'Why not?' asked Tigor, broke free.

'You'll see! Now be quiet and come along!'

The other members of the family followed Sagatel, who, with the sheep, descended a few wide stone steps that led down from the back of the cloister to some bushes. Numerous brightly coloured rags had been tied to the nibbled twigs, to symbolize the wishes and prayers of devout women and children. In their midst, though, was a stone slaughtering bench, buzzed around by flies, with a rough corrugated iron roof put over it. Seda's father quickly led the sheep on to the stone expanse, laid the animal out on its side, dropped on his knees across its neck and forequarters, and a moment later, slit its throat. The blood issued from its carotid artery in thick spurts. The sheep made no cry, not even a groan. Its hind legs, though, kicked out wildly. They were still twitching rapidly when the head, but for a few strands of sinew, had been severed from the body. Tigor felt a sharp surge of nausea in his mouth, fled back up the stairs to the cloisters. He didn't see the butcher sawing off the lamb's forelegs. Didn't know that the sacrificial beast was still trembling once its head was fully separated from its body, and Seda's smiling moustached father had tossed the skull away in a great arc, sending it bouncing down the rocky hill like a ball. The body went on trembling and quivering minutes longer as it bled.

Aristakes had followed Tigor, found him huddled on the floor of the church. 'But all this is put on for your benefit, this sacrifice! Towards the success of your enterprise! The one you wanted to perform on behalf of us all, who are forbidden! You are our one ray of hope! The three old ones, Samvel, Artem and Medji, will instruct you. They will initiate you in our secret knowledge.' Aristakes laughed. 'A child you are! Well, what we commonly refer to as a man, that you decidedly are not?! . . . Admittedly, there are surviving elements of heathenness still among us. But no people on earth adopted Christianity and made it the state religion as early as we did. In the Year of Our Lord 301. Show me what other people did that! In 301, your forefathers were still little better than chimpanzees!'

Tigor didn't budge.

A class of schoolchildren was taken through the church, eight- and nine-year-olds who surrounded the stranger. Caution and curiosity visibly fought in them. One asked: 'Where you come from?'

'You astronaut?' asked another.

'I'm a teacher,' said Tigor.

When he returned to the butchering place with Aristakes, a skinned carcass was hanging from a large butcher's hook. Seda's father stashed the bloody skin in the boot of his car.

Medji called out to Tigor: 'Me, I also didn't look!'

Then the group clustered round him, wished him good luck and offered him encouragement, shook his hand. Sagatel gave a short speech, which Aristakes translated selectively, lest Tigor be frightened off by its religious zeal. 'He says, you are the one chosen by the forces of destiny to find the remains of the Ark ship for us. He says, the Elders, the descendants of Noah's family, will give you strength and knowledge. He says, in the fertile Ararat plain, which is spread out before our eyes, a delivered people have already once undertaken the first steps towards a new beginning . . . He blesses you, and he blesses your ancestors . . .'

'My thanks to him,' whispered Tigor. 'But you had no right to tell him fairy tales . . . I'm not the man you take me for.'

The mirror manufacturer translated Tigor's rebuttal: 'He tells us that he is prepared to take on the sacred duty we have offered him.' He pointed in the direction of the – invisible – double peak, clasped his friend's shoulder. 'Now you are on the wrong side of the frontier,' he said. 'But when summer draws to an end, you will cross into the country that was once called Hajastan, and you will climb the mother of all mountains. You see where the border runs among the river meadows. That, my brother, is no ordinary death-strip, it is the line of demarcation between us Christians on one side and the enemy peoples on the other. Our enemies choke us on all sides. Here before our eyes are the Turks of Turkey. To my back are the Turks of Azerbaijan. In the south are the Turkic peoples of Nakhichevan, which word "Nakhichevan" signifies "the landing place", that country also belonged to us, before the Turkic peoples stole it from us . . . Only to the north do we have half-brothers in the good Georgian people . . .'

Samvel, the blind elder, groped for Tigor's eyebrows, his nose, cheeks, lips, stroked him with his rough hand. The chosen man let it happen.

'You look *so* worried!' cried Medji, made her excuses, she had to go back to Yerevan, back to bed, otherwise her chronic fever would break out again, that she had carried about with her ever since her visit to John Barrymore's weekend hacienda in Palm Springs, in the desert of Southern California, forty-five years ago now. If she overtired herself any time since then she would without fail get a high temperature and the shivers.

The family of seven got back in the little car that had carried them up, when the sheep had travelled in the open boot.

'That class of schoolchildren we ran into earlier, what about if I . . .' He stopped. The idea seemed very far-fetched. He was no longer sure whether it was a good one.

The mirror maker was washing his hands close to the shambles. The water came out of the pipe a few drops at a time. 'What are you telling me?' he asked.

'Nothing. Wasn't anything.'

'Now don't tell lies. You wanted to talk to me about that class of schoolchildren . . .'

'Oh, just nonsense . . . I was thinking if I could teach the children . . . maybe that would make me want to stay on a while . . . I'm sure it's not possible anyway . . .'

'. . . not *possible*?! There's hardly anything we need so much as outstanding minds, perhaps also teaching the children a little English!' Aristakes burst forth, 'for in future, I believe, we will be ever more closely entwined with the English language . . . And with the new forms of mathematics, still more! Quite apart from that, it would constitute an enrichment of our urban scene to be accommodating you here with us, to exchange ideas with you would be my entire pride and joy! . . . I must telephone Minister Edilian immediately!' He ran around in circles like a headless chicken. Tore up the steps to the cloister, after a long search found the porter of the monastery. Learned from him that Khorvirap was not connected. Allowed ten minutes to pass before returning to Tigor.

'It's in the bag,' he claimed, all out of breath, 'the Minister hails your international co-operation initiative, of which the children of our workers are to benefit. In view of the current precarious financial situation of our Republic, your gesture of solidarity will have to be strictly on a voluntary basis: we are, Edilian reminded me, much more densely populated than most of the Soviet Union, while having less water and less cultivable soil than the other republics. Comrade Oganessian, he said, we are, I hardly need to remind you, barely able to feed our own people. We have very small mineral deposits. Our modest financial plan for the next five years dictates that any surplus must go to our brothers and sisters in the disputed territory of Karabakh (within the borders of the Republic of Azerbaijan, and thus surrounded by our enemies). We see ourselves facing a completely unfamiliar situation: every day our brothers and sisters in Karabakh come to us with new needs and new desires. Whatever it is they ask for from us,

we are determined to help them, at whatever the cost to ourselves
. . . Many of our teachers, Edilian said, have gone to Karabakh in
the course of the last few months, which only makes this surprising development more welcome to me . . . We are agreed then:
you are to teach English to some junior classes of boys and girls in
Yerevan. And in addition, if humanly possible, some of the very
basics of mathematics?!'

Tigor appeared more cheerful than for some months. The men
shook hands. Aristakes took the lamb's carcass off its hook, and
managed to secure it to the sidecar. Back in the city, he first
dropped off his exhausted friend outside his hotel. He then went
on to the nearby Education Ministry on the corner of Alaverdian
and Tchaikovsky Streets, there, in front of the main entrance, he
shouldered the headless sheep, climbed up several flights of
stairs to the top of the building, and knocked on Samson Edilian's
leather-padded double door. Set the meat down beside a pair of
red telephones on some of the newspapers that covered the entire
desk. And finally, seated under a relief of Marx and Engels that
went on for several yards, gave voice to his request.

'. . . it's in the bag,' the Minister replied without any hesitation.
He was an athletic-looking young man with sandy hair. After eloquently thanking him for his generous gift, he continued: 'I welcome the initiative of your friend, which will benefit the children
of our workers. Thank him, on my behalf, for his gesture of solidarity. Is he of Armenian extraction, your friend? . . . No? That
complicates things a little, but we'll still find a solution. I'm sure
he'll get a residence permit from Moscow, as his is an international initiative. The times have changed out of recognition. What
yesterday seemed unimaginable is fact today. Please be sure to
stress to your friend the precarious financial situation of our
Republic! I hope your friend – what's his name, by the way? – will
be good enough to call on me later today. I will use him in the
Haghtanak School on Babayan Street. Do you know it?'

The very first evening after his arrival in Paris found Abraham
Porter strolling to the return address Tigerman had written on
the envelope containing his calculations about the tides in
Delaware Bay: 176, rue d'Assas. (The research assignment from
the Navy had been awarded to the postgraduate students, they

were due to begin on the work in the following semester.) The student could not find his professor's name written anywhere, neither on the ground floor on any of the letterboxes, nor on any of the apartment doors up and down the building. He rang all the bells, but no one would let him in. Through a series of locked doors, he tried to explain what he was after. No one had any knowledge of the person he was asking for. He climbed right up to the attic, to the maids' rooms under the eaves, and knocked on all the doors there too.

Once he'd explained to her what he'd come about, Madame Murat, the senior park warden of the Luxembourg gardens, allowed him into her attic room, and poured him out a glass of champagne which he, however, refused. '. . . a present from my staff . . .!' she said, and refilled her own glass. Madame Murat suggested to the American, to whom she took an immediate shine, that he might try his luck at the Théâtre de l'Odéon, the *cintriers* would surely be able to help him, she hadn't seen Monsieur Tigor for several days now herself. She told the stranger in great detail all about her latest mishap. She had had her bag snatched the night before at the Métro station of the Gare de Montparnasse, and lost her year's travel pass, family photographs and some cash. She made no allowances for the fact that Abraham's high school French was wholly unequal to understanding her rapid monologue. In the end, he had to ask Madame what the Odéon was, and above all what '*cintriers*' was supposed to mean.

He had to overcome a certain amount of shyness to take the few steps from the small hotel where he was staying, Des Deux Continents, to the Théâtre de l'Odéon. Napoleon greeted him courteously, asked him no questions, and ushered him straight into the building. Abraham had been given a map by Madame Murat, and climbed up to the *cintriers'* room, felt completely ridiculous, had no idea what he was doing, looking for Tigerman inside a theatre.

Not even Hakim, who at this point wasn't even aware that his friend had left, was able to help the American. He sent him down to Mrs Hathaway.

Abraham spent a whole hour in her office, gave vent to his grief and rage, learned from her that his professor had indeed spent several months working as a rigger in the theatre, a fact that seemed completely to unhinge him. '. . . but where is he *now*, the motherfucker?!' he screamed.

The theatre deputy manageress gave the student the address in the rue Monsieur le Prince, advised him to get in touch with the former housekeeper of the deceased Arnold Bohm. A Portuguese concierge was washing the stairs and singing when he entered the building. Esmelinda led him up to the top floor. They knocked on Agueda's attic door together. She didn't answer. After a few knocks, a grumbling was heard within. Agueda refused to open. The Portuguese girl then accompanied Abraham back down to the first floor, to the apartment of the lawyer, de Sagarra. His wife was at home, and asked the gigantic basketball player into her sitting room. The Armenian woman knew Tigor's probable whereabouts, but regretted that she unfortunately had no address for him, or the name of anyone in Yerevan who might be able to get in touch with him. At that, Abraham understood the true reason for Tigor's peculiar behaviour over the last few months. His teacher, there could be no doubt about this, had become embroiled in some espionage affair. All at once Tigor's outrageous farrago of lies turned out to be a carefully contrived cover story.

From the same telephone box from which Tigor had so often called him, Abraham now called Marina, his girlfriend, and Evan, his best friend. They had clubbed together with other students to pay for their friend to fly to Europe, convinced he would be successful in securing the return of their errant favourite professor. Both Marina and Evan laughed when he told them sadly what he had managed to find out. Espionage, they each said, independently, was all in the past, Tigerman was undergoing a grave personal crisis, which was prompting him to flee to impossible places. It was with difficulty that they managed to dissuade him from taking his suspicions to the American Embassy in Paris.

Accompanied by Marie-Antoinette, he climbed up to the rigging once more a few days later, and informed Hakim of the sad truth. The *cintrier* heard the news with consternation. His show of shock was not without talent, given that he had received a letter from Yerevan that morning. In it, Tigor had apologized for leaving without saying goodbye, and promised to keep his Odéon colleagues abreast of what was happening to him. '. . . however,' his letter concluded, 'should you be approached by a student of mine, by the name of Abraham Porter, I happened to glimpse him arriving just as I was leaving, you must tell him you have NO NEWS, he's looking for me, and is perfectly capable of following me all the way here too! Please help me to elude him! In old seamanly troth, Your T.'

Abraham went back to Madame Murat. She comforted him, toasted bread for him, spread with soft goat's cheese, and, after she'd run out of champagne, gave him cheap red wine from Cahors, out of unlabelled bottles. And Abraham ended up staying with her, and stayed for several days. The park warden, who visited a fortune teller twice a month, a woman by whose advice she did absolutely everything, had laid cards not long ago that strongly suggested that a powerful, humourless man would appear in her life, and make her reasonably happy.

On four mornings a week, Tigor now taught mathematics and English in the primary school in Babayan Street, in cramped, squalid classrooms that reeked of cold sweat, chalk and ancient wooden benches. In the introduction to the English textbook he started off by using, though he cast it aside soon enough, the author designated his oeuvre 'as a means of communication in the cause of socialist patriotism and proletarian internationalism'. The classroom walls were graced by the inevitable picture of Lenin and faded reproductions of photographs of Ararat.

Tigor's pupils were aged between six and ten, and they took to their new teacher, whom they called the American. More problematic were relations between the stranger and his new colleagues. Most of the ladies and gentlemen in the teachers' common room were violently opposed to Tigor's appointment, didn't altogether understand it even. He never actually came up against his opponents: they avoided him, and he did nothing to seek them out. The syllabus was not significantly different from that in the States: in Yerevan as well the youngest classes were instructed in the basics of set theory, and the beginnings of group theory, and nine-year-olds were expected to be able to calculate the area of a triangle. Tigor was able to teach the material with ease, to begin with, even without verbal communication with the children: most of them understood the symbols he wrote on the blackboard, the formulas and equations. In the last quarter of an hour of each lesson, he would tell them about growing up in Europe, describe life in North America, ask his students about their parents, their dreams and their fears. The fact that the language barrier appeared to be so easily surmounted surprised the school directors as much as the children themselves. Some of them got to be fairly fluent in English quite quickly. Seda, Medji's granddaughter, was one of his best pupils, often reciting nursery rhymes and songs, her favourite was 'Peter, Peter, pumpkin-eater, had a wife and couldn't keep her. Put her in a pumpkin shell, and there he kept her very well!'

Not since he had first begun to give lectures (Tigor had made his debut on Abel's theorem, that extraordinary additional principle of the elliptical integral, that was dearer to his heart than any other series in mathematics), had he felt so happy and so stimulated as now, when he was living as a primary-school teacher in Yerevan. He took the grimness of the metropolis, the stench of the air, the filth of the streets, all in his stride. He hoped he would be able to find the source of his inner turmoil, and find the paths that would take him to renewed calm and understanding.

'... but why *here*, of all places?' old Medji asked him, more than once.

Every month he went along on class excursions to the basilicas and monasteries of the country. He visited Makaravank and Khoranashat near the Georgian border in the North, he travelled over extravagant potholes to the churches of Haghpat and Sanahin, overlooking thickly wooded valleys. While the south of the country was barren and desert-like, the northern half of the Republic – which Aristakes dubbed the Armenian Switzerland – was green and fertile.

Seeing as he was working for no wage, Minister Edilian had arranged for Tigor to move into a suite at the Armenia. He had a broken-down piano there, and four outsize armchairs, and a bathtub that was twice as big and three times as wide as himself. Over the next few weeks, Sophia, the chambermaid, became his mistress. He often watched himself, in the full-length bedroom mirrors, holding the pale young woman, who was frail and slimly built, in a much-too-violent embrace. It had been at her prompting that he had first touched her, kissed her, penetrated her. It would never have occurred to him. He endured her loud, almost incessant coughing and her chain-smoking. He allowed her to dig her long, somewhat crumbling fingernails into his back. After a few days, he began biting them off, and within a few weeks, they were all gone. Sophia, sitting up in bed, and swaying back and forth like a child, begged him to hit her. In this, he was unwilling to accommodate her. Did, though, dribble wax from a burning candle over her belly and thighs, before – always in the same position – mounting her scrawny body. When the girl had to go back to her parents in the steppe-like south-east of the country at the beginning of the summer, Tigor wouldn't have been able to say with any confidence what colour her eyes were.

Tigor generally spent his afternoons in the factory that Aristakes managed as a state enterprise. He had chosen one of the shard-strewn storage rooms for himself, and turned it into a kind of office, complete with rickety desk and worn chair that was leaking its foam-rubber padding. This was where he prepared his lessons, wrote down the most important things that happened to him in his logbook, or read weeks-old American newspapers that visitors had brought into the country. Arnold's little short-wave radio kept him in touch with world events: he listened to news almost every hour, moving from station to station, though the BBC's World Service remained his firm favourite.

On Mondays and Wednesdays, the three elders came to visit him in his room. Aristakes often joined them, translated what Medji, Artem and blind Samvel were saying. When Oganessian was unable to get away to their meetings, Medji took over the role of interpreter.

'The world was created in six days,' blind Samvel began one day, toyed, while he spoke, with the bullets in his ammunition belt, 'not in symbolic days, as is sometimes said, whereby one day is equal to millions of years! No, each day as a day of twenty-four hours, ordinary hours, ordinary days. And the seventh day was a day of rest. And every blade of grass, every piece of amber, every fly, every marmot, deer, orang-utan and human being: all of them were immediately there, just as we know them today. The trees stood there as fully grown trees, with many annual rings, from the beginning. The mountains, the rocks, if we had been able to measure them with the equipment we have today, would already have been millions of years old, to every appearance, even though they had only just been created. Even these so-called fossils that are found under the ground, and the skeletons in caves were lying there from the beginning, like props in a cleverly detailed stage set. And the stars, the galaxies, even the diamonds under the ground, which I used to deal in, they too, they were complete from the very beginning. Like Adam on the day of his birth: a grown-up.'

Medji and Artem berated Samvel, Aristakes too had a go at him. What was he thinking of, spouting that kind of nonsense? What was Tigor, the man of science, supposed to think? Why confuse their champion with this? 'Don't pay any attention!' Oganessian beseeched his friend.

'. . . your wish is my command,' the elder went on, 'so, the little fish noticed, according to you believers in the theory of evolution, that there wasn't all that much interesting food for him in the water. He spent the next two to four million years converting his fins into little feet. Then, because he wanted to eat still more, and also be better protected, he needed wings to get up into the treetops. So what did he do? He waited another five million years for his little feet to turn into fluffy, colourful feathers. And a few million years after that, the wings had turned into a giraffe. Some people say: well, it wouldn't have happened like that. It was all in leaps and bounds. Freaks of nature. And all at once there was an *ear*!'

'Now, that's enough of that . . .!' protested Aristakes.

'Well, why don't we consider the ear: strategically placed, one of them either side of the head, with little whorls and hollows, to entrap sound waves and conduct them down to the eardrum. Drum – like a calfskin drum?! Hardly! Finer than one tenth of one millimetre, and with minute pieces of cartilage attached to it, a freak of nature, you believers in evolutionary theory would call it, to amplify the sounds of the world and conduct them into the inner ear. Where the nerve impulses are triggered, in the twenty to thirty thousand hair cells of the acoustic nerve! All of it self-evidently chance and merest freak of nature, as you believers in evolutionary theory would say . . .!'

On another afternoon, Artem, the former geologist, told Tigor of the oral tradition of the ten tribes, whose last descendants were Samvel, Medji and himself. In the remote future, this according to a prophecy from the year 69 BCE, a stranger would visit their country from the direction of the sunset, a man of science, who would succeed in finding the remains of a ship that had been sought for thousands of years, a ship which, according to the legends of many different peoples, had survived the Great Floods, and had come to rest on the highest peaks of Hajastan. '. . . this oral tradition that has been handed down to us,' he said, 'must be taken as literal truth, there is no doubting it, it takes its origins from the time of the legendary Tigran II, king of kings, who, in the year 95 before the Birth of our Saviour, founded the Kingdom of Greater Hajastan, and moved the capital city of his enormous empire to the geographical centre . . .'

Tigor interrupted the elder: 'You said he was called *what* . . .'

'Tigran II, the Great and the Wild, the son of Artavazd,' replied Aristakes, in place of Artem. 'He conquered Sophona, Cappadocia, the Empire of the Seleucids, Cilicia, Phoenicia and Palestine. Under him, for the only time in our history, we became a world power!' It seemed that the strange closeness of the great monarch's name to his own struck no one but Tigor. The etymology of his surname was from the Latin Tigurium, a word for hut or shack which, in Triestine dialect, had evolved into Tigojer. Tigor's forefathers had been called Tigojer, they had been small-holders, living on the edge of the city. Tigor, astounded and moved, was careful not to alert the company to the similarity between the two names, the legendary ruler's and his own.

The family tradition, Artem resumed, was now dying out. None of them, Medji, Samvel or himself, had brought children into the world, and the children and grandchildren of the other seven tribes had fallen victim to the genocide at the beginning of the century, which had cost two million lives. The stranger, so the prediction went, would come to them 'without any territory'. What was meant by that, however, was not that he would be there without any real estate as was only to be expected in the case of a stranger here, but that he had undertaken the journey to Hajastan without exactly knowing the true reason or 'grounds' for his visit.

'In other words: that person would feel sort of drawn towards us,' Medji clarified. Her voice was smoky and low.

Tigor often spent his evenings with her in the dingy dining room of his hotel. A combo of old men played foxtrots and tangos. He listened to memories of her years in Hollywood as Errol Flynn's secretary. '. . . Flynn just *loved* me. But not once did he dare touch me!' She had been friends with the scriptwriter Salka Viertel, who had written *Queen Christina* for Greta Garbo. Medji described the sadomasochistic lesbian relationship between Garbo and Frau Viertel with particular unsparingness and indelicacy. She also reminisced about a meeting with Walt Disney when he was working on *Fantasia*. She had been present, Medji said, when Disney's associates (among them her husband of the time) had first shown their boss the sequence that combined a movement of Beethoven's Pastoral Symphony with Arcadian images of winged horses and pretty female centaurs. When the lights went on again in the screening room, Disney had turned round to his people and raved: 'Gee! This'll really put Beethoven on the map!'

She didn't care for people, Medji often said, 'that ugly, ugly species'. Only animals seemed unconditionally lovable to her: 'Have you ever seen a cat die?' She asked Tigor: '. . . and what makes you tick?' guessing at quite other motives for his presence in Yerevan than those he gave, a suspicion that she would occasionally voice directly. Each time, Tigor would laugh at her and then ask her to dance with him. He intimated to her that he really didn't want to undertake the ascent that was expected of him now, only took part in their afternoon get-togethers so as not to offend Aristakes.

'. . . but then why are you here? I don't get it . . .'

'And you? Why are *you* here?' he retorted.

Because she wanted to be buried where she had been born; the only thing she had, the only thing that no one had been able to take from her was her homeland, and the feeling of being attached to a certain place in the world. And then she emptied her glass, because wine was her great passion; one or two bottles an evening, that was normal consumption for her.

In general, he didn't much care where he was, Tigor stated. He would have to reconnect his inner wires before he was capable of deciding where he wanted to settle. That said, he derived enormous and quite unexpected satisfaction from his teaching at Haghtanak School.

'. . . so you're becoming a saint, or what?'

She didn't take Tigor for the chosen one her relatives tried to see in him. Strangers 'without any territory' must arrive in Armenia on a daily basis, she argued, besides she had her doubts as to the truth of the so-called family tradition: in her opinion, it was nothing more than a pious old wives' tale. 'The poor guy, what has he done so he has to scrabble around up there for us?' asked Medji. 'Why are you chasing that infirm man up the mountain?'

'It is part of the tradition,' said Samvel, 'that the chosen one receives the instruction to find the Ark in his dreams. And that he will resist, and try to refuse the lofty calling . . .'

'And who wouldn't?' replied Medji. 'And he hasn't had any dreams of the sort either. Or am I mistaken?'

Tigor said nothing.

Aristakes insisted: 'I sense that he is the one we have been awaiting. To find the Ark, a man needs to be as pure as a child. And that is our visitor, from the nails of his feet to the hair on his head. I sense it.'

'How do you sense something like that?' Medji wanted to know.

'. . . you trust your instinct . . .'

'Instincts are just a man's excuse for bad actions,' the old lady tartly replied.

The Oganessian twins spoiled their friend. They vied with each other to spend more time with him. On Sundays, Aristakes often took him out to Lake Sevan, where they went fishing together in the searing June heat. 'Unfortunately, my brother has remained a Communist at heart,' he lamented, rowing the frail craft over the water. 'Any domain that protrudes even one iota from the materialistic world view to which he clings with berserk tenacity, to him is anathema, never forget that!'

Aristakes' wife, Anna, would prepare their catch over a small pine-needle fire. While she cooked and then while they ate, the mirror maker would cover her with kisses: he would kiss her on the hair and brows, on her temples, neck and shoulders, kiss her on the cheeks and chin. Anna was small and curvaceous. Her lips were always painted a deep red. Her dyed hair was crimson. She liked to wear dark-red snakeskin boots that Aristakes had brought back for her years previously from Europe. The fish was always impregnated by a different scent, because Anna collected expensive French perfumes, and wore a new one each month.

On weekday evenings, Aristakes introduced Tigor to the mysteries of mirror making. 'Mirrors', he would enthuse, 'are devices for extending the world. Mirrors are devices for changing the world. Imagine a room without a mirror. And now imagine the same room with a mirror. The huge difference, can you feel it, can you see it? It's a difference that changes dimensions, is it not? The mirror, and surely you will bear me out in this, brings together the here and the beyond.' He taught Tigor how flat, flawless glass was made. At the same time as his visitor, he told the surly workers, who regularly turned up for their shifts two or three hours late, to grind down the hot slabs of glass on the enormous work tables, and then polish them down with iron oxide. He allowed Tigor to make an oval vanity mirror all by himself, to cut the glass, mix the silver compound, but then the elaborate silvering processes and the noxious tin vapours were too much for the novice unaided. Aristakes took over for the final stages, and then proceeded – to the open incredulity of the workers – to describe the outcome as a successful piece of apprentice work on the part of his pupil.

Johann Wolfgang took Tigor up the volcano Aragaz, not far from Leninakan, pointed out to him, at a considerable altitude, excavations of roughly hewn flintstones, whose age he reckoned to be in the order of eight hundred thousand years. '. . . Gah!' he groaned, in the course of one of their numerous excursions together, 'my brother and his ark-mania! I beg of you not to be taken in by him! It's a torment through which he puts almost every friend he has. Since we were boys, he's been dreaming of finding that ship. And even then I was pouring scorn over him. Digging is *my* profession! And I tell you: there may well have been flood waters, even here on Aragaz, which, incidentally, is at the heart of a great earthquake peril for our country. Even on Mount Aragaz, they find shells and they find sea-salt, but no higher than a few dozen metres up. But please don't come to me with a thousand metres, and a ship packed with mammoths and lions that's supposed to have landed yonder, on Ararat! Oh, my dear brother! He's a rakish fellow, you know, you should be wary of him, some of his friends are almost underworld types. Perhaps you did not know that? There are thugs among them . . . So, be wary!' He sang, chest puffed out, bathed in sweat: 'Hajastan, you earthly paradise, you cradle of mankind, my beautiful mother-land, O Hajastan!' In the glove compartment he kept a revolver. '. . . we have to be forearmed,' said Johann Wolfgang, 'when we drive through the settlements of the Azerbaijanis that lie scat-tered over our Armenian soil . . .'

Tigor occasionally accompanied Aristakes to a gloomy restau-rant on Abovian Square, outside which the erstwhile weightlifter liked to strut back and forth for an hour or so a day, to receive the greetings and the acclaim of the inhabitants of the city, among whose most distinguished citizens he certainly reckoned himself. It was his regular haunt, where he liked to have large groups of people congregate around him, then to hold lengthy orations, appealing to them to go out on the streets to demonstrate for the return of the Armenian province of Karabakh – which he called Arzakh – from the neighbouring Azerbaijanis. The greater these future demonstrations (up to that point there had not been any popular agitation for the reclaiming of that exclave), the greater the international attention it would receive, and the more insis-tent the pressure on Moscow finally to come to a decision about it. 'Our future,' he cried out, as incendiary as any tribune of the people, 'our future will be marked by great storms before we safely reach port! We have only to be nice and quiet, nice and well mannered and meek, then we will experience further injustices. In the history of our people, it has never been any other way. Seventy years ago, our newborn babies were snatched from their mothers' arms by our enemies and stuffed into sacks. A few miles on, the murderers emptied the sacks in front of the mothers, and told them to claim their babies. In that huge crowd, no mother could find her little one. And so those monsters stuffed the howl-ing little boys and little girls back into the sacks, and drowned them like puppies, and burned them and dashed their brains out, and spitted them like pigs and roasted them. For hundreds of years we have been oppressed, and through it all we have remained quiet and neutral. When we were spoken to, we looked at the ground. Enough of that now . . .! The world will only listen to courageous people . . .! The world will only listen to shameless people!'

The men round the table, fearless-looking types, applauded for minute after minute. They cried out: 'Long live Aristakes, you hero of our homeland!'

Tigor continued to attend the afternoon sessions in the mirror factory. Medji was always present too, but she refused to play any part in the passing on of ancestral wisdom, not infrequently dismissing it as 'pure rubbish'. It had been left to Noah, Tigor learned from Samvel and Artem, to build a ship, mightier than any ship that had ever been, mightier than any ship that would ever be. At the time of Noah, there were men and women that grew to be twenty feet tall. Their children were born on the day that they were conceived. Infants could stand up, walk and talk on the day they were born. People lived to be hundreds of years old, hunger and thirst were unknown, they lived almost as they had in paradise. Men were so strong that lions and panthers were no more of a threat to them than flies. The weather was pleasant and spring-like all the year round. Heat and cold were unknown. Increasingly, though, the heavenly powers were neglected, people said to one another: what do we need the heavenly powers for? Are we ourselves not all-powerful . . .?! Their behaviour had become increasingly promiscuous, too, even the animals were given to sinning, cocks coupled with ducks, dogs with wolves, cats with tigers. Lying and stealing had become second nature to mankind, even though theft is the crime, more than any other, that ruins civilizations.

And so Noah, a righteous man, had been chosen to build an ark for himself and his family. He was four hundred and eighty years old when he began to build the ship. And he was six hundred when the flood began. The great ship was hewn from cedar wood, and Noah caulked it with pitch, inside and out. For a hundred and twenty years he continued to build it, in the hope that people would flock to him, while he was cutting the wood and nailing the boards together, to ask him: What are you doing,

Noah, tell us! But all they had done was laugh at him, and not one of them had asked: Noah, tell us what it is you're doing? Had they asked him, Noah would have replied: You yourselves and the whole world are on the brink of destruction, to punish you for your endless depravity. Unless you change your ways, unless you put aside evil, the powers of heaven will show you no mercy, and the Flood will come! The people of those times were great magicians, however, and they weren't afraid of the powers of heaven. When the Ark had been finished, six hundred metres long, and three storeys tall, and divided into four hundred compartments, the powers of heaven gave mankind one last week to consider, paradisal days in which no one came to their senses. Noah himself had not believed that the flood would come, but when, on the seventeenth day of the second month of the one-thousand-six-hundred-and-fifty-sixth year after the creation of the world, the heavens opened and the waters fell, and the level of the water was already up to his ankles, and he had seen the angel of death come flying towards him, then Noah too began to believe in the Flood, and he brought himself and his family to safety aboard the ark, and with them all the beasts, at least one pair of every sort.

Thereupon the giants did indeed cluster round the ship, seven hundred thousand of them, baying to be admitted. But when Noah had turned them away, and called out to them: You had one hundred and twenty years to repent, then they tried to climb up into the Ark, but they failed. Forty days and forty nights, the waters fell from the heavens, and each drop was first boiled in Hell. When the giants came in contact with the drops, their skin began to blister and peel off them. Also, water came issuing from the earth, boiling. At that the people took their children and their babies, and crammed them into the openings of the earth to stop the waters. With their children's flesh, they blocked all the wells. But the water that fell as rain continued to rise, its level went up day after day for one hundred and fifty days. Far and wide, the land was cracked apart like a pot, and the storms made haste to submerge even the tops of the mountains, and to obliterate the human race. The destruction that came from the heavens reached even one hundred ells into the soil, no trace remained of the generations that had lived before the flood, even their bones were dissolved as though they had never been. Only the fishes survived. The fishes had not sinned.

'. . . how could the fish survive if the water was boiling hot? Why were Noah and his family the only ones who weren't giants? Or were *they* giants too?' asked Tigor, and Medji nodded mischievously. Artem and Samvel never responded to remarks of that sort.

On the top floor of the Ark dwelt Noah with his wife and his three sons, and their wives and their children, Tigor learned from the mouths of Samvel and Artem. They had the prettiest of the birds and dogs and cats with them, and ever since these creatures have been the preferred pets of mankind. On the middle floor they had put all the other animals, from ants to rhinoceroses, and from tapeworms to baboons, of some species only one pair, of others as many as seven. On the lowest floor, the dung was collected, and the stench on the Ark was unendurable. For each animal, Noah had brought along its requisite fodder, and some food was grown on the Ark itself, dates and olives grew there, along with apples and oranges. He had taken seeds from every plant in the world, to be replanted once the waters had receded. When the flood finally began to abate, it went down at the rate of one and a half hands' breadths a day. And the Ark, which had drawn eleven ells of water, had landed on the slopes of what was then the highest mountain of the world, the Massis. It took months more before Noah and his family and the animals they had taken with them could finally leave the Ark. How was it possible that the dove that Noah released had returned with an olive branch, when all the vegetation in the world had been destroyed? The olive branch came from Paradise, whose gates Heaven had opened by its own recent exertions. And Noah, who knew where the olive branch had come from, knew that there must be some dry patches of earth by now, because the dove wouldn't have been capable of flying to Paradise and back without a rest. But when the survivors left the Ark for the first time, they set foot on an earth that bore not the remotest resemblance to the earth they had left a year before.

'Do you know how Noah began the replanting of the world?' It was the only story from her ancestral horde that Medji cared to divulge. 'With wheat, perhaps? Or rice? Or barley? Not a bit of it!

The first plant he put in the ground was the vine. Just then Satan appeared beside him. "Would you like me to help you make the vine grow well?" asked Satan. 'Yes,' replied Noah. Then Satan went away, and returned with a little lamb in his arms. He slaughtered the little lamb, and let it bleed to death over the vine. Then he went away again, and this time he came back with a lion. He slaughtered the lion, and let it bleed over the vine. Then he brought a monkey, and slaughtered it, and drenched the vine with monkey's blood. Finally, he came back with a pig, and he killed that, and poured a libation of pig's blood over the vine. That marked the beginning of the rule: if you drink a little glass of wine, you'll be mild and peaceful as a lamb. If you drink a bottle, you'll be a lion, bragging about all the deeds you mean one day to perform. Drink two bottles, you'll dance around like a monkey. But if you drink three bottles, you'll vomit, and roll around in muck and filth like a pig . . .'

'. . . the life of the new race of men', continued the blind Samvel, undeflected from his purpose, 'became so much more laborious than that of the generations before the Flood! The new men were forced to call Heaven in aid, in their pain and difficulty. They had been brought low, and it served them right. They came to depend on the rain, and the sun and the seasons. Nothing has been certain since or fixed on this planet . . .'

'. . . we are at the gates of another millennium now,' whispered Artem. 'The memory of the great Flood knits the epochs together . . .'

'You must find the Ark – for us,' Aristakes implored his friend. 'Up there, on the glacier, the wooden splinters are lying even now, as far as the eye can see! It is destined for you, you are the first man who will come up with the proof that what is written in these books is the truth . . . You will acquire the strength of a new Messiah in this world, people will hail you as a new Saviour. Not to mention the treasures from the stores of Hajastan that we will present you with, once you have accomplished your mission . . .'

Three quarters of a year had passed since Tigor's flight from the conference centre in Trieste. It was now the height of summer. The pall of dirt that hung over Yerevan had become so thick that there was not a single day on which it was possible to see Ararat from the city. The temperature measured forty degrees in the shade. In the sunny back yards of the houses, children built little sand heaps in which they baked eggs. The school year had four more weeks to run. The boys and girls besieged their stand-in teacher, he was on no account to leave, as he occasionally had let drop he would, he had to come back and teach them again next year. Their parents brought cakes, meat and fruit to him in his hotel, Seda's mother kept sewing him short-sleeved polyester shirts in yellow-and-green stripes.

Minister Edilian summoned Tigor to his office one morning during school hours. He had just received word, he said, that next week an American astronaut (he wasn't sure of the man's name) would be paying a brief visit to the Soviet Republic of Armenia. 'I'd like it if you, Jack' (which was what he'd called Tigor ever since first meeting him – he liked to cultivate an American aura, and even put his feet on his desk) 'looked after our guest a bit. My own English is pretty respectable, wouldn't you say, but even so, Jack, I'd like you to be there when I meet with the guy.'

Tigor suggested inviting the astronaut, whoever he was, along to the Haghtanak School, he was sure the children would be impressed by such a man.

'Neat idea! But what about you, Jack? Aren't you impressed?' Edilian asked.

'I can't believe it, I've been trying to speak to this man for the past fifteen years, you wouldn't *believe* how happy this makes me!' cried Aristakes, when he heard of the impending visit of the astronaut. 'I'm certain I know who it is, no question, I've written to him in America, care of NASA headquarters, and written letters and left telephone messages with the US Embassy in Moscow, and in all that time I have heard not one peep! This is the man who has been looking for the Ark on three separate occasions, purely to demonstrate the literal truth of the Book of Books! I can tell him where to look! I can tell him! And he's coming here to *us*! Do you think it's because he received my messages?!'

In the school, ordinary lessons were suspended, and the junior years were taken together for four classes. In the playing-field-sized dining room, with Medji interpreting at his side, Tigor spoke about the history of manned space travel, talked about

Yuri Gagarin and Alan Shepard, the first of the solitary warriors to be catapulted into the universe, stuffed into the hollow cones at the apex of their fire-spitting monsters. Years before, he had conducted a study on the heat-resistant qualities of a certain metal foil, and his conclusions had led to the material in question not being persevered with for the space shuttle, then at the planning stage. At the time, Tigor had gone into the history of space travel in some detail. He talked to the children about John Glenn and Alexei Leonov, Valentina Tereshkova and Gus Grissom, described the successes and failures of both the American and the Russian space missions, and their culmination in the Apollo project and the flight of the lunar ferry Eagle, when, for the first time, two men had been landed on the moon.

'. . . and James Benson Irwin, whom you are going to meet in a few days' time, was the commander of Apollo 15, in summer 1971,' Tigor concluded his account. 'Irwin spent three days and nights on the moon . . . Try and think of what questions you'd like to ask him. Irwin was described as having returned from space with feelings of deep humility and gratitude. With the certain conviction that our blue planet was the outcome of a well-considered cosmic providence. My friend Aristakes, whom you all know, particularly asked me to mention this last point to you . . .'

The silence in the room was only broken by the ticking of two clocks, facing each other on opposite walls.

Tigor and Aristakes were both part of the welcoming party that met the astronaut at the Zvartnotz airport a few days later. In four black limousines fitted with white lace curtains, they first proceeded to the Edjmiadzin monastery, very close to the airport. The official visitor was accorded a private audience by Vazgen I, the spiritual leader of the Armenian people. The man of God set before his guest sweet grapes and freshly picked apples and pears. 'Forgive me for being so blunt, I'd like to ask you this,' His Holiness began in a perfectly pleasant manner, 'do you seriously believe in the existence of Noah's Ark. Don't you – as we all do, in our heart of hearts – think of it as nothing more than a charming fairy tale?' The astronaut bowed his head politely before the old man. And left the room, without giving Vazgen I an answer.

He gave no clue later as to what had transpired between the churchman and himself. His secretary, however, was a little puzzled at the short duration of the audience of James B. Irwin.

A young monk conducted the group of visitors around the large and imposing monastery. A gold-and-diamond set of the thirty-six letter Armenian alphabet was kept in a safe. 'These letters are the soldiers that defend us against our attackers!' proclaimed the monk, a pointed black hood covered his head. A separate vault contained – to the astonishment of the visitors – the state emblem of the Soviet Socialist Republic of Armenia, cast in pure gold. Large diamonds garnished the hammer and sickle, surrounded the red star burning over the outline of Ararat. '. . . out of gratitude,' said the young cleric, matter-of-factly, 'under the Soviet system, our people is prospering for the first time in living memory. Without their help, we would still be living in holes in the ground, as we were after the First World War. Conditions then were worse than any in Dante's Hell. Our situation only improved after our Russian saviours helped us to rebuild!'

The astronaut was intent on seeing one particular item that was kept in Edjmiadzin, which had been the real reason for his visit. In a small chapel in the monastery, so he had heard, was kept a rough, two-foot length of timber which travelling merchants had found centuries before, a piece from Noah's Ark. Irwin requested that the glass case in which the relic was exhibited be opened for him. Grigor, the monk, pretended not to understand. It took an intervention in Armenian from Minister Edilian to induce him to get the keys to the case. Aristakes took advantage of the hiatus to introduce himself to the astronaut, which he did in incomprehensible agglomerations of sentences. He dragged Tigor across, practically forced him into conversation with Irwin. 'You must! And tell him all I have told you, to do with the likeliest places to search!'

Irwin, wearing dark-blue polyester overalls and a white peaked cap secured with an elastic strap round the back of his head, appeared milder and friendlier than Tigor had expected. An iron-grey fringe of hair tumbled over his brow. His tanned face was etched with deep vertical furrows. Good-humouredly, he spoke of the three heart attacks he had suffered in the last few years. Even when he'd been standing on the moon, he had felt his heart acting strangely, missing the occasional beat. He had supposed these irregularities had been brought on by the chemical composition of his space diet.

Ignoring the strict warnings of his doctors, he had nevertheless in the past week climbed Ararat, to mark his sixtieth birthday. Equipped with oxygen tanks, and accompanied by eight experienced mountaineers, he had succeeded in climbing further than ever before, reaching the summit, five thousand metres above sea level. Every thirty seconds, Aristakes begged Tigor for a translation of what Irwin was saying. '. . . even though we failed once again to find any trace of the Ark,' the astronaut said, 'my faith in the scriptural account of the Flood has not been diminished at all, if anything strengthened. We'll be back . . .'

Grigor opened the glass case. And Irwin began by photographing the exhibit, then held it gently between his fingertips. An object that reminded Tigor of a *poutre*, the characteristic wooden beams to be found in so many Parisian apartments, he had probably last seen them in Arnold's salon.

The astronaut closed his eyes and remained motionless for a minute. The low drone of two military-transport planes taking off from Zvartnotz filled the little chapel.

Later, as it was getting dark, there was a more intimate reunion in Irwin's suite at the Armenia: Edilian, Aristakes, Tigor and Brian Lauder, Irwin's young secretary from Washington, whom the astronaut had not introduced until now. Irwin had politely declined the mayor's invitation to attend a performance of Verdi's *Otello* at the Yerevan Opera. It was probably on account of this perceived snub that the mayor and his deputies for their part decided not to see the visitor again. Minister Edilian seemed to be annoyed too, because now he opened the conversation with the remark that those pieces of wood that had been found over the centuries on Ararat were in all probability from the ruins of ancient pilgrims' or settlers' huts – '. . . or am I wrong?' Edilian gave the impression of being set on injuring the American; he looked pleased with himself, and there was something cruel about his smile.

Irwin listened attentively to what the politician had to say. Left it to Brian Lauder to give his answer to that often-heard, often-

143

repeated argument. 'Think of the example of Troy,' the secretary said, 'who would have imagined that the fantastic city that Homer describes in his *Iliad* actually existed? And that it was only by grace of one man's burning zeal and unshakeable conviction that the reality behind the dream was proved once and for all.'

Seized by the idea of finding the ultimate proof that the Old Testament was 'lock, stock and barrel', as he put it, an accurate account of historical events (a perception that was clearly and unshakeably rooted in his mind from the time of his lunar mission), Irwin was presently organizing a great diving expedition: 'We want to look for the Egyptian chariots on the bottom of the Red Sea. For those chariots in which Pharaoh's army chased after the children of Israel, before the waters crashed over the heads of the pursuers. Before the millennium, we plan to find the Tower of Babel, so we can take some of that masonry, a few of Pharaoh's chariot wheels and any amount of fragments from the Ark, and ship everything back to Colorado Springs where, as you might know, I make my home. And then, at the end of 1999, we aim to start up "BibleLand" . . . We'd be delighted to invite y'all to the opening, in the heart of the state of Colorado . . .'

But he wouldn't be able to attempt Ararat again for another few years, the astronaut explained, the area around the double peak was simply too hazardous at present: Kurdish rebel forces were engaged in a bitter guerrilla war with regular units of the Turkish army. Irwin stressed that he and his party, who had once again been climbing the mountain of mountains without official knowledge or clearance from the government, had escaped death only by a whisker. They had stumbled upon a concealed rebel encampment, and the only reason they hadn't been killed on the spot was that an army patrol had happened to be in the immediate vicinity, and the slightest sound would have given away their location: '. . . they waved the barrels of their Kalashnikovs at us furiously to get us to clear out . . .' The account of that moment was the first and only part of the evening's discussion that Tigor imparted to the hapless Aristakes.

The children at Haghtanak School didn't want to let the astronaut go. Dense knots of boys and girls surrounded him. He had spoken of his lunar flight for a few minutes, but for over an hour of his four expeditions to Ararat. He answered the questions that were put to him as thoroughly as he could. Only after another two hours did he succeed in finally tearing himself away. In front of the crumbling grey building, its windows for the most part broken or patched up, Irwin and Lauder took leave of their hosts. The astronaut had requested to be accompanied to the airport by Edilian alone. Aristakes pressed into his hand a sketch of Ararat that he'd made himself, rather resembling a child's drawing. The mirror manufacturer had marked the three likeliest spots with large X's. Lauder and Tigor hurriedly exchanged addresses: 11,144 Walnut Street for 111 Arlington Avenue, though neither of them were places where their respective occupants were often to be found.

When Irwin climbed into the limousine, Seda was standing behind him. 'Excuse me, mister,' she said softly, 'please . . .'

The astronaut was on the point of shutting the door.

'. . . a moment!' Seda propped her elbow on the hot metal door frame. In front of all the other children, she said, she had not dared tell Irwin a dream she'd had the previous night. In it, she had clearly seen the village of Nalband, where she had been born; the snow-covered ground, the fields, even the surrounding hills had given the impression of being somehow crooked, 'as if broken', and a water tower had fallen on to the roof of a tractor, and then in her excitement, Seda spoke a few sentences in Armenian. The dream, which Seda said had frightened her badly, had ended with James Irwin, on board a large aeroplane, landing in the middle of the village, and slowly, painfully slowly, trying to straighten out all the crooked and broken things.

When Irwin finally settled back in his seat in the limousine, he pushed the lace curtain aside, and waved briefly to Seda.

Ararat

One morning, Abraham Porter, who was spending the university holidays at his mother's house in Camden, New Jersey, received a special-delivery letter summoning him, to his utter bafflement, to the office of the Rector of the Archaeological Institute of the University of Pennsylvania in Philadelphia, the day after tomorrow. In the event of his failing to appear, he risked his status at the university.

Also present at that meeting on the eighteenth floor of the administration building, in addition to the author of the summons, Professor Joshua Dellman, were the President of the University, Reuben Davis, and the two Deans of the Mathematical Faculty. The student, who was known to have been a particular favourite with his professor, was asked what contact he had had during the past several months with Giacopo Tigor. '. . . I thought he was *dead*?!' came Abraham's response. It was a difficult lie to tell. Perhaps, if he told the university authorities the truth, he might even save Tigor from some situation in which his life was at risk. Porter was warned that his academic career would be 'in severe jeopardy' if he was telling anything less than the truth. It was known from an unimpeachable source that Tigor was not dead at all, but had disappeared for some reason best known to himself. Davis described him as psychologically frail, irresponsible to an almost criminal extent: '. . . in my personal view, he's a dead man anyway. But I want justice done, do you read me, Porter?' To lend weight to his words, the one-armed President brought his knuckles down sharply on the desktop.

Abraham stuck to the story that he had heard nothing whatsoever regarding his teacher's absence during the past nine months. And, in keeping with the good old American tradition, he was believed. He wasn't to know that an archaeologist from Malmo had gone back on his word. Nor was he told that detectives in the university's employ had long ago succeeded in obtaining from Tigor's bank details of recent account activity, including the amounts, the timings, and the destinations of the transfers he had made, most recently to Yerevan, the capital of the Soviet Republic of Armenia.

The night before the final day of school, six days had elapsed since the astronaut's visit to Yerevan, and Seda saw her heavily laden teacher in a dream. He was climbing, fatigued, through difficult terrain. Sometimes the angle of his ascent was so steep, it seemed to tip him and the burden he was shouldering, right out of his skin, and a sort of phantom pendular second self swung behind him. The twofold wanderer climbed higher and higher, found himself on a snowy peak, under glacier-heavy banks of clouds. He failed to see Seda, even though she was running along behind him, sinking at times into the snow, and calling out 'Hey, mister!' He climbed up and up, not stopping, as though cables had been attached to him, reeling him in gently but implacably towards some unknown place.

When the handing out of report cards had been concluded in the late morning, Seda came along to say goodbye. It was very noisy in the playing-field-sized dining room, and the children standing around teased Seda and laughed at her. So Tigor took the girl by the hand, and led her up to the teachers' common room on the first floor. There they sat at a large wooden table. Its surface, deeply incised and etched, was strewn with crumbs, fruit-pits and rinds, all of it left over from that morning's end-of-year buffet for the Haghtanak faculty, to which the support teacher had not been invited.

He shuddered, and the feeling grew stronger as Seda told him her dream, and the little hairs on his neck stood up. He trailed his fingertips through a puddle of lemonade, drew little liquid arrows, every one of them pointing to the child. That night, he had dreamed something very similar himself. Once again, he saw cables and masses of snow. Again, he felt his shoulders give a painful and involuntary lurch, as though his body were leaning out of his skin.

Tigor stayed behind for quite a long time in the common room; Seda had run out to her mother, who was waiting for her at the school gates.

He took a taxi to Nor Aresch. Aristakes, half naked and

150

extremely hairy, was perching cross-legged on top of a desk that had been knocked together from rough planks. He was on the telephone. '. . . I'm just trying . . . You look like you've just had not one but two heart attacks! For days I've been trying to get Edilian to help me get back in touch with the American,' he explained, holding the receiver jammed between chin and collarbone and slipping on a shirt in a poisonous shade of green. 'Then he, armed with my information, will make the sacred discovery. So simply the sad story will be resolved. He in your stead will find the grail. For me, for us, for our people. Every strengthening of our people is a step in the right direction . . . And we need such strengthening now, this very minute! Are you ill? What is the matter? . . . No answer from the Minister! Or is he refusing my calls . . .?'

'. . . I am ready.'

'Excuse me?' Aristakes' face looked painfully contorted.

'I am ready. This whole story – to me, it's nothing but mumbo-jumbo really . . . a mirage . . . but I finally want to get to the bottom of it . . .'

'Like one of your theorems that needs to be brought to a satisfactory conclusion?' Still, Aristakes was not jubilant, unsure whether he'd understood Tigor's suggestion aright.

'You've been very kind to me, all of you . . .'

'. . . you want to go and climb the mountain of mountains, because we've given you good things to eat and to drink?!'

'"*Le cœur a ses raisons que la raison ne connaît pas*," as Pascal put it very aptly.'

'*Who?* What's that? Didn't grasp a word . . .'

'Blaise Pascal, born on 19 June 1623 in Clermont-Ferrand . . .'

'. . . but before you do anything else, you need to get some strength back!' Aristakes wasn't sure what to do, what to think, where to begin. 'Can't have you this broken down! What have you done to yourself, Mary and Joseph? I'm so happy! Permit me to hug you!' He jumped down off the table, threw his arms aloft, in the manner of a weightlifter at the end of a competition. And embraced his friend far more forcefully than for several months previously.

He would leave as soon as possible, Tigor said.

'. . . out of the question!' Aristakes laughed. 'This must be celebrated! You are my entire pride and joy!'

All his pleading and insisting to Oganessian that he didn't want his departure to be celebrated (above all, he dreaded having to watch another lamb being slaughtered) echoed away ineffectually. Tigor hadn't yet left the office, and already Aristakes was beginning to invite family and friends for Sunday afternoon. '. . . an intimate gathering!' he said as an attempted sop to the unhappy Tigor between calls.

'Three hundred and fifty are attending, if not many, many more!' called the mirror maker as Tigor arrived at the festive place, along with Seda and her parents, who had given him a lift out of the city in their car. 'And how long did it take me to organize? Not even forty-eight hours! Come! Come along, we've been waiting!'

In the shade of the apple and pear orchards of the Ovannavank Kolkhoz, around long tables that were laden with things to eat and drink, on the ground, on cloths and blankets and on the grass, people were eating, drinking, singing and dancing, and all in the intense heat, and buzzed around by great swarms of mosquitoes. All those whose acquaintance Tigor had made over the course of the past several months had come, and with them their families and friends. Families of farmers from Lake Sevan and a seminary of priests from Sanahin to the north of the Republic, and the entire junior part of Haghtanak School, with parents and grandparents, swarmed round the American from Europe who had just begun to put down frail little nerves of roots among them in the Caucasus. Tigor strolled through what looked like a huge garden, found the three elders sitting together in the shade of a tall pomegranate hedge. There was so much noise, they could only wave to each other. Johann Wolfgang invited him to sit with his family under parasols, and share their plastic picnic mat. Tigor stopped with them a while, surrounded by dishes, plates, cups, among scraps of vegetables and quartered lemons. They poured him coffee that Silva had brewed alfresco, and gave him brandy with it, a whole water-glass full, which he managed to empty into the grass while no one was watching.

The director of the kolkhoz was a cousin of the Oganessian twins. In spite of the intense heat, Garnik Khatissian was wearing a black suit and collar and tie. He didn't remove his jacket until a group of young men in colourful clothes from the neighbouring village had called to the dance. They played flutes, knee-fiddles and tambours. The dancers held hands, ten or twelve of them in a ring, whirling round and round faster and faster, as the flutes trilled higher and higher. The heat pressed down on the earth like a hot iron. The mosquito bites swelled and itched.

The young woman who had been dancing next to Tigor, she was wearing a thin turquoise dress and couldn't have been much older than eighteen or so, asked him while they had stopped for a moment to catch their breath, who he was. Rather astonished that she didn't know, he told her. She didn't understand him, it was too noisy. An aura of heat from her body spread over him, a smell of hay and sweat and soap. The music started up again, even louder and faster than before. Tigor was caught up in the ring of dancers. He felt as though he were floating high above this collective garden, and was surveying the country once more, this continent, alien and familiar, that had adopted him with such warmth, and let him live in its midst like a cherished in-law. He alighted on the grass once more.

Ever since their arrival, Seda had been trailing him everywhere. When the musicians paused for the first time, and Tigor was squatting exhaustedly on the ground, she came over and leant her head against his shoulder. 'Give me a kiss!' she said. He pretended not to hear. 'Kiss me! On my lips!' said Seda. Tigor started telling her about *Alice in Wonderland*, described the moment when Alice (Seda looked not unlike the girl in Tenniel's celebrated original illustrations) took her place in the big arm-chair at the head of the tea table. 'Alice looked all round the table,' he quoted, 'but there was nothing on it but tea. "I don't see any wine," she remarked . . .'

'. . . stop it already! Kiss me!' Seda scolded. And she kept badgering him until Tigor went with her to the far end of the kolkhoz, where they were out of sight of the celebrants. There, behind blackcurrant bushes, he knelt down in front of her and kissed her on the mouth, more carefully and tenderly than he had ever kissed a woman in his life.

'These mosquitoes, they must be Turkish mosquitoes!' cried one of the musicians, 'they must have been despatched against us by our enemies, by the numberless enemies we have all over!'

'. . . from the numberless enemies we have all over!' shouted

Garnik Khatissian. The words spread like wildfire. Then, just as suddenly, quiet was restored under the fruit trees. Tigor felt spectacularly hungry and thirsty. He ate fruit, vegetables, bread and cheese indiscriminately, every mouthful tasted delicious, it was like Candyland, or as though he'd been fasting for days. He was so distracted by eating, that he barely noticed the speed with which a small rostrum was being knocked up right next to him from pieces of hardboard. A group of men, Garnik and Aristakes among them, were already forming themselves in a queue to address the assembled masses. Baffling, where so many flags had sprung from all at once, great, heavy lengths of material, crudely stitched-together stripes of red, blue and orange, the national colours of Hajastan. The possession of such a flag, or being seen with one, had been forbidden for the past sixty years, on pain of death. The circles of dancers had turned into flag-bearers and wavers of tricolours.

Tigor tried to get as close as he could to the girl in the turquoise dress. He had prepared a short sentence meaning to invite her back to his suite at the hotel for the night. Seda helped him to find her again. She was standing close to the stage, waving a flag. Already the first of the speakers, a young army lieutenant, was beginning. The improvised public-address system gave out yowls of feedback. They had all forgotten about Tigor.

Four days later, the Oganessian twins took him to the airport. The other side of the park, by the large Spendiarov Opera, the streets were choked with huge crowds. Johann Wolfgang, at the wheel, was cursing and hooting, he would have quite happily ploughed through the masses of people that were coming from all directions. But the mirror maker wound down his window and called out words of encouragement to the protesters: '. . . it's really happening! We've done it! We won't give up now!' he roared. He shook hands by the dozen, and waved to the demonstrators, as though at the epicentre of a political rally that was being put on for his personal benefit. Ideally, the tiny Lada would have had a sliding roof that Aristakes could have pushed head and shoulders through, and addressed the masses. Entire school-classes were marching, and workers' delegations were gathering under the banners of their particular factories. Tigor guessed at the purpose of the commotion, but nevertheless, cautiously, almost tone-lessly, inquired: '. . . What's all this about?'

Johann Wolfgang merely shrugged.

'General strike!' cried Aristakes.

'. . . for what? Against what?'

'General strike!' even louder, more boisterously.

'. . . in aid of what?' Tigor insisted, felt keen revulsion against the surge of patriotism that was sweeping Yerevan.

'General strike!' screamed the mirror manufacturer.

They passed a line of young women, all with their arms linked behind their backs – it looked like a tightly braided pigtail. The sea of people frightened Tigor. In the round square in front of the opera there were already something like a hundred thousand. As many again were converging on it from the surrounding streets. A thousand parasols had been opened. Everywhere chains of people were forming, as they linked arms with one another. Suddenly, as from one monumental voice, the chant broke out, echoed all over the city: 'Arzach! Arzach! Arzach!'

'. . . confounded fools!' shouted Johann Wolfgang, 'Savages and ignoramuses intent on having their one and only dream too quickly realized! You will drag us all down into misfortune! We will be plunged into bloodbaths on account of you!'

They watched from the car as the mass of people, like a single organism, raised their arms in the air and clenched their fists. They punched the air to the rhythm of their chanting.

Inside the tiny vehicle, Aristakes too was chanting the word of the multitude. 'Finally we've taken the plunge!' he blurted out, smacked fist into palm, kept his eye on the rear-view mirror for as long as he could, while the demonstration slowly receded behind him. '. . . It's all happening! We're taking to the streets with our cause! And I can't be there with them! Arzach, I'm sure you know, now that you've lived among us for so long, Arzach – I've told you myself too, though you never pay any attention to what you're told – Arzach is our region in the Karabakh moun-tains, where our brothers and sisters dwell under permanent threat, in incessant fear of pogroms, since Arzach is situated the other side of the border with the Republic of Azerbaijan, since 1923 when the Stalin pig took away our territory and gave it to the enemy . . .'

'My dear brother, you must understand, is most regrettably a rampaging irredentist,' Johann Wolfgang gave his view of his twin's opinions. 'It is fortunate indeed that you are now leaving us, and will not be drawn into this maelstrom of nationalistic sentiment!'

'. . . the reincorporation of the province of Arzach into the motherland must remain our loftiest aspiration,' Aristakes carried on regardless. '*At last*, this step is being taken that I've dreamed of for all these years! Our farewell will have to be speedy: I must not miss the climactic scenes on Opera Square, which today we will rename Freedom Square! Or perhaps Adranik Square, after the celebrated heroic commander of our army, when we were an independent republic, in the blissful years 1918 to 1920!'

'. . . what you are promulgating here is ultra-nationalism of the most dubious militaristic slant . . .' Johann Wolfgang muttered angrily.

They said their goodbyes in the little airport ticket hall, amidst piles of dirt and debris. '. . . who would have dreamed of such developments, four calendar months ago,' said Johann Wolfgang, 'when on this selfsame spot I bade welcome to the delegation of my Scandinavian colleagues, and beheld you, today my friend, for the very first time!'

Aristakes urged him to hurry, not only because he was impatient to get back to Opera Square, but on account of the considerable delay they had experienced in reaching Zvartnotz.

Seda and her parents, and Medji had also turned out to say goodbye, but there was barely time for that, the crew of the huge jet were waiting for Tigor.

'So, you've got my drawing on you,' said the mirror manufacturer, he spoke extremely rapidly. 'It will be a very simple matter from there to make the discovery. To find the Ark, as you know, one must be as pure as a child. And that you are, my angel, from head to toe. Be courageous, my hero – and don't disappoint us!'

'Write me letters, I'll write back!' asked Medji.

'. . . write me letters, I'll write back!' called Seda. And Tigor kissed her on both cheeks. Ran out onto the tarmac without looking back.

*

He had informed Igor that he only had five hours in Moscow, but hoped to see him, if the Balt was able to pick him up from the domestic airport and drive him across to the international one.

'. . . so, are we headed back to the States?' the driver greeted him, picked up his heavy bags. 'I've been so happy for over a week now, it's bursting out of me!' Tigor thought it was the prospect of seeing him again that had made Igor so happy. 'But you'd better talk first,' the driver went on, 'because then it'll be my turn, and then you won't be able to get a word in edgeways!' The Friday afternoon traffic was so heavy that they managed only a funereal pace along the Garden Ring, the ten-lane orbital highway. And when his passenger seemed a little reluctant to speak of himself and his own plans, Igor's desire to communicate burst forth. Recently, he said, he had received an official letter from Lomonossov University, containing the astonishing proposal that from the beginning of next semester – though of course on a trial basis, and with no contractual guarantees to speak of – he was to resume lecturing at the Mathematical Faculty: 'I'm sure you can imagine what that signifies to me . . . I am infinitely happy about it. In all the days of my life, I never supposed I would receive such a clear reparation and rehabilitation. For the occasion of my re-engagement, I'm selecting one of my dearest themes: Henri Poincaré. Probably with a strong emphasis on the fixed-point theorem, and the three-form problem. Beyond that, I'm planning a particular study of space, I will teach mathematical astronomy, because I've become convinced that the coming century will see the discovery of extraterrestrial intelligence, a discovery which will revolutionize the perspectives of the planet and its inhabitants in a way that no previous discovery ever has. For that reason, we must be certain to understand the laws of space, no subject will compel attention so much as our realization that we are not alone in infinite space . . . And then the two of us, we will exchange results to the end of our lives, from one side of the globe to the other, we will wander from university to university, and we will exchange regular visits, both professional and private in character, and I can't say how *happy* it all makes me . . .!'

When Tigor then told him of his destination, Igor's initial reaction was to suppose that his colleague was pulling his leg. He laughed, even though he didn't find it an especially funny joke. His passenger repeated that he was flying on to Eastern Anatolia that very day, said it so sorrowfully and matter-of-factly, that the Balt finally had no alternative but to believe him. For what reason, he enquired, was he undertaking such an expedition? But Tigor didn't reply.

'Maybe you're just a little short of sleep, my good friend,' said Igor, 'then you will reconsider. It might easily cost you your life, the climate there is among the worst in the world. Of course, some degenerate aristocratic family in Armenia has filled your head with this nonsense. Just spend a few days here, with me, in my place, you'll calm down, we can sort out one or two matters in relation to Poincaré together, and then you can return to your chair. The turn-off to my street is just one or two kilometres from here, I'll drive you straight to my modest apartment on Volokolamsk Chaussée . . . You know nothing in the world beats teaching the young!'

Tigor replied brusquely that he had no intention of going back to Igor's house with him. '. . . let's say . . . I've become embroiled . . . in this . . . quest – that I have to complete . . .' he said. 'That's all there is to it. You know how you feel obliged to solve every problem that you are posed . . . In this business, I'm even going into the camp of the enemy, who predict that all scientific thought is a dead end . . .'

'Those assembled gurus and charlatans!' scolded the Balt. 'Why don't you tell me what this is really about! To my perspective, the lepers are those who seek to make the unproven and unprovable their Golden Calf! With their obfuscation, they wreck everything that we – you too! – have established in the sciences with years and lifetimes of effortful devotion . . .!' He did not take the Volokolamsk Chaussée turn-off from the motorway.

Igor took advantage of the remaining time spent in the over-crowded cafeteria of Scheremetevo Airport to make a further attempt to convince his friend not to carry on with his mystifying journey. The air conditioning blew such a cold blast over them, it was as though they were both clambering over broad glacier ridges in icy silence.

'I beg you,' said the driver, when he could think of no further arguments, 'allow me to be your Sancho Panza. In future, I'll accompany you everywhere you want to go.' Tigor smiled, but failed to understand what the Balt was proposing. He was largely unfamiliar with world literature. Hadn't read Cervantes, or Tennyson or Yeats or Keats, nor yet Pushkin, Tolstoy or Dostoevsky. He only knew Novalis, because Novalis had been his mother's idol. He had read a little of Italo Svevo at secondary school, to please Arnold, who thought Svevo was incomparable. He knew passages of *Alice in Wonderland* off by heart, because he greatly admired the logician and mathematician Charles Lutwidge Dodgson, who called himself Lewis Carroll and had made use of his specialized knowledge 'to carry the art of nonsense to a peak,' as the *Encyclopaedia Britannica* had it. The *Britannica* really was Tigor's favourite, and more than everything else that he had left behind, he missed its twenty-four volumes in their white leather bindings.

It was not until the final moment of parting, when Igor was waving him off through the thick glass partition, that Tigor was overcome by the certain knowledge that he should have given in to his friend. Panic bloomed in his pores. He even thought he was committing an irreparable error, but the point of no return was already behind him with the passport-control booths: it would be to show himself unbearably vulnerable, he thought, if he did try and turn back even now. He gritted his teeth, turned away from his escort and disappeared, bathed in sweat, into the labyrinthine tunnels of the departure hall.

In Istanbul, he didn't even leave the airport, within a couple of hours he was on his connecting flight to Erzurum. It grieved him, on the particularly turbulent flight which occasioned him not the slightest fear, that he had left Igor. He felt deeply homesick. It grieved him that he had left Yerevan. Felt homesick for Aristakes and Johann Wolfgang, for the children at Haghtanak and their parents. He pined for the dancing, flag-waving girl in the turquoise dress. He missed Seda's cautious kisses, felt homesick for what he thought was probably the ugliest city in the world.

Behind Erzurum's enormous mosque was the bus terminus. Tigor had no eyes for what was going on around him, he barely saw the small, East Anatolian town, ringed by high mountains. The bus that carried the traveller to Dogubayazit took a day to cover a little more than two hundred kilometres. The steep Tahir pass needed to be overcome, an ascent during which the ancient, crowded vehicle was never very far from mechanical failure. Then it was almost walking pace to Agri and thence to Dogubayazit. It was night when Tigor arrived. The handful of hotels were full, and with much effort and luck he secured a ground-floor room in a small eating-house. He didn't see Ararat until the following morning. The upper part of the mountain was swaddled in clouds. It had taken him two and a half days to get from Ararat to Ararat.

He knew that it was forbidden to go up the mountain without official permission, never mind alone. And it never occurred to him to ask for permission. Begging children accompanied him on his errands, he bought nuts, raisins, quantities of dates, also dry sausages and zwieback. He purchased a down sleeping bag, several changes of thermal underwear, and some lined mittens. He was rather surprised to see so many travellers in Dogubayazit, there were people with rucksacks everywhere he went. In a shop where he was buying a powerful and absurdly heavy torch he got into conversation with a bronzed couple.

'We're from Scotland . . .' said the woman.

'Inverness, way up north,' said the man, more precisely.

'And we're going up Mount Ararat tomorrow!' added the woman.

'With a group,' said the man.

'Care to join us?' asked the woman.

For a moment, Tigor thought he couldn't breathe. Just as after the fall into the deep end of the empty swimming pool at the edge of Revoltella Park. Unable to breathe for several seconds, just like then, my fifth birthday, thought Tigor. Breathe! How simple of me to assume – breathe! – that I would be the only one climbing the mountain!

How could I allow myself to be pushed so far? The notion of scaling the summit along well-trodden footpaths! Camping out at night with eighty or a hundred others, amidst garbage piles, as if on some Adriatic singalong! Why didn't I grab hold of the last boathook and listen to Igor's forceful arguments! I feel as though

I'd been brainwashed, he said to himself. Rage and hurt flooded his body like flashes of lightning.

'. . . you all right?' asked the woman.

In the displays in the shop windows (surrounded by geometrical arrangements of sun creams) there were colour photographs of the summit of Ararat, with waving, laughing hikers, posing beside a wooden, wheelbarrow-sized replica of Noah's Ark. By evening, Tigor had encountered more and more of these people, sitting outside every café, on every terrace, rucksacks packed and at the ready, chalk-pale faces and arms glistening with oil. Across their noses they had slathered an extra couple of fingers of protection. On the roof-ridge of an incomplete multi-storey shell, a sign had been fastened that read: 'Welcome to Noah Country'. Right next to it squatted the wretched tin-roofed wooden shacks of the local inhabitants. Computer rock howled from loudspeakers in tiny bars. Guides offered their services on the dusty main drag. They wore big reflector sunglasses, and were leaning against the walls, one leg drawn up, boot-soles pressed against the wall. Their walkie-talkies, which they took up the mountain with them, spluttered and wheezed, just like a radio-cab in the big city. Pack-mules kicked around on the asphalt, they cost ten dollars a day to hire. Hand-painted wooden signs offered motorbikes for rent. The travellers waited and sat tight, like locusts that also like to foregather in large numbers before going on pillage.

At dusk, Tigor found himself in the middle of a car park full of articulated trucks. The drivers stopped off in Dogubayazit on their way to Persia. Tigor stood stock-still among their cabs. When it was dark, he tore the piece of paper that Aristakes had given him in tiny pieces. It had contained his hand-drawn plan of where to find the Ark, with a big X in the top right hand corner. He was talking to the girl in the turquoise dress, who lived in the Ovannavank Kolkhoz, not far away, but on the other side of the River Araxes: 'I get so scared', he was saying to the girl, 'to be sitting inside myself and looking out, like being in a building and looking through the window. It frightens me so to be me. Do you understand? My ideal construction of a self would be a living reflection of me, a second, identical self – a double of me. That would be the friend I so badly miss. He would laugh when I laughed. Cry when I cried. When I reach out my hand to him, he would reach out his hand to me . . .'

For two hours he had been walking on the freshly tarred road, muttering to himself, barely noticing that he was walking through the night. The sky was turning pinky-green in the breaking light. There were women carrying hay bales on their backs across wide fields. Large yellow plots of flowers interspersed the plains on which wild horses were grazing. Mosquito swarms were accompanying Tigor, had been since minutes after dawn. A herd of mares trotted past him, causing the ground to shake. A rusty army tank approached, the wheels churned noisily; no sign of any crew. The mountain Massis, the Mother of the World, moved closer, soared nakedly into the sky, bigger, higher than any he had ever seen, he who had grown up in the shadow of the Alps. He thought he could make out the Khorvirap monastery on the horizon. '. . . brought for you, the sacrificial animal!' he heard Aristakes' intense whisper, 'for the success of your mission! You are our only ray of hope!' I alone! thought Tigor, with the bitterest taste in his mouth.

Near the little hamlet of Aralik, he started to climb. The first day, he followed a narrow nomads' path in the restricted military zone along the northern flank of the mountain, completely off limits to civilians. He clambered over great lumps of basalt and sheer runs of lava up until nightfall. He saw no one. Was surprised at the calm, regular beating of his heart. His physical strength seemed to grow with every obstacle in his path. He kept his eyes trained on the ground, saw Trieste and Philadelphia, the plant room and the rigging loft, school and university, in view. Engaged in debate with Aristakes, insulted him, allowed the mirror man to reply, attacked him again, listened to what Oganessian had to say for himself, and cursed him. A herd of sheep, several hundred strong, stood densely pressed around their leading animal, made no move as Tigor approached them. He had to wade through the soft creaturely pool like a stretch of deep mud. He was stung badly. The snakes that had been a particular terror to him in the plant room, here he saw them slipping across his path at hourly intervals. The higher he climbed, the deeper he sank into the labyrinth of his brain.

He spent the first night in a cave, scorpions scuttled across the floor, Tigor remained oblivious. The second night, he bivouacked out in the open, on a mildly unstable expanse of scree. Thunderstorms and cloudbursts blew over him, he wasn't bothered by the weather. When a savage wolfhound leapt at him, he instinctively parried its leap with a movement of his arm, graceful as a ballet dancer's. The creature crept away behind a shiny smooth block of lava, whimpered, licked its sprained paw. On the third day, fog obscured the visibility. Tigor climbed without a break. That evening, he reached the lowest terminal moraine of a mighty glacier tongue, whose meltwater formed little streams. The cloven ice colossus lay a little higher up. Next morning, he would carry on up there.

Beneath his temples, in the interior of the mountain, he heard the roar of underground rivers. In the fish market in Trieste, he saw the creels full of crabs, how they clambered over and under one another, hacked away at each other in a fight to the death, splintered their armoured shells and pincers. He surveyed a large, live salmon, with snow-white scales, bedded on shavings of ice. Held a hand up in front of his face (fish being particularly frightened of human eyes) and with his other hand took it carefully into his head, and with him on his journey.

In the first light of day, he spotted a man he hadn't been aware of the previous night, asleep quite close to him. He was wearing a grey-green uniform, and had his back turned to him. In spite of the temperature – at night, it was several degrees below zero – he didn't bother with sleeping bag, blanket or even headgear. Tigor boiled some water, mixed up some of his rather evil-tasting instant soup, and then called out to the soldier. Ate and drank his own breakfast, then, not having had a reply from the man, warmed the soup up again, and gave him another shout. He waited another half-hour before going over to wake him up. When he did so, his equanimity abruptly left him, Tigor was afraid he might black out as he leaned over the dead man. Both his eyes had been put out, and pus was filling their large dark sockets. His upper teeth and the whitened gums were exposed, the killer had cut off his victim's upper lip and tongue. A sight that Tigor, feeling thoroughly ashamed of himself, couldn't see enough of, once he'd got over his initial shock. He left the place and came back to it, came back to it a second time and a third, hunkered down by the body a fourth time, wallowing in his disgust.

He was getting nearer and nearer to the ice carpet. Sisyphean blocks of frozen lava tumbled down through his brain. Tigor was climbing up into his own biography, steeper and more hazardous than any mountainous terrain. He despatched the fish with the snow-white scales down through his throat into his thoracic cavity, asked the cold-blooded creature what it saw there. His heart was healthy, he learned, it was pumping hard. Also the network of veins was working satisfactorily. His belly was a limestone cavern.

At the centre of a narrow declivity was a small lake full of mirror-pure glacier-melt. Two men and a woman were standing on a jagged rock promontory. The woman's thick, beautiful hair was blowing in the gale. When Tigor came up to them, they promptly surrounded him, talked in quiet gutturals at him, held a small rusty knife under his nose. He held his hands up, felt like an actor who had to concentrate not to spoil a scene by bursting out laughing. Then the men lit into him, stripped the rucksack off his back, ground their heavy boots in his face and testicles, stamped around on his body as though trying to put out a carpet fire. Punched him in the solar plexus, but by that stage Tigor was unconscious. The unveiled woman knelt down next to him, held the knife at his throat in one hand, and felt for his carotid artery with the other.

The leader of the group had his twentieth birthday that day. He had become separated from his friends, having stayed behind to look at the herd that was grazing in another valley nearby. Early that morning, his father had given him some eighty sheep. Now he was feasting his eyes on the sight, glorying in the feeling of having become a wealthy man. He would have stayed with his herd even longer, had not the wail of low-flying fighter planes shattered his feelings of bliss.

'. . . whap! skrash!' he called, as he caught up with his band, who were just in the process of sacrificing an enemy of the people to their revolutionary struggle. He was only sorry not to have a soldier he could torture, like that officer three days ago, who had fallen into their hands. '. . . whablam!' screamed Yilmaz, and straddled the unconscious man, index fingers together, pointing down at him like an imaginary pistol barrel. Then slowly lowered the make-believe weapon, issued the order that the man be permitted to live. The Peshmerga warriors protested that the latest resolution of the committee of 'fighters who stare death in the face' could on no account be overridden. Mosul, the raven-haired one, had felt for some time that Yilmaz was becoming unreliable, now she threatened to call for him to be replaced at their next meeting. She knelt down to give the *coup de grâce*. Yilmaz held her back forcibly. From the breast pocket of his black goatskin jacket, he pulled out a fountain pen. It was the pen that Tigor had given him and the two other young men on the street corner in Yerevan on the first day of his stay in Armenia. To begin with, the young Kurd had only owned parts of it, but in the course of numerous bartered transactions, he had gradually taken their parts off his two comrades. To Yilmaz, this splendid object had the status of a charm.

Why should a chance meeting several months ago be any sort of justification for sparing the tourist's life, Mosul wanted to know. The commander leaned down to her, put his arms around her shoulders. She broke away. Moved off with the two others. They climbed down to the base camp, three hundred metres down. The wind carried the woman's expletives back to the spot where the attack had taken place.

Yilmaz stayed behind with the casualty, tried to make him a softer bed, covered him up with clothes that he took out of Tigor's rucksack.

He came to the next morning. Saw nothing but fog, felt completely frozen. His whole body hurt, most of all his cheekbones. Gave a start when he saw a man with a moustache, his head wrapped in a large black-and-white patterned woollen cloth, kneeling beside him. '. . . I friend . . .' said the Kurd. Tigor didn't understand what had happened. He didn't recognize the man. Woke up, hours later, Yilmaz was dangling the fountain pen in front of his eyes, his mother's present to him for his twenty-first birthday.

The injured man tried to describe the appearance of the trio who had ambushed him. '. . . goodness gracious . . .' replied Yilmaz, he had recently come across the expression in one of his comic books. Tigor mentioned the mutilated soldier too.

'Goodness gracious me . . .!' came the response from Yilmaz.

On the second day, the pain had lessened, and the swellings gone down a little. The Kurd had given him the use of the tent in which the shepherd lived who tended his flock and that of his father. The shepherd had been transferred down to the base camp, and Yilmaz looked after the sheep himself, until Tigor was fully recovered, with the help of a dog he called Beast. He made tea for Tigor, who was lying on a camp bed, gave him sheep's milk and cheese, and the rescued man, gradually getting his strength back, began to torment his rescuer with every conceivable question, to which he never got an answer.

'. . . but how did you get to Yerevan?!' insisted Tigor, for the fifth time now.

The Kurdish people, Yilmaz finally conceded, above all the Kurdish rebels, came and went across the boundaries of four countries, as though Kurdistan were already the sovereign nation state of their dreams. They would not acknowledge the existence of any national boundaries within their territory. At that time, he had met up with two friends who belonged to the small Kurdish community in Armenia, and had discussed, with them and their fathers, possible supply routes for urgently needed goods. 'Kurdistan means mountains. Rivers. Good faces. Freedom . . .' However, the enemy was mighty, he added. The enemy buried his victims alive. And he forced the relatives of the condemned man to watch the execution-cum-burial to the bitter end. 'If we do not fight, they will *melt* us . . .' he added. Only then did Tigor grasp that Yilmaz might have been the killer of the soldier. He said nothing, for fear of getting an answer he didn't want to hear. However, the idea that this Peshmerga might have something to do with the three characters who had beaten him up, that did not occur to him. And Yilmaz averred that the criminals, if they were ever identified and caught, would be hauled up before a people's court.

'. . . shazzak! Whap! Whump!' he cried, as though to lend further substance to his promise. And raved about his idol Spiderman, the saviour of the human race, who, all in a matter of seconds, could weave nets, and unspool steel cables and unbreakable fibres, to fight evil and smooth the path of good.

*

He had something he wanted to show him, said the Kurd, early on the morning of the third day of Tigor's convalescence. They scrambled up narrow vertical fissures, and scree from the terminal moraine. They reached the sheet of ice, made their way cautiously over the mighty glacier, which crept through the narrow, funnel-shaped valley, at the end of which was the hollow on whose perimeter Tigor had spent the past couple of days recovering from his injuries. The convalescent found it hard going over the ice. He didn't want to walk any more, he couldn't manage another step, and still he kept following his young guide. Yilmaz stopped for him every minute, occasionally grasped him by the wrist to pull him up.

'. . . I dug into the earth,' whispered Tigor the first time they paused for any length of time, 'in the plant room and in the Luxembourg gardens, dug deep, cut through roots, ripped open the earth, searching, dug with a persistence that astounded me . . . instead of excavating myself . . . Even as a child, I was a stranger to myself. Sometimes the walls of my own nursery looked quite unfamiliar to me . . .'

'Arrggghhhh!' went Yilmaz. 'Yeeargh!'

'. . . later on, I became obsessed with the idea that I had to make a contribution to mathematics . . . make a name for myself! Fame creates order, you know? It's like an anchor in the sea of chaos . . . Even though I only really chose mathematics for the discipline of my life, at the instigation of Gino . . . You must go on, said Gino, he was the rigging master in the Giuseppe Verdi Theatre in Trieste, but then maybe you don't even know what a rigging master is? You must go on and study mathematics, Gino said, once you've finished school! And so I ended up studying mathematics for *his* sake! And my somewhat esoteric specialism in the field of probability studies, the so-called snowflake constant, only became my subject because that had been my tutor's subject, and he persuaded me to take it up where he left off . . .'

'You need a woman, my good man,' said Yilmaz slowly, with much head shaking. 'I will never be able to understand the West, however hard I try . . .'

'One of the few independent steps I've taken in my life', Tigor went on, 'was the flight from the conference centre in Trieste . . . I'll tell you more about that on some later occasion . . .'

'. . . quoosh! . . . yeech!' wailed Yilmaz.

'. . . my attempt to live in the woods, a sort of rehearsal for some subsequent post-civilized age . . . And then the Odéon was my own initiative as well . . .'

'Are you telling *me* all this, or yourself?!'

'. . . but after that I had a relapse: I allowed Chabanian to drive me to Yerevan. And then I let Aristakes talk me into going up Ararat . . .'

'. . . you let what?' asked Yilmaz.

Tigor's exhaustion was such that he could barely stand upright, but still they climbed on, over the steep, compacted ice. From time to time, the rubbing of the glacier against the edge of the rocks produced a quiet creaking, and that was the only sound in the chill air. A steep vertical shaft opened up before them, for a few minutes they rested at the edge of the crevasse. Descended into the wide moulin, washed by meltwater into an irregular flight of steps. The glacier walls shimmered in the broken, glassy blue light. Pointed ice stalactites hung down overhead. Pillars of névé soared up metres high.

Having reached the bottom of the glacier, they made their way along a cave-like passage that led them into deeper darkness. They were now underneath the glacier, in a dark, volcanic grotto. If they followed this connecting passage for a few miles, Yilmaz claimed, they would come to a whole network of passages that would finally take them through the earth's mantle into the molten magma at the heart of the planet.

'Ahora!' cried Yilmaz. Tigor switched on his torch. To him this descent into the earth's interior felt like one of those dreams in which, while dreaming, he knew he was dreaming. The passage glimmered in green and silver. He dreamed: as soon as I wake up, I'll ask my benefactor to take me underneath the glacier . . . He had fallen asleep on his feet. Yilmaz took the torch out of his hand, shone the light on the path. Tigor whispered as he woke: '. . . take me underneath the glacier . . .' And he opened his eyes. Yilmaz was telling him about a volcanic eruption of Ararat, some hundred and fifty years ago. The streams of lava, according to him, had torn through the glacier, split the valley, and buried a town by the name of Ahora. The passage they were walking in ran parallel to the site of the erstwhile catastrophe, Yilmaz explained. Heads bowed, they felt their way forward.

All at once they were standing under a lofty arch. The dimly discernible contours suggested the outlines of blocks of masonry. Yilmaz led Tigor further. 'The city of Ahora!' the terrorist shouted out, enthusiastically. Wood splinters in the cathedral-sized hollow that the lava masses had spared. Wood splinters as far as the torch could show.

'. . . good? . . . wow?' asked Yilmaz.

Tigor found the broad, empty pediment of a statue, that had the figures 140–55 chiselled into it, and below that some characters from the Armenian alphabet. Above the letters a map had been etched with elliptical and wave-shaped contour lines that gave the whole thing the appearance of a spider's web. In the top right corner of it, a little cube had been drawn. Tigor spent a long time kneeling in front of the stone. He knew the significance of the letters and numbers on the stone pediment. They were the name and the dates of Emperor Tigran II.

The ice, old and dirty, furrowed by an impossible number of lines and creases, looked to him now, as they were standing up on top of the glacier again, like the epidermis of a venerable elephant. Tigor slept until nightfall. In his dream, he ripped every flower, every leaf out of the ground, along with the earth that clung to the frail roots, bit through small insects, without noticing. He stood in front of the dilapidated wall of a chapel. There he vomited so hard it hurt him to the root of his penis. Only when he awoke did he begin to understand what had happened to him that afternoon. Nobody, not even Aristakes, would believe him.

'. . . zonkk! powwow! skrash!' yelled the terrorist into the moonlit night, and the sounds were reduplicated by a powerful echo. They were bivouacking on the edge of the glacier, on top of an ash-grey erratic. Ate up the provisions that Tigor had bought so plentifully in Dogubayazit. In theatrical cascades of sentences, he thanked Yilmaz for having granted him the experience of Ahora.

'You really need a woman, my good man . . .' growled Yilmaz. By daybreak at the latest, he needed to be back with his flock, he said. Reproached himself for not having told base camp of his whereabouts long ago. Regretted having taken this act of friendship upon himself, and having spent the past four days away from his people.

Tigor talked unceasingly about the map that was etched into the pediment of the statue, at the edge of the buried town of Ahora. Yilmaz accepted Tigor's notebook and a fine felt-tip pen (the fountain pen had run out of ink months ago), and by the light of the torch, and from memory, he sketched an exact copy of the map. At the centre of the drawing lay the crevasse into which they had made their descent. On the right hand side, towards the top, Yilmaz sketched a fingernail-sized cube in perspective. That place did not lie more than half a day's march away from where they were, he claimed.

Tigor pointed to the cube. 'What's this?' he asked.

'You know! Don't ask!' Yilmaz laughed.

'What is it?'

'You know!'

'. . . you don't believe it really exists, do you?'

The Peshmerga didn't reply.

'. . . please, take me there tomorrow,' beseeched Tigor.

'I'm busy killing. Tomorrow no time!'

'. . . busy *what*?'

'Never mind . . .'

'What do you kill?'

'My sheep.'

Tigor pointed at the map: 'Please take me there tomorrow!' He pulled four fifty-dollar bills out of his pocket. Yilmaz took the money, and drew a couple of crampons, a pickaxe and a long, stout rope in the notebook. He explained that they couldn't carry on with the climb without that equipment. He would fetch the things tomorrow morning, and would be back in twelve hours, at the latest. At sunrise he left. Tigor was amazed at the surefootedness – like a mountain goat, he thought – of Yilmaz descending.

The glacier glittered in the bright sun, the colour of it lightened to baby blue. Later the weather turned. Everything was swathed in fog. Tigor was waiting. Slept sitting up. Evening fell. The night began stormy, and Tigor, in his down bed, froze as he had never frozen in his life. The blackness ate oxygen. In odd minutes of calm, there was a lunar stillness. The torch batteries were used up. Shafts of lightning lit up the ice like headlights. Thunder uprooted rocks. One rumbled just past Tigor's sleeping place, almost crushing him, he had no idea of it. His lungs ached with cold.

When it grew light again, Tigor knew he would return to Trieste, and make his life there. That was a foregone conclusion. Trieste, the city on the edge! Walking in the Karst, permanently encountering frontiers! He would inform Abraham, beg his forgiveness. Turn the Walnut Street apartment over to him, with the books and records and furniture and his personal effects. He would teach at the high school where he had been a pupil, and had taken his final exam on 5 June 1965. The day that Ed White in his astronaut's oxygen-drenched silver suit had climbed out of a Gemini capsule and undertaken a twenty-two minute space walk. Tigor resolved that as a middle-school instructor of mathematics, physics and chemistry, at the Maria Theresa Gymnasium on the Via Bonaparte 88, he would be strict. However difficult and contradictory this might appear, on the one hand he would enjoin his charges to lead disciplined lives, and on the other he would bring them up never simply to do what they had been told. 'Make your own way in life!' he would teach them. 'Don't do things to try and be well liked. The decision about what you do with your lives once you're finished with school is completely and utterly yours!' On his shoulders he felt the cold, dry breath of the Bora which blew down onto the city from the Karst mountains. From the teachers' common room you could make out the old harbour and the Molo Venezia, and the sea beyond. He saw himself after classes, sauntering through the dark crooked little alleyways that smelled always of cats' piss, down to the Piazza Unità, one side of which opened out to the sea. He would sit out on the terrace of the Café Degli Specchi, drink his mocha and spend hours of the afternoon browsing through the newspapers.

As evening came again, Tigor knew that Yilmaz would not return. The following morning, it started to snow. Tigor followed the map that the Kurd had drawn for him, not really knowing why he was climbing again. He didn't eat or drink. Caught snowflakes on the back of his black glove, studied the disappearance of the lacy crystal skeletons. He took the pocket magnifying glass out of his jacket, inspected the snowflake nets. Immaculate hexagons, lattices, screens, perfectly symmetrical, star-, plate- and pencil-shaped and fern-like at their extremities. Over the course of nineteen winters, he had caught them in a polyvinyl ethylene solution, on a black cardboard plate, at four degrees below zero centigrade, to take pictures of them and compare them to the thousands of classic photographs by Wilson W. Bentley, and those of the Japanese scientist C. Nakaya in his work, *Snow Crystals*.

He observed one crystal that had landed on his leather mitten, keeping half an eye on the second-hand of his watch, counted off the ninety-six seconds that, according to Tigor's Constant, need-ed to elapse before an identical hexagon would appear on an area of maximally ten square centimetres. But even if the miracle had happened, he wouldn't have been able to prove it, he had no microscope on him and no camera. He couldn't even make a note of it; Yilmaz had taken his felt-tip.

He felt as though his body was leaning out of his skin, that's how heavy his rucksack had become. He climbed further, with-out a break, ever steeper and ever higher. The crunching and rolling underfoot, the great rocks that scraped and furrowed the mountain, the gigantic ice carpet across which he was moving, became more oceanic with every step. He had the illusion of striding over the foam-crusts of the sea, of gliding from wave-peak to wave-peak. He packed himself into the skin of one of his students, a real Southern California kid, surfin' down there in Laguna Beach somewhere, letting it all hang loose, real laid back, with the girls and all. The colder he felt, the more determinedly he danced over the waves. Surf crash. Blazing warmth in the tips of his fingers. No thirst at all. *Après moi le deluge.* 'I, Prometheus-like, chained to the Caucasus!' He didn't know that Prometheus meant 'the one who thought ahead'. Knelt down to offer a small-er target to the wind. No head protection. No rope, and no net. Apollonian nets, named after Apollonios of Perge, 262 to 190 BCE, Apollonian nets, Mandelbrot tells us, are self-inverse. The net can be drawn in a single stroke of the pen. The pen will cross certain points twice, but never in the space of a single curve. Therefore we may conclude: the Apollonian net can be tied from a single rope . . . Or is Mandelbrot mistaken? Is Tigor's Constant the right answer?

The wind relented. The cloud cover broke. There was a view all the way down and across to the monastery of Khorvirap. 'I'm just tired,' Tigor said to himself. 'I'm not panicking. I'm just tired . . .' He unrolled his sleeping bag, crept into the down with all his clothes on. 'It's possible to breathe more deeply in the cold,' he whispered. 'We're salmon without eyelids, going to the ends of the earth to spawn. Return from oceans to the rivers and streams where we were born. Shuttle between fresh water and salt water without hesitating. We're wanderers between worlds.'

As he woke, neither hungry nor thirsty, he knew that any further break would cost him his life. Lying on the ice produced such heavenly lassitude. Why go on? Why not lie down on the ice and sleep? 'Sleep, just sleep,' he said to himself, repeated the words like a mantra. Ate snow, crammed his mouth full, and the more snow he gulped down, the thirstier he became. Climbed higher, at times up to his knees in it, then slithering back yards at a time. Dumped his rucksack, made a mental note of the spot, to find it again on his way down. Don't stop! How healthy my heart is in fact, Tigor deluded himself, I never knew that. He looked up into the sky, thought he saw a rainbow to the north-east. A wide-bodied jet looping round for a landing in Yerevan. Tigor counted the stripes and colours of the spectrum, whispered: '. . . broken light of fire and water, You connect Heaven and Earth . . .' Lay down on the ice, spreading his arms as though in flight.

Climbed out of the capsule, crossed the Caucasus and Mongolia, half obscured by clouds. He adjusted the orbit, while the spaceship slowly dipped into the night-side of the earth. Such a long flight! The horizon was a pale blue stripe, above that a darker blue, and then deep blue, broad bands of colour leaking into the black dome of the universe. The pale blue turned orange and red, sank into night. Lightning, in the form of diamond pinpricks of light, over Japan and the island of Sakhalin. Minutes later the sun rose again.

The two soldiers who were crossing the Ahora glacier on routine patrol a few days later came upon a frozen corpse. He was on his front, arms spread out, like wings. With the tip of his machine gun, the younger of the two raised the man's head slightly, while the older bent down over him. He found a passport in the snow, picked it up, flicked through it, put it in his pocket.

'Nationality?' asked the younger.

'Tourist,' replied the older.

To save themselves the trouble of conveying the corpse to Dogubayazit, the men scraped snow over Tigor. They made no report of their find.